*Strip me of my Inhibitions.*

"Can you see me now?" she asked.

"I see you perfectly. Strip for me, Sandy."

A shiver of anticipation rippled through her body.

"Come on, baby. Don't be afraid. Undress for me."

She put her fingers on the first button of her blouse, slowly undoing it. Her fingers slid to the second button . . . and the third.

"Honey," he grumbled, "if you don't hurry up and take that damn blouse off, I'm gonna come down there and rip it off you myself."

She smiled, pleased to know she had some power over him, after all. . . .

# Bad Girl

## MAYA
## REYNOLDS

HEAT

HEAT
Published by New American Library, a division of
Penguin Group (USA) Inc., 375 Hudson Street,
New York, New York 10014, USA
Penguin Group (Canada), 90 Eglinton Avenue East, Suite 700, Toronto,
Ontario M4P 2Y3, Canada (a division of Pearson Penguin Canada Inc.)
Penguin Books Ltd., 80 Strand, London WC2R 0RL, England
Penguin Ireland, 25 St. Stephen's Green, Dublin 2,
Ireland (a division of Penguin Books Ltd.)
Penguin Group (Australia), 250 Camberwell Road, Camberwell, Victoria 3124,
Australia (a division of Pearson Australia Group Pty. Ltd.)
Penguin Books India Pvt. Ltd., 11 Community Centre, Panchsheel Park,
New Delhi - 110 017, India
Penguin Group (NZ), 67 Apollo Drive, Rosedale, North Shore 0745,
Auckland, New Zealand (a division of Pearson New Zealand Ltd.)
Penguin Books (South Africa) (Pty.) Ltd., 24 Sturdee Avenue,
Rosebank, Johannesburg 2196, South Africa

Penguin Books Ltd., Registered Offices:
80 Strand, London WC2R 0RL, England

First published by Heat, an imprint of New American Library,
a division of Penguin Group (USA) Inc.

First Printing, September 2007
10 9 8 7 6 5 4 3 2 1

HEAT is a trademark of Penguin Group (USA) Inc.

LIBRARY OF CONGRESS CATALOGING-IN-PUBLICATION DATA:
Reynolds, Maya.
    Bad girl/Maya Reynolds.
        p.    cm.
    ISBN: 978-0-451-22210-7
    1. Single women—Fiction.   2. Voyeurism—Fiction.   3. Dallas (Tex.)—Fiction.   I. Title.
    PS3618.E976B33 2007
    813'.6—dc22          2007004001

Set in Centaur MT
Designed by Ginger Legato

Printed in the United States of America

PUBLISHER S NOTE
This is a work of fiction. Names, characters, places, and incidents either are the product of the author's imagination or are used fictitiously, and any resemblance to actual persons, living or dead, business establishments, events, or locales is entirely coincidental.
    The publisher does not have any control over and does not assume any responsibility for author or third-party Web sites or their content.

# Acknowledgments

I have many people to thank for helping to bring this book to life. Special thanks to my wonderful agent, Jacky Sach, and to my marvelous editor, Tracy Bernstein.

Also thanks to all the people who critiqued for me along the way: Jeanne Laws, Linda Lovely, Marie Tuhart, Maria Zannini and all the writers of the Irving Writers' Connection.

And, finally, thanks to my loved ones, especially my father. When I was a teen, he offered to match my part-time job's salary if I would write instead of working for a summer. I didn't have the courage to take the leap then, and I'm sorry he didn't live to see a novel of mine in print. I miss you, Daddy.

# Chapter One

Sweet Cheeks rode his stationary bicycle, his back to Sandy. His tight ass moved rhythmically up and down and side to side as his muscular legs pedaled furiously. The bike's whirling noise and his heavy breathing muffled the sound of her footsteps behind him.

He wasn't wearing anything except bike shorts. Sandy admired his broad shoulders, now shiny with perspiration. Although he was only two minutes into his routine, his hair was already plastered to his head, the long, dark curls clinging to his face and neck.

She slid one hand across his damp back to squeeze his left shoulder. His deltoid muscle was as hard and firm as the rest of his body. She leaned forward and kissed his right shoulder.

He tasted hot and salty. Sandy clenched her thighs together as she felt the rush of moisture between her legs that always accompanied the sight of his nearly naked body.

Sweet Cheeks stopped pedaling and turned, pivoting to pull her toward him while remaining perched on the bike.

When she moved into the vee between his thighs, his bulging cock pressed against her naked belly. She arched, stretching and rubbing against his erection, eliciting a moan from him. His hands shifted to her ample hips, where his fingers kneaded her fleshy ass, encouraging her to continue what she'd started.

His gaze was fixed on her bare chest, and she took a deep breath. The movement raised her nipples, displaying her full breasts to advantage. Her lungs filled with his musky man scent, which was amplified by exercise and his excitement at seeing her.

Beads of perspiration clung to his chest, and she leaned forward to capture a single droplet with her tongue. When she licked him, his muscles convulsed. Sliding her hands to his rear, she cupped those sweet ass cheeks, trying to insert her fingers between his body and the bike seat.

He nudged her backward so he could step off the bike. His large hands encircled her waist and he lifted her—as easily as though she were a size 6, not a 16.

She wrapped her legs around his hips, bringing her aching cunt in line with his cock and making it nearly impossible for him to free himself from his bike shorts on his own. Still clinging to his body, she tried to help him remove the pants. They were both frantic, their movements jerky and awkward.

When the garment fell to the floor, he stepped out of it and shifted her weight in order to get his hand between their bodies. He fumbled for a minute, trying to maneuver himself into the creamy channel that already dripped with readiness for him.

She squirmed eagerly, licking and nibbling at his ear. The tip of his thick cock pressed against her, promising fulfillment.

When he entered her, she let out a little gasp of pleasure and bowed her back, raising her breasts so he could reach them with his mouth.

He filled her completely. . . . They were two bodies with one mind and one purpose. She undulated against him, increasing the friction. His groan brought an answering sigh from her.

He staggered, struggling to retain his hold on her. Stumbling forward, he anchored her body on the wall.

The unforgiving plaster pressed against her bare shoulders and buttocks as he pounded into her. She clutched at him, not caring if she scratched him with her nails, knowing it would only excite him more. She needed to reach her peak. . . .

A horn sounded abruptly from the street below, shattering her vision and denying her climax. He stopped pedaling.

Sandy blinked into the eyepiece of the telescope as the familiar fantasy slipped away.

Across the street, the object of her lust reached for the sports drink sitting on the table next to his bicycle and tilted his head back to swallow the liquid.

"Damn." Sandy shook her head to clear the fantasy's lingering image, smiling ruefully. "You need to work on your staying power, Sweet Cheeks. You let me down."

Unknowing, her gorgeous neighbor resumed his exercise routine.

Sandy swiveled her telescope to scan the front of his building again.

Beyond her balcony, Uptown was coming alive for the night. If she leaned over, she could look down and see people drifting in and out of boutiques, eating at outdoor cafés or standing in line for tickets at the art house movie theater down the block.

Her sixth-floor condo was just north of downtown Dallas, in the shadow of the skyscrapers that dominated the north Texas sky.

Sandy focused on the apartments directly across from hers, checking to see if any of her regulars were home yet.

Her spying on the neighbors had begun accidentally a few months earlier, but during that time, she'd become attached to many of the people who lived across the street. In a curious sort of way, she felt like their guardian, keeping an eye on them to make certain everything was all right. She'd even intervened once by calling the police when she'd thought someone was in danger. Of course, she'd called in the report from a pay phone down the street.

Yes, there were Mr. and Mrs. Kinky, the young couple on the fifth floor. They were in their kitchen preparing dinner. Knowing them, dinner would be part of the evening's foreplay.

Mr. Dominant, the penthouse tenant, wasn't home yet. She frowned and wondered if he was traveling again. He'd been gone a great deal recently, and she half hoped he was moving out. His sexual escapades made her queasy, but she couldn't stop herself from watching.

Unlike the open latticework balconies of the apartments across the street, Sandy's balcony was solid brick. She hadn't furnished it with hanging plants or wind chimes or anything that might draw attention. The only item on hers was a tall ficus tree. The hundreds of dark green leaves quivered in the pleasant September air and, more importantly, helped to conceal her telescope. Her customary black slacks and lightweight black pullover—selected for their slimming effect—helped her to blend in with the shadows.

An evening breeze blew a strand of black hair across her eyes.

She brushed at it impatiently, wishing she had tied back the shoulder-length curls.

Her hands trembled, and she felt the fluttering of excitement in her belly from her fantasy workout. It was the same each weekend. No matter how often she spied on her neighbors, the thrill never waned.

More tenants returned home and switched on their lamps. The flat face of the building across the street resembled a checkerboard with alternating squares of light and dark. She slowly rotated the body of the telescope, trying to find activity. Mrs. Blue Hair, the elderly woman on the fourth floor, had been sick lately. Sandy was glad to see she was feeling well enough to host her Friday-night bridge group. Three other women sat at a table in the living room, playing cards and chatting.

She checked Mr. and Mrs. Kinky's apartment again.

"Oh, wow! Hey, guys, that's some gourmet meal you're whipping up there."

The good-looking young couple was stark naked, lying on their sides in the sixty-nine position on a Chinese black lacquered dining table. The wife was busy sucking her husband's penis while the husband masturbated his wife.

Sandy shook her head. "You two are unbelievable. Every time I think I've seen it all, you raise the bar another notch." She tightened the knob to focus on the action and smiled as the wife reached orgasm with a mouth-open scream. "You go, girl."

Mr. K.'s hips moved more rapidly now, and using one hand, he tried to press his wife's head closer toward his erection.

Mrs. K. was in no condition to meet his needs. Sandy saw the young blonde's face go slack. For the moment, the wife was in her own world. Her husband's dick slipped out of her mouth.

"Oh, oh. He's about to explode," Sandy whispered.

Sure enough, his cock began spewing ropes of cum everywhere.

Mrs. K. resurfaced, came alert and made a grab for her husband's wildly pumping penis, but it was too late. He bathed her with his cream.

"That's one virile man," Sandy said to herself. She continued to watch, a little worried that Mr. K. would be annoyed with his wife for not maintaining her hold on him and swallowing his semen.

To her relief, the young couple began to laugh. As they scrambled to sit up on the table, they held on to each other for support. The blonde wiped the cum off her face and neck and smeared it on her husband's chest. He leaned forward and licked her lips.

"That's it, guys," Sandy encouraged. "Celebrate each other."

The sight of the happily married couple made her feel wistful and even more alone than usual. It had been so long since she'd been part of a couple. Her sense of isolation brought her back to this balcony again and again. Sometimes she felt more connected to these anonymous neighbors than to anyone else in her life.

Satisfied that her young neighbors would be fine, Sandy shifted the body of the telescope again. She did a quick survey of the building to check on the anorexic model on the third floor and the elderly gay man on the fifth floor.

By nine o'clock, the penthouse tenant whom Sandy called Mr. Dominant returned home. A beautiful brunet woman Sandy had never seen before accompanied him. They sat on leather chairs in his living room, sipping wine and talking.

Sandy tightened her focus on the girl, who looked about twenty and had the porcelain skin and perfect features of an expensive doll. "Dolly, that's what I'll call you," she muttered. The woman's polite, attentive, yet somewhat blank expression suggested she was no stranger to the D/s world of Mr. Dominant.

Unlike the stationary biker, Mr. Dominant was not the big, bodybuilder type. He was a slim five-nine with a Mediterranean complexion and dark, wavy hair. His charming smile almost disguised his rather cruel mouth.

He leaned back against the leather cushions and studied his guest before barking a short command. Sandy saw his lips move and watched the girl stand and begin to unbutton her blouse.

Dolly never took her eyes off Mr. Dominant, who remained seated, watching as she slid the shirt off her shoulders. The black, lacy bra she wore drew attention to her smooth, white skin and made her look more vulnerable.

Sandy saw Mr. Dominant's lips move again. In response, Dolly unbuttoned her skirt. She pushed the material down over her hips until the garment puddled at her feet. Her sexy thong matched the bra.

Sandy wondered what it would be like to stand almost naked before a man sitting in cold judgment of her. A tremor rippled through her body at the thought. Did Dolly know what came next?

Dolly stood passively and waited. From past spying on Mr. Dom, Sandy knew his partner would take no action without being told to do so. Her heart began to beat faster, and she wondered if the girl felt half the tension she did.

He spoke again. Dolly leaned forward and reached behind her back to unhook her bra. As she freed the last hook, the lacy scrap fell off, and her breasts tumbled forward.

Dom stood and snapped out a command. The woman removed her panties, then stepped forward and knelt before him.

Sandy shivered. The sight of a naked Dolly at Dom's feet, staring worshipfully up into his eyes, disturbed her. At the same time, it was unquestionably erotic. Sandy opened and closed her fist, resisting the temptation to touch her tightening nipples.

Dom reached out his right hand to cup his companion's cheek. Dolly pressed her face into his hand and kissed it.

Dom shifted and slid his hand into Dolly's thick brown hair. *If she's a true submissive, she likes to subjugate herself to a master,* Sandy reminded herself, but when she saw him tighten his grip, she couldn't help whispering, "No, don't."

He seized Dolly by the hair and dragged the girl off her knees. She hung there, suspended in air between his fist and the floor, her face twisted in pain.

Still fully dressed, Dom pulled his nude captive across the room by her hair toward an ottoman in front of the fireplace. He shoved her in the direction of the oversized piece of furniture, and Dolly obediently crawled onto it. She knelt on top of the ottoman on her hands and knees with Dom towering over her.

Sandy knew what was coming. She had seen Dom place a submissive on the ottoman before. She squeezed her thighs together, savoring the feeling of warmth uncoiling between her legs.

He walked to an umbrella stand near the front door. After removing what appeared to be a rattan walking cane, he returned to stand behind Dolly. Sandy could not see his face and did not know if he said anything before he raised the cane and brought it down on Dolly's bare buttocks.

The girl arched her back as the rattan connected with her skin. Dom immediately raised his arm and brought the cane down in another wide arc, slapping it hard against Dolly's ass.

This time, Dolly lurched forward and fell halfway off the ottoman.

Dom shook his head, threw the cane on the floor and stomped away. Dolly turned toward him with a pleading expression, but didn't say anything.

He marched over to his desk and opened a drawer. Sandy knew what he kept in that drawer. Her shoulder muscles knotted with anxious tension.

The ringing of her telephone distracted Sandy from the scene across the street. For the space of another ring, she debated whether to answer it. If it was her mother, a nonresponse would start a cycle of calls every twenty minutes until Sandy picked up—even if it took until two in the morning. *Better get it over with now.*

She rushed toward the living room, brushing past the closed drapes, and picked up the phone on the fourth ring—right before the answering machine kicked in.

"Hello," she said breathlessly.

"You've been a bad girl, Alexandra Davis," a male voice greeted her.

"Who's this?" she demanded. It had to be one of her brothers or a friend.

"This is Justice." He paused, and Sandy tried to decide if the caller was her older brother, Matt.

"You've been spying on your neighbors. How do you think they'd feel if they knew?"

Sandy's heart stuttered. *No! This couldn't be happening.* No one could have seen her. She'd been too careful.

"I don't know what you're talking about," she replied in her coldest voice. "I'm going to hang up. If you call me again, I'll report you to the police." She slammed the receiver down.

OhgodOhgodOhgod! She bit her lip and stared at the phone. What if someone *had* seen her? Maybe someone knew. Reality came crashing down. If this came out, she could be arrested. She'd lose her job. No agency could have a sex offender employed as a social worker, going into homes with families. And her mother! Oh, dear heaven, what would her mother say?

Sandy forced her mind to function through the mounting panic. First, she needed to get the telescope off the balcony. She needed to sit down and think this through. . . .

The phone started to ring again. Sandy stared at it like a field mouse cowering before a snake. She made no move to pick it up. It rang a second . . . a third . . . and, finally . . . a fourth time.

The answering machine kicked in, and Sandy heard the male voice from before. "It's no good, Alexandra. You can't hide from Justice. If you don't believe me, go check outside your door. I'll wait."

# Chapter Two

Sandy's stomach muscles clenched. She looked toward the door and took an involuntary step backward. Was this a trick? Maybe he was waiting out there to grab her.

Almost as if he'd heard her thoughts, he said, "This isn't a trick. I'm not out there. Leave the chain on and look. I've left something for you."

She gnawed on her lower lip as she walked toward the door and looked through the peephole. No one outside. Didn't mean anything. He could be standing beyond the peephole's range of vision.

"Go ahead, Alexandra. Look," the voice from the machine encouraged.

Sandy unlocked the dead bolt, but left the safety chain in place. She eased the door open.

A large brown envelope sat on her welcome mat. She stretched her arm through the crack in the doorway, but the space wasn't wide enough for her to reach the envelope.

"Come on, Alexandra. I don't have all night."

She swung around to glare angrily at the phone. His calling her "Alexandra" made it worse. "Alexandra" was the name used by her mother, her boss and her gynecologist. All the connotations of "Alexandra" were negative.

Making a sudden decision, Sandy unlatched the chain, opened the door, grabbed the envelope, pulled back inside and slammed the door shut. It rattled in the doorframe.

"Good girl. Now, why don't you make yourself a strong drink before looking in that envelope? I'll call you back in a few minutes." The dial tone replaced his voice.

She stared in horror at the telephone. How had he known she'd opened the door and taken the envelope? Was he standing at the end of the hall, watching with a cell phone? *Sweet Lord, maybe I'd better call the police.*

Sandy staggered across the room toward a chair and dropped into it. If she called the police, what would she say to them?

No, she needed to think first. She needed to get that damn telescope off the balcony. She needed . . . a drink.

Standing, she rushed toward the small brass-and-glass serving cart that did double duty as her bar. She seized the first bottle she came to—Baileys Irish Cream. Still carrying both the bottle and the brown envelope, she headed for the kitchen to find a glass.

She poured the liquor with a trembling hand and then stared at the envelope lying on the marble countertop.

It was a plain brown nine-by-twelve envelope with a single clasp. There were no markings on it, not even her name.

After taking a deep swig of the Baileys, Sandy opened the envelope. A group of photos bound by a rubber band fell out.

Picking up the packet, she removed the band. She flipped through the pictures, and bile rushed into her mouth.

All of the photos were shots of her balcony. They had been taken with a telephoto lens and an exposure setting for low light. The photographer had been somewhere across the street—above the sixth floor because he had shot downward into her balcony.

In every picture, the telescope was obvious. So was Sandy. There were photos of her looking out from behind her draperies, carrying the telescope out to the balcony, adjusting the settings. It was clear that her telescope was not directed toward the night sky; it was almost level.

She stared in horror at images of herself looking into the telescope while rubbing her breasts and—sweet mercy!—with her hand inside her slacks, touching herself.

Her employment contract had a morals clause. Even if she wasn't arrested, these photos were enough to get her fired and, perhaps, take away her social work license.

Sandy slid off the barstool and raced toward the bathroom, getting there just in time to vomit up the contents of her stomach. She knelt in front of the commode, gagging and retching. So much for the stiff drink to settle her nerves.

She was washing her face when the phone rang again. This time, she didn't hesitate. She walked straight to the telephone and picked it up. "What do you want?" she snarled.

"Alexandra, Alexandra," the voice said in an admonishing tone. "You sound so angry. Now you know how your victims will feel once they realize what you've been doing. How you've invaded their privacy—"

"I asked, what do you want?" Sandy interrupted.

"Justice. Like I said before." The voice became businesslike. "There's something waiting for you downstairs at the desk. Go get it. I'll call you back in twenty minutes."

"I'm not going any—" Before she could finish the sentence, he hung up again.

Sandy stalled for nearly five minutes. She went out to the balcony and retrieved the telescope, bringing it inside and putting it away in the bedroom closet. After brushing her teeth to clear the nasty taste from her mouth, she checked her appearance in the bathroom mirror. Her face, pale at the best of times, was now bleached of all color. Sweat beaded her forehead, and her hands were trembling.

When she ran out of reasons to delay, Sandy called down to the security desk to ask if there had been a delivery for her. Russell, the night guard, confirmed there was.

She couldn't stand the suspense any longer. Picking up her keys, she left the condo and carefully locked the door behind her.

Even the gentle movement of the elevator made her want to throw up again. She swallowed and spent the rest of the short ride practicing deep breathing.

Russell greeted her with a smile. There were two boxes sitting on his desk. Both were wrapped in plain brown paper. One was large and square, while the other was longer and shallower.

Sandy tried to sound casual when she said, "Hi, Russell. Is one of these mine?"

"Hello, Ms. Davis." Russell was the first security guard she'd met when she moved into the high-rise six months earlier. Middle-aged and friendly, he was always willing to help a tenant.

He grinned. "I was just getting ready to telephone when you called down. You must be celebrating Christmas early. Both of these are for you."

"Both?" she squeaked, looking at the tops of the boxes. Sure enough, ALEXANDRA DAVIS was printed in block capitals on each wrapper. "Did you see who dropped them off?"

"Nope. I was helping Mr. Caruthers from the third floor carry his groceries in. When I got back, they were waiting here. One of them is pretty heavy."

She tried lifting the boxes. The shallow one was easy to lift, but the other, larger box weighed at least twelve pounds.

"Thanks, Russell. I think I can manage."

"At least let me carry the big one to the elevator for you."

She didn't put up a fight, wanting only to get upstairs as quickly as she could.

When the elevator reached six, she carried the boxes to her condo. Once safely inside, she put them down and glared at them. No matter what they contained, it wasn't good news.

She decided to start with the shallow one first. After finding a steak knife in the kitchen, she cut the strapping tape that secured the package.

Midway through opening the box, she thought of fingerprints. If she decided to call the police, she should probably preserve his prints and not leave hers.

Dropping the knife, she went back to the kitchen, where she grabbed a pair of latex cleaning gloves. She returned, wearing the gloves, to finish removing the brown paper wrapper.

The box underneath was white cardboard and had a typed message taped to its top. *Open the other box first.*

By now, Sandy was wired so tight, she screamed at the box, "Stop telling me what to do!" Tears of frustration ran down her face, but she obeyed, shifting her attention to the second box.

This box had a note, too. It read, *Good girl. Open me first.*

"Bastard," she snarled. With trembling fingers, she slit the tape across the top and opened the flaps.

Inside were several items, each carefully packed in Bubble Wrap. Sandy lifted the first one out and began to unwind the protective layers.

"Oh, God. No."

It was a video camera.

The camera came with attachments and an instruction booklet. There was also a modular telephone with an array of more-than-standard buttons.

The implications of the camera terrified Sandy. She was not going to perform for this sick bastard. The photos were bad enough. If she gave him videos, she'd never be free.

She should call the police or maybe one of her brothers. If she came clean, perhaps she could get some help in finding this madman and expelling him from her life.

The phone rang again, interrupting her thoughts. She snatched up the receiver. "Who are you?" she demanded, her voice rising to a screech.

"Call me Justice," he replied. "Because that's what I'm going to get. Justice for all those people you exploited. Now, have you opened both boxes?"

"Just the camera and phone. I am not going to——"

"You're going to do exactly what I say," he snapped. "If you don't, the police will be on your doorstep in fifteen minutes. Open the other box."

Sandy closed her mouth so hard her teeth clicked audibly.

She shifted the receiver to her shoulder and grabbed the second, smaller box.

When she'd opened the flaps, white paper peeked out. She reached in, removed the top item and tore off its tissue wrapping.

Inside was a red satin, flowered jacquard bustier with black lace accents. It had a lace-up front and garters.

"No, no way," she whispered into the receiver.

"You'll look beautiful in it. I can't wait to see those big gorgeous breasts filling that up." Justice's voice had gone low and gravelly. "I'm getting hard just thinking about it."

Sandy was so shocked, she forgot to be scared for a moment. She licked her lips nervously. No man had ever said anything like that to her before. And she'd never owned anything so . . . sexy.

She checked the tag of the bustier. Sixteen. Exactly her size. How did he know? And what would it look like on?

Appalled to realize she was even thinking about it, she cried, "I won't do this."

"Yes, yes, you will, Alexandra. I'll—"

"It's Sandy," she butted in. "I hate 'Alexandra.'"

"Okay, Sandy. Tell you what. We can leave the rest of that box for later. We've still got work to do. Let's start with the telephone."

She hesitated. He'd already made it clear that he'd report her if she refused outright. She needed to buy some time to figure a way out of this mess. If she pretended to be totally cowed, maybe he'd be lulled into a sense of complacency. Besides, even if she did film herself, it didn't mean she had to hand the video over to him.

For the next fifteen minutes, Sandy obeyed Justice while operating on autopilot. She had to remove her cleaning gloves in order to follow his instructions to replace the phone in the living room with the one he'd sent. Justice explained that the new phone had a hands-free speaker feature that would permit them to talk without her having to hold a receiver. She cringed at the implication that her hands would be busy elsewhere.

"Can you hear me now?" he teased after she pushed the speakerphone button.

"Yes, I can," she answered, irritated to find her lips curving into a small smile. He was blackmailing her, but his teasing and flattery as they worked were clearly intended to seduce her into forgetting he was the enemy.

She looked at the phone again, speculating about Justice. Could he be one of the tenants from the building across the street? His voice sounded educated and authoritative, as though he was accustomed to being in charge.

She glanced toward the living room draperies, now securely closed. From the angle of the photos he'd taken of her, she knew they were shot from across the street above the sixth floor. Mr. Dominant's penthouse was on the seventh floor, but it couldn't be him because she had been watching Dom the first time Justice phoned.

"Good. Sandy, I can't stand it any longer. I need for you to put on that red teddy."

Sandy's breath caught in her throat. He really expected her to do this. She should be disgusted. But at some point in the last half hour, her body had started to respond to the low, intimate sound of his voice. That voice was the stuff of her fantasies. Warm, sexy, even tender.

"It's a bustier," she corrected automatically, shaking her head to dispel the dangerous, invasive thoughts.

"That's right. The teddy is the one without all the wires, isn't it? We'll get to that one later." His voice was silver-toned and seductive. "Put it on, baby."

The sound of the endearment hung in the room, making Sandy's heart beat faster. Only a short while ago, she had felt chilled with fear; now she felt flushed, hot. What was wrong with her? What was he doing to her?

Sandy fingered the satin and lace material of the bustier. She could pretend to be doing it. He wouldn't know. He couldn't see her, after all.

"My cock is hard just thinking about you. Help me out here."

Sandy's sex clenched at his words; her panties were soaked. Was he big? The question popped into her mind unbidden and, with it, an image. A man seated, his face in shadow, his thick shaft jutting proudly from between splayed legs. Waiting for her.

"All right," she said. "I'll put it on."

"Tell me what you're doing, everything you're doing." His voice was lower now, little more than a rough growl. Sandy felt her own excitement growing in response.

"I'm . . . removing my pullover," she mumbled, grabbing the hem of her shirt and yanking it up over her head.

"You're wearing black. You always wear black. It makes your skin seem even more pale and perfect."

"My ass is huge," she complained. Given her situation, it was a ridiculous statement, but she couldn't stop the familiar feelings of inadequacy that came with the thought. "I'm too fat."

"No, you're not, baby. You're Rubenesque. Three hundred fifty years ago, your body was the standard of beauty. You need to learn to appreciate all those lush, dimpled curves. I do."

His words calmed and emboldened her. Rubenesque. She liked the sound of the word. Sandy unbuttoned her slacks and removed them. "I'm taking off my pants."

"That's the girl. Now your bra. What color is it?"

"Flesh-toned." She grimaced. For once, she wished she were wearing a hot, lacy bra like the ones in the lingerie catalogs.

"Oh, baby, you need to wear black to contrast with all that luscious skin." His breathing sounded harsh. "I want to suck your breasts until you come. Have you ever come just from having your nipples sucked?"

"No," she whispered, afraid to admit how little experience she'd had.

"Too bad. Sounds like you've been running around with the wrong guys. Now your panties. Are they flesh-colored, too?"

"Yes," she lied, unwilling to describe the plain white cotton underwear she was actually wearing.

"Okay, Sandy. Slide them down. Now I want you to touch your pussy for me."

Sandy stifled a gasp. No man had ever used that word with

her before. It was the word reserved for her fantasies—forbidden, sensual, lonely fantasies. Despite her fevered body, she shivered. Her imaginary world was merging with her real world. Where would it take her?

"Pretend that it's me fingering you, making you wet. Can you do that?"

Mesmerized by Justice's voice, Sandy lay down on the couch and spread her legs. She slipped two fingers into her cleft and wasn't surprised to find herself dripping. It was that voice. He had the sexiest, most erotic voice she'd ever heard.

"I . . . I'm touching myself," she said out loud.

"Good, sweetheart. So am I. I had to open my pants and let my dick out because it was getting too tight in there."

"What does it look like?"

Her question met with silence, and Sandy felt herself blush. What was the matter with her? She didn't even know this man, and she was asking him to describe his cock. *He's blackmailing me, for Pete's sake.*

"What does *what* look like?" She heard the smile in his voice.

Whether it was the wickedness of what they were doing, or the sound of his voice, Justice's teasing emboldened her. "Your dick," she said boldly. "Describe it to me."

He inhaled sharply. Sandy smiled to herself, pleased to have surprised him.

"It's about eight inches long. I'm not circumcised, so it's thicker than most guys'. It's hard as a pike, and the tip is all purple with wanting you."

Sandy's breath caught at the image. "I wish I could see it," she breathed.

"I wish you could, too, baby. But, for now, reach into that box the bustier came in, and you'll find another gift from me."

# Chapter Three

andy sat up and stuck her hand into the box. Her knuckles brushed past layers of tissue and cardboard. "Is it inside another box?" she asked.

"No. Go all the way to the bottom. You'll find it."

She did. The minute her fingers curled around the hard length, she pulled it out. "It's a vibrator."

"No, honey. It's a dildo. Eight inches long and two inches wide—just like mine."

Sandy examined the dildo, her heart rate increasing. It was huge: black rubber with a curved body and a bulbous, mushroomlike tip. "Just like mine," he'd said. She ran a finger along the length, thrilling at the lifelike feel of veins and ridges. She could pretend that this was real, that this was Justice she was holding in her hand. The thought made her sex twitch.

"I want you to put it inside your pussy and pretend it's me."

She squeezed the tip. It gave, but not very much. "This is awfully big," she said in a small voice.

Justice didn't answer for several seconds. When he did, his voice was gentle. "Sandy, are you a virgin?"

She was instantly offended. "Of course not. I'm thirty-two. Do you think there's something wrong with me?" Okay, so she was overweight, but did he think she was a freak?

"No, sweetheart. But I needed to be sure. Listen. Just lie back and listen to me for a minute. Will you do that?"

"All right," she muttered, still annoyed with him. She shifted her body on the cushions, trying to get comfortable.

"I want you to take that dildo and rub it against the outside of your pussy. Just rub it back and forth while I tell you what I'm doing."

Sandy forgot her annoyance. She followed his instructions, wrapping her right hand around the circumference of the dildo and moving the rounded end along her slit. His words came back to her: "hard as a pike" with a tip that was "all purple." Her sex thrummed with excitement as she imagined his cock touching her flesh, his hands separating her thighs.

"I'm leaning back in my chair, holding my cock and wishing it was me instead of that rubber dick teasing your sweet lips." Justice's voice flowed over her like a length of fine silk. "I'd rub my dick back and forth over your pussy until you begged me to fuck you. But I wouldn't."

"You wouldn't?"

"No, not until you came for me once. That way, you'd be wet and welcoming when I slid inside your tight little hole." His voice was barely above a growl now. "I'd push in and out just a little at a time, until I felt you starting to come again. That's when I'd shove myself in so that we could come together."

Sandy pictured him leaning over her. His shoulders would be broad and tanned; his hands would be gentle and knowing. His face would be filled with love. . . .

She relaxed into the cushions of the couch and reached down with her left hand to part the lips of her labia. With her vagina exposed, she ran the dildo along the inside of her pussy in a gentle, rhythmic motion.

"Talk to me, Sandy," Justice growled. "What are you doing?"

"I'm getting the dildo wet," she answered.

"Yeah, my dick is leaking juice, too. I'm so ready for you."

Sandy caught her breath, excited by his raspy voice. Her vulva was weeping, and the dildo's bulb was slick with her fluids. She tried to insert the tip into her vagina and gasped at the contrast between its hardness and her softness.

"I wish I could taste your pussy," Justice said. "I'll bet you taste sweet. Like cinnamon candy."

Sandy trembled, and her muscles clenched on the thick rubber tip pressed against her entrance. She tried to imagine Justice's head between her thighs while he licked her. Excitement swept her. "What color is your hair?" she asked.

He laughed. "Wondering what I'd look like going down on you, baby?"

"Yes," she whispered.

There was no laughter in his voice when he said, "My hair is dark brown. I keep it cut short because it gets too curly otherwise.

"My tongue is long and hot and dying to lick you all over."

She wanted his mouth. She wanted his cock. She wanted this damn dildo inside her. Now. Taking a deep breath, she pushed it in.

Everything else fell away. Nothing else mattered. All feeling in her body became concentrated on that one place.

"Talk to me," Justice urged.

Sandy ignored him. The dildo was past her entrance, and she was adjusting to the intrusion. She shifted, and the discomfort suddenly morphed into pleasure. Friction ignited her nerve endings, spreading warmth down her thighs past her knees to her toes. She moaned, "It's in."

"That's my girl. Oh, baby," he groaned. "Shove my big hot cock all the way into that sweet little pussy. Let me fuck you, baby."

Listening to his magical voice, Sandy rocked her hips back and forth, moving the artificial penis at the same time. Ripples of delicious sensation washed over her. "Ohhh," she sighed.

"Honey. You did good. I can feel your tight little hole, and it's making me . . ." Justice voice trailed off. Sandy could hear him panting while he masturbated.

Eager to keep pace with him, she began moving the dildo faster up and down inside her vagina. The warmth that had begun in her genitals spread over her entire body. "It feels so nice."

"Yeah," he panted. "So nice."

Sandy plunged the rubber phallus in and out, each stroke faster and more confident than the last. Fluid lubricated her sheath, making movement easier. She bent her knees and pressed her bare feet against the arm of the couch. That spark of heat was now a blazing inferno. She clenched her ass and thigh muscles, wanting to savor every sensation. She could smell the musky scent of her own arousal. Justice's panting added to her excitement. She imagined him thrusting into her, her nails scratching down his long, muscular back. She closed her eyes—the better to fix an image of him in her mind.

"Are you ready to come, Sandy?" The strain in his voice was obvious.

"Not yet. I want this to last." She licked the sweat off her lips.

"Ooo-kay. I'll wait." His words didn't match the rhythmic grunts she could hear. "Oh, baby, I want to fuck you so bad. I want to bury myself in your flesh."

"I want that, too," she gasped. The heat in her belly felt like a burning lump of charcoal, searing her insides. She began to arch her body in an effort to reach for her orgasm.

"Sandy, I can't wait." His voice was urgent and demanding. "Come with me. Nooooowwww!"

His words pushed her over the edge. The thought of him losing control, and the knowledge that she was responsible for him losing control, excited her past reason. Sparks of light shot across the darkness behind her closed eyes. The colors would be next.

"I'm coming," she cried as the rainbow burst free of its prison of black.

Sandy's world exploded in a smear of bright colors and streaks of lightning. She bucked, swinging her hips back and forth in counterpoint to the phallus. Her vaginal muscles clamped down on the dildo, vainly trying to milk the artificial penis. Liquid gushed from her body, bathing the dildo and her right hand.

She'd never experienced so intense an orgasm. During her teenage years, she'd endured the clumsy groping and untutored fumblings of boys her own age. She'd been twenty and in college before she had her first orgasm. Since that first time, she'd had several relationships, but had never enjoyed the kind of passionate sex her girlfriends talked about. Nothing had prepared her for this moment. It had just never occurred to her that a disembodied voice and a piece of hard rubber could provide the most shattering climax of her life.

Justice's voice intruded. "Are you okay, Sandy?"

She was still trying to catch her breath. "Uh-huh," she gasped. Aftershocks coursed through her body.

"Baby, that was terrific. And it's only going to get better for us."

*For us.* His words hung in the silence between them. Sandy felt the hazy afterglow dissolve as reality set in. For "us"? There was no "us." She didn't even know his name and wouldn't recognize him on the street. He was blackmailing her.

Sandy sat up. When her juices began to leak out of her pussy, she lunged off the couch. She staggered toward the bathroom, holding the dildo in place with one hand.

"Sandy, talk to me," Justice called, his voice losing its pleasant fuzziness and taking on an edge.

In the bathroom, Sandy stepped into the tub and pulled the rubber penis out from between her legs. She felt a sense of loss wash over her body as she withdrew it. The dildo's exterior was coated with pussy juice. She dropped it into the tub.

Her cleft was still dripping and she grabbed a towel to mop herself dry.

"Sandy, where are you?"

She looked toward the living room and Justice's voice. Stepping out of the bathtub, she retrieved her robe from its hook behind the door. Once she had it on and the belt tied around her waist, she felt better, less shamed.

"Sandy!" Justice sounded more insistent.

"I'm here," she responded as she returned to the living room.

"What's going on, honey? You liked this. I know you did."

"Yes, damn it. That's the problem."

*"What's* the problem, baby?"

His continued use of endearments grated on her. "I'm not your baby, Justice. I'm your victim. What do you want?"

He let the silence sit between them for a moment before he said, "We just shared something great, and now you're pissed about it—is that it?"

Sandy felt the warmth of the blush that swept from her neck to her cheeks. "That's not what I'm saying."

"Then what are you saying, Alexandra?" he asked in a cool tone.

His use of the hated name flayed her. Every frown and reproving glance she'd received in her life had been accompanied by the name "Alexandra."

"I don't know what you want from me," she wailed. "I'm scared."

His voice softened. "Baby, you don't ever have to be scared of me. I'd never do anything to hurt you. Have I hurt you yet?"

"No," she whispered.

"Then give me a chance, Sandy, and give yourself a chance, too. You don't have to be on the outside, looking in all the time."

Suddenly cold, she hugged herself. Tears ran down her face, but she didn't remember starting to cry. In less than an hour, without physically touching her, this man had gotten inside her head and under her skin. He asked for her trust, but didn't give her any reason to trust him.

"I don't know what to say to you," she whispered.

"Then don't say anything. Let's stop for now. You've had a rough night and need a break. It's Friday. You can sleep late in the morning. What if I call you again tomorrow evening at seven thirty? We can talk some more then."

Sandy realized he was right; she was exhausted. All she wanted to do was crawl into bed and pull the covers up over her head. "Okay."

"Will you do two things for me?" he asked, still in that gentle voice.

She was immediately suspicious. "What?"

"There's a new Baroque exhibit at the Museum of Art. I read about it in *D Magazine*. Will you go see it tomorrow?"

He'd done it again. Completely disarmed her. "Why?"

"There are paintings by Rubens in that exhibit. You need to see them. And when you look at them, remember that I see you the way Rubens saw his models."

She didn't know how to answer that; instead of responding, she asked, "And the other thing?"

"Put the two boxes I sent you away for tonight. But tomorrow afternoon, when you get home from the museum, go through that second box and look at the items inside."

She felt an almost overwhelming sense of relief. Neither thing he was asking sounded difficult. She could agree, hang up and go to bed. "Okay," she said for a second time.

"Good girl. Get some rest. And promise me you won't peep anymore tonight."

"No, I'm going to bed." She didn't think she'd ever touch that telescope again.

"Good. Tomorrow will sort itself out. Good night." He hung up before she could answer.

She stood and looked around her living room, too tired to think. Turning, she walked toward the bedroom and the blessed oblivion of sleep.

Zeke Prada stared at the telephone. He wasn't sure what he'd started. And he sure as hell didn't know where it was going.

He'd been staking out the building across the street for three weeks now, and it was beginning to get to him. Watching a douche bag like Victor Cabrini abusing women was eating away at his soul. More than once, he'd wanted to race across the traffic on McKinney, break down the penthouse door and beat the living crap out of that wiseguy bastard.

Zeke was an undercover vice cop on loan to the organized-crime task force investigating Cabrini. The task force had a condo on the eighth floor in Sandy's building, where they maintained 24-7 visual and audio surveillance on Cabrini.

The night the operation began, Zeke had gone across the street to Cabrini's building to make sure that the stakeout post wasn't visible. He borrowed the keys from security, climbed to the roof and took a position above Cabrini's penthouse.

He could still remember every detail of that night. After weeks of scorching temperatures, the heat wave had broken, giving Dallas its first signal that summer would soon be gone. After he'd ascertained that Cabrini wouldn't be able to see the task force's observation post, he'd lingered on the roof, enjoying the pleasant evening.

It was purely chance that Sandy Davis chose that moment to quit peeping for the night. Her furtive movements as she carried the telescope back into her condo caught Zeke's attention.

His cop's intuition told him exactly what she'd been doing. Still, when he returned to the stakeout post, he didn't report her voyeurism to his partner. His excuse was that he had no proof she'd been spying. For all he knew, she could be an amateur astronomer observing the night sky.

Because of the seriousness of the Cabrini investigation, the stakeout members were putting in long days. Teams of two worked twelve-hour shifts, four days on, three days off. Zeke waited until his next free night to return to that rooftop and check out Sandy's balcony. This time, he brought along a camera with a telescopic lens.

By then, he'd had four days to observe Cabrini in action with his sexy little submissives. None of their bondage/discipline games aroused him as much as Sandy did—alone in the dark touching herself.

Once more he neglected to report the voyeurism. He told himself that, technically, he was off duty and would turn in the report once he got back to work. In the meantime, he spent his off-hours running a check on her identity and background.

By the time he returned to duty again, Zeke knew Alexandra Davis: where she worked, shopped and banked. He even knew her credit score. He'd been curious as to how a social worker could afford so expensive a condo. It turned out that she'd inherited a tidy little sum when her father had died a few years earlier.

He wasn't sure what it was about Sandy that intrigued him so much. Maybe it was the dichotomy: During the day she was this prim little do-gooder, while at night, she turned into Batgirl—dressed in black and hiding in the shadows.

Zeke began looking forward to his off-duty time so he could spend those days following and watching Sandy. He soon realized she was as isolated as he was. She had a few girlfriends with whom she went shopping and to the movies. She went out to dinner one night with some guy. But mostly, she remained alone, on her balcony watching others. He'd spent long hours trying to imagine what she was thinking out there by herself in the dark.

He knew he needed to shut her down. As the task force closed in on Cabrini, Zeke couldn't risk the mobster spotting her and realizing he was under surveillance.

Zeke was no longer kidding himself that he would turn Sandy in. His growing obsession with her scared him. By mid-September, he knew he couldn't delay any longer. He needed to develop a plan to frighten her into quitting her voyeuristic hobby, and he needed to get on with his own life.

Zeke's uncle owned an electronics store and loaned him the video equipment and telephone he needed to scare Sandy straight. The task force had a set of her building's master keys, and he'd made his own copies. There was a vacant condo on the sixth floor, two doors down from Sandy's. After setting up base in that space, Zeke called her on his cell phone and watched from behind the front door as she snatched the envelope of photos off her welcome mat.

But something went wrong.

Not at first. His scheme had worked. He was abrupt and threatening, and she was clearly terrified. And then, without warning, he'd departed from the script. He'd intended to bully her with obscene demands, not seduce her.

Zeke knew what had thrown him off stride. It was the mental picture of Sandy holding that damn bustier in her hands. Suddenly he was touching himself and asking her to do the same.

Maybe Cabrini's bondage and discipline fantasies had stirred him up more than he realized. Maybe he'd gone too long without sex. Maybe he was cracking up. All he knew was that the thought of plunging his dick into Sandy's moist heat nearly undid him.

Her ready acquiescence excited him, while her insecurity touched his heart. But he couldn't fix her. He wasn't a psychiatrist, and she had enough money to hire her own damn shrink anyway.

He'd wait until tomorrow morning, knock on her door and tell her the truth.

Zeke shook his head in irritation. What the hell was he going to say to her? He'd forced her into virtual sex. If she reported him, he'd be fired for sure.

No, there was no way he could admit his identity to her. He needed to forget this whole thing. He'd already scared her. She wasn't going out on that balcony to spy on her neighbors again.

He needed to wait until she left her condo in the morning, let himself into her place with his master key and collect the video camera and telephone. Once he returned the equipment to his uncle Max, he needed to walk away. He'd forget about calling her tomorrow night. She'd come home to find everything gone and then wait for his call, worrying that he was going to turn her in to the cops. Eventually, she'd realize she was off the hook.

But there were a couple of problems with that plan. First, Sandy would be terrified by his easy access to her condo. She'd probably change the locks and spend sleepless nights worrying that he'd return to rape her. Or maybe she'd decide that the reason he didn't contact her again was that she was too unattractive. He hated the idea of adding to her pain. She was insecure enough already.

The second problem hit closer to home. Their little exercise in phone sex was among the best he'd ever had. He prided himself on his control and couldn't remember the last time he'd lost it like that. Probably not since he was seventeen and so full of testosterone that he spent his days walking around with a third leg.

Just thinking about Sandy made his cock stand up and salute. The truth was, he didn't want to walk away.

What the fuck was he going to do? How was he going to get out of this mess without hurting either one of them?

# Chapter Four

Sandy woke at nine thirty on Saturday morning feeling more relaxed than she'd been in weeks. She lay sprawled among her pillows, thinking about the previous night.

She'd always been a careful person, organized and controlled. Nothing at all like that woman last night who'd stripped naked and masturbated with a dildo while talking dirty with a stranger over the phone.

The thing was, she couldn't remember ever being that excited before—even when she'd been in bed with Josh.

Sandy had dated Josh Shaw for about four months until he broke up with her—right before her thirtieth birthday. He started dating her younger sister, Tricia, three weeks later. Now he and Tricia were engaged, a little piece of news that had been worth a weight gain of another fifteen pounds.

She hadn't been to bed with a man since Josh. It wasn't that she'd been in love with him; in fact, she was fairly certain she wasn't. But she'd still been crushed by his rejection and his subsequent embrace of her petite sister. Sandy couldn't help but wonder if her being overweight had been a turnoff for Josh. Since he'd left, the thought of undressing in front of a potential lover had been more than she could bear.

Maybe that was why last night had been so fantastic. She'd been able to enjoy all the excitement with none of the shame. Well, at least none of the shame until it was over.

Eager to forget that moment, she jumped out of bed and headed toward the shower. She had errands to run, and she was having lunch with her friends Dora and Leah at noon. If she had time, she might even stop by the Museum of Art and take a peek at that Baroque exhibit.

Sandy was already seated in D'Maggio's garden atrium with a view of the entrance when Leah Reece breezed in. The maître d' and waitstaff leaped to serve Leah—unlike when Sandy had arrived and had to wait several minutes for someone to notice her.

It wasn't Leah's style to follow passively behind the maître d'; she came striding toward Sandy with the host following in her wake like a tugboat behind a sleek oceangoing sailboat. Leah's blond good looks and confidence attracted attention from other diners, especially the men.

It had always been this way. Sandy and Leah had met in junior high when Leah transferred in during the middle of the school year.

The daughter of millionaire magazine entrepreneur Tex Reece, Leah was a lanky tomboy, uninterested in the usual teenage girl pursuits. Instead of rock, she listened to jazz. Instead of cheerleading, she'd signed up for the school newspaper. Within days, she'd become a favorite target of the small clique of teen girls who dominated the ninth-grade social scene. Leah's indifference to her ostracism only inspired the queen bees to ratchet up their efforts to torment her.

By the end of her first week in the new school, the other girls were avoiding Leah, obedient to the dictates of the populars.

Unimpressed by the nasty comments and snide looks cast her way, Leah had carried her lunch tray to the table where Sandy sat alone, reading a novel. "Mind if I sit here?" she'd asked. The two had been friends ever since.

"Hey, girlfriend," Leah greeted Sandy now. "Been waiting long?"

Sandy shook her head. "No. How are you?"

Leah slipped into the seat held for her and accepted a menu. "Busy as ever. You?"

On the way to the restaurant, Sandy had struggled with whether to tell Leah and Dora about Justice. If anyone would listen without passing judgment, it was Leah. At the same time, Sandy winced at the thought of describing her peeping activities to anyone else.

Dora arrived before Sandy could decide whether to share her secret or not.

Theodora Perkins was the bouncy auburn-haired real estate agent who had helped Sandy find her condominium. During their house-hunting forays, the two had become friends.

The women ordered lunch. Sandy followed her friends' lead and ordered a grilled chicken salad instead of the Monte Cristo sandwich she'd been eyeing on the menu.

"So, how are things at *Heat?*" Sandy asked after the waiter left with their orders.

*Heat* was Leah's baby, her claim to fame. A popular online magazine targeting the twenty- to thirty-four-year-old Gen-Y demographic, *Heat* boasted cutting-edge articles and chat rooms where subscribers could post photos and meet in the virtual world. Against her father's advice, Leah had started the zine with an inheritance from her grandmother. She was both the publisher and the executive editor.

"Things are great. Kadeem Brickman's agreed to be my guest art director for April."

"Kadeem . . . you mean the black movie director?" Dora's eyes widened.

Leah nodded, grinning. "Yup. He's contracted for a five-day shoot with the overall theme of 'power sex.' *Slate*, eat your heart out." She reached for a breadstick.

"Power sex?" Sandy frowned. "What's that?"

Leah rolled her eyes. "You know, dominance and submission. Bondage and discipline."

Sandy almost dropped the glass she was holding. Her mouth worked soundlessly while she tried to think of something to say.

Dora jumped in. "Oh, Lord, Leah. You're not really going to devote a whole issue to bondage and discipline, are you? This is Dallas, heart of the Bible Belt."

"Don't kid yourself, honey," Leah said. "BDSM is alive and well in Big D." She snapped the breadstick into two pieces.

Sandy's mind skipped to the previous night and watching Dom and Dolly. It was the perfect way to introduce the subject of her peeping and Justice.

Leah was still talking. *"Heat* is all about popular culture, and BDSM is a part of that culture. Besides"—she brought a piece of the breadstick to her mouth and ran it sensually across her lower lip—"this is the first time Kadeem's ever done a magazine spread. With the combination of his name and the subject matter, I'll blow my competition away." Her red lips curved upward. "Can you imagine Daddy's reaction?"

Sandy winced. Tex Reece was the prototype of the politically conservative, business-savvy Texan. She could well picture his reaction to the news.

"And, I've gotta tell you"—Leah lowered the breadstick— "I'm really looking forward to meeting this guy. He's the hottest thing I've seen in ages. I could eat him with a spoon." She glanced at Dora. "Enough about me. Have you nailed that good-looking boss of yours yet?"

Dora shrugged, and Sandy's heart ached for her. For the past year, Dora had worked for a licensed Realtor named Greg Stanford. When she'd suggested they see each other outside of the office, Greg had made it clear he didn't believe in fraternizing with his staff. Although Dora pretended to laugh about it, Sandy suspected the wound went deeper than her friend was willing to acknowledge.

Dora kept her voice light. "Nope, and it doesn't look like I ever will." Obviously wanting to change the subject, she looked toward Sandy. "What's up with you?"

Once again, Sandy teetered on the brink of indecision. She wanted to tell them about Justice. But what if they freaked out? Sandy knew her friends. If she thought Sandy was in danger, Leah would take steps to protect her, including calling the police.

In that instant, Sandy finally admitted to herself just how much she was looking forward to talking to Justice again. She wasn't going to do anything that might interfere with another call from him.

Besides, Leah and Dora were always urging her to take more chances. Well, tonight she was going to do just that.

Zeke returned to the main gallery of the Dallas Museum of Art for the second time in ten minutes.

He'd followed Sandy to lunch at D'Maggio's and had taken a corner table off to the side, where he wouldn't be noticed.

During the three weeks he'd been tailing Sandy, he'd seen her with both of these friends before. They had been giggly and playful together, obviously very comfortable in one another's company.

Today, Sandy seemed quiet and thoughtful. He wondered if she was debating whether to tell her friends about last night.

If she'd considered sharing, he didn't think she'd gone through with it. There were no shocked expressions, no urgent whispers. The conversation didn't seem to be anything but light chatter.

While Leah attracted most of the eyes in the room, it was Sandy's face that held Zeke's rapt attention. For not the first time, he reflected on how much she reminded him of the statue of the Madonna to the left of the pulpit in the Catholic church where he'd served as an altar boy. Her flawless pale skin, heart-shaped face and huge eyes were the embodiment of innocence.

*Maybe that's it. Maybe it's because I know about the sexy dark side of her beneath all that innocence that she turns me on so much.*

Whatever it was, he could barely look away from her face while she ate. He relived their phone conversations in his imagination and felt his cock stir to life.

Lunch lasted barely an hour. Afterward, he'd followed Sandy while she'd run several errands. It was now after three o'clock, and she'd finally pulled into the underground garage beneath the DMA.

Because he knew where she was headed, Zeke had stopped off at the men's room and then taken a leisurely route to the main gallery. When he'd looked in the first time, the room had been filled with elderly people—obviously part of a tour. He'd quickly scanned the room, determined Sandy wasn't there and taken another loop through the museum.

This time around, the geriatric art lovers had moved on, and Sandy was standing in front of a large oil by Rubens.

Zeke stood in the arched doorway, wishing he could get a better look at her face. He took two steps into the room.

When Sandy turned to her right to view the next painting, he looked down quickly at the brochure he'd picked up at the entrance. He pretended to be studying it while she drifted around the room.

She stopped in front of the largest painting in the exhibit. It was Zeke's favorite: Bathsheba bathing on the roof of her house.

The figure of Bathsheba dominated the center of the painting. She was nude, her skin pink and glowing. Two attendants knelt before her: one with a ewer of water and the other with a towel. In the near distance, King David stood on the roof of his palace, watching.

Rubens had painted Bathsheba in loving detail. Her light brown hair was pinned up, with graceful tendrils trailing to her shoulders. A strand of beads circled her forehead, giving the impression of a pearl tiara.

Bathsheba's breasts were exquisite: full and round with pale pink nipples. Zeke's mouth went dry as he looked from Sandy's porcelain face to the sumptuous breasts of the woman in the painting.

The irony of King David observing the naked woman from the rooftop was not lost on Zeke. He remembered the first night he'd seen Sandy from across the street. All his actions since that moment had seemed preordained somehow. He wondered whether David had felt the same compulsion he was experiencing. *Of course, he must have. He schemed to kill Bathsheba's husband, didn't he?*

Sandy's face was rapt. Her cheeks were tinted a delicate rose color. He wondered if she was thinking about David watching Bathsheba, too. She moved closer to the painting, and Zeke saw a museum guard take a step in her direction.

Sandy didn't touch the painting. She just leaned toward the canvas as though mesmerized by it. Zeke felt his erection pressing against the confines of his pants. He folded his hands on his stomach with the brochure dangling, covering the front of his jeans.

After what seemed an eternity, Sandy shook her head as though waking from a dream. She glanced around with a guilty expression and moved to the next oil.

*Let it go, Prada,* Zeke warned himself. *No good can come from this. Get the hell out of here, and stop mooning over her. You're not going to call her tonight. If this goes wrong, you could lose your job, your career, and maybe even end up in the slammer. And you know what happens to cops on the inside.*

Sandy moved to a bench positioned in front of a small pair of matching paintings. For the first time, he could see her nipples outlined against the fabric of her blouse.

*Shit! She's as turned on as I am.*

He gritted his teeth against the sudden impulse to walk up and lean over to whisper in her ear.

*What the hell do you think she'll do if you come up behind her like that? She'll scream bloody murder, and you'll be on the six o'clock news with a headline reading "Sexual Stalker Cop." Get out of here now.*

With reluctance, he moved toward the doorway, casting one last hungry look at the figure sitting with her back toward him.

Sandy stomped around her condo, looking for something to throw. It was eight ten p.m. Justice had said he'd phone at seven thirty, but he hadn't called. She should have known. Even her sexual blackmailer didn't find her interesting enough to pursue.

Hot, angry tears filled her eyes. She glanced toward the kitchen, thinking about the half gallon of Rocky Road ice cream in the freezer.

The ringing phone interrupted her pity party. She rushed to pick up the receiver. "Hello."

"Sandy," Justice's voice greeted her.

"Where have you been?" she blurted out before she could stop herself. "You said you'd call at seven thirty." She winced at the whine in her tone.

"I know, sweetheart. I'm sorry."

"Where were you?" God, what had come over her? She

sounded like a woman who'd been stood up by a date. This was her blackmailer, not her lover.

"Right here, trying to decide whether to call you or not."

"Why?"

He hesitated before saying, "Ask me again another time. For now, tell me about your day."

Sandy sighed, happy just to be talking with him again. She refused to allow herself to examine how important he had become to her in less than twenty-four hours. "I did some shopping and had lunch with friends."

"Did you go to the museum?"

"Yes." She gathered her courage. "Those paintings. Is that really the way you see me?"

"Tell me what *you* saw in those paintings." His voice was rich and seductive—like a warm caress down her spine.

"There was a painting of Bathsheba in the nude. She was so beautiful. I mean, all of Rubens' women had thick waists and stomachs, but they looked so sexy."

"You mean they had lots of curves and glowing bodies—just like you."

Sandy's heart swelled at his words. Did he mean it? Was it possible? Or was he mocking her? "Do you honestly find . . . plump women sexy?" she asked.

"I find *you* sexy. Did you look in the second box this afternoon?"

"Yes. I couldn't believe some of that stuff."

"Did any of it excite you?" His voice was lower now with a richer tone.

"The teddy. I've never seen anything like it. I didn't know they made—"

"Sandy," he interrupted. "Let's hook up the camera and then you can put the teddy on for me."

She didn't hesitate. Even if she filmed herself, it didn't mean she had to give him the finished video. Punching the speaker-phone button, she said, "Tell me what to do."

Justice had her remove the camera from its box and plug in the long attachment cord. Then he suggested she get a step stool and a screwdriver.

When she returned to the living room, he told her to climb up to the central-air-conditioning vent in the ceiling and un-screw it.

Sandy climbed on the step stool. "I don't understand. What am I doing up here?" she asked.

"You'll see in a minute," he assured her.

Using her screwdriver, she removed the overhead vent. A length of black electrical cord fell out of the space, hitting her shoulder.

"There's a cord up here," she said in surprise.

"That's right, honey. When you plug that cord into the cam-era, we'll have direct feed between us."

"Direct . . . ? You mean like a closed-circuit television?"

"Exactly. I'll be able to watch you from here."

"Where's here?" she demanded. "Are you in this building?"

"Stop asking so many questions, woman, and plug in the damn camera."

Sandy stepped off the stool. She hadn't anticipated this. All along, she'd figured she could make the videotape, but not give it to him. A closed-circuit system meant Justice had a monitor and—probably—a recorder set up somewhere nearby. Once she hooked up the camera, there was nothing to stop him from filming everything she did.

"I don't know about this," she said.

"Come on, baby. I'm dying to see you. You *want* me to see you, don't you?"

"I'm not Paris Hilton. I don't want videotapes of me floating all over the place."

"I'm not going to tape you, honey. I just want to watch you pleasure yourself."

"Forgive me if I don't believe you," she snapped.

He didn't argue. "Sandy, when you were going through the box today, did you find the mask?"

"Yes." She'd wondered about the elaborate piece of artwork with feathers and spangles; reminiscent of Mardi Gras, it would cover most of her face to the tip of her nose.

"If you won't believe me when I say I won't record this, you can wear that mask, and no one will recognize you even if there is a tape."

Although her intellect said not to do it, Sandy's intuition screamed at her to take a risk for once. For a short time last night, she'd been a different woman. Brave, sensual, exciting. She wanted to be that woman again. She wanted to trust Justice. To make him beg, to hear him moan—first in supplication and then in surrender.

Sandy walked over to the box and rummaged around until she found the mask. He was right. She could conceal her identity with this.

"If I change my mind, you won't argue with me?"

"Absolutely. If you try and can't do it, we'll forget all about the camera."

Sandy still wasn't sure she believed him, or that she even cared if he was telling the truth. *Her* truth was that she felt more alive than she had in months, in years. Her blood was racing, her body tingling, anticipating the pleasure to come. She didn't want to lose that feeling.

It took nearly forty minutes before the camera was set up. Sandy's fingers were clumsy in their excitement. She kept dropping things and having to get down off the step stool to retrieve the screwdriver or a fallen screw. Justice was patient, never raising his voice, never pushing her to hurry.

"You went through a lot of trouble running wire all the way down to this condo," she commented. "How did you do it?"

"I'm a resourceful kind of guy."

"Why not just have me make a videotape for you?"

"Because then we couldn't have simultaneous orgasms. I want to come while I watch you climax."

His words made her stomach muscles contract. Once more, he'd given voice to her most secret fantasy. This was so surreal. She squeezed her thighs together, enjoying the sensation of the silky material brushing against her sex. Her labia were wet, her body responding to the promise of things to come.

She picked up the mask, slipped it on and moved in front of the camera. After taking a deep breath, she flipped the switch that turned the camera on.

"Can you see me now?" she asked.

"I can see you perfectly. Strip for me, Sandy."

A shiver of anticipation rippled through her body. She stared at the camera lens like a rabbit caught in the glare of a flashlight.

"Come on, baby. Don't be afraid. Undress for me."

She put her fingers on the first button of her blouse, slowly undoing it. Her fingers slid to the second button ... and the third.

"Honey," he grumbled, "if you don't hurry up and take that damn blouse off, I'm gonna come down there and rip it off you myself."

She smiled, pleased to know she had some power over him, after all.

When the blouse was completely undone, Sandy turned her back to the lens without removing the shirt. Looking over her shoulder toward the camera, she began to unzip her slacks.

"Sandy! Turn around and face me," he commanded.

"This is my show, Justice. If you don't like the program, change the channel." Her boldness surprised Sandy. She had never taken charge of a sexual situation before.

"You still haven't taken that damn shirt off," he griped.

"Patience." She smiled mischievously.

After undoing the slacks, she let them drop to her ankles. The shirttails covered her ass.

"Are you still with me, Justice?" she asked.

"I'm dying here. This isn't the way I pictured this moment."

"You can't always have things the way you'd like," she replied.

Sandy reached up to remove the clip holding her hair back. She freed her curls, shaking the shoulder-length tresses out.

"Oh, honey," Justice moaned.

Slowly turning to face the camera, Sandy held the two edges of her blouse together, concealing her body.

"How are you doing, cowboy?" she asked.

"Holding my breath, baby. Let me see those beautiful tits. Please."

Sandy gave silent thanks to the impulse that made her don Justice's black teddy earlier in the evening. She opened the shirt, giving him a glimpse of the black lace, but keeping her hands strategically placed to hide her breasts.

"Damn! You're wearing it," he groaned. "I'm getting hard just seeing all that lace."

"Good," she encouraged. "That's what we want." Turning sideways, she began to slide the blouse off her shoulders.

"Damn it, Sandy. Turn around. I want to see you."

Smiling inwardly, Sandy let the blouse fall to the floor. She swiveled to face the camera's eye, covering her nipples with two fingers from each hand.

When Sandy had first seen the teddy, she'd been shocked to realize there was no material to cover the breasts—only reinforced silk underneath two open holes through which the wearer's bare tits would protrude.

After she put the garment on, she found her naked breasts completely encircled by bands of lace and held up by the teddy's shoulder straps. She'd been thrilled with the sight of her own body in the lacy garment, her breasts thrusting out. She looked seductive and sexy.

"God, Sandy, you're beautiful," Justice breathed. "Let me see your nipples. I've been wondering what color they are."

"What color do you think?" she asked in an arch tone.

"I've seen women with brown nipples and red nipples, but I think yours will be pale, pale pink."

Pleased beyond words, Sandy dropped her hands, revealing her pale, pale pink nipples.

"Awwwww. I knew it," Justice whispered. "Damn, they're gorgeous. I want to suck them so bad."

Sandy ran her fingertips over the nipples, squeezing and tweaking them until they hardened.

"Honey, drag a chair over in front of the camera so you can sit where I can see you." he pleaded.

Sandy pulled an overstuffed chair across the hardwood floor into the camera's line of sight. She perched on the edge of the seat and waited.

"Good. Now lean back."

Sandy followed his instructions, slumping backward into the forest green upholstery.

"Now spread your legs and raise them over the arms of the chair."

Sandy could already feel her sex throbbing. Exposing herself to Justice this way was the most daring thing she'd ever done.

Justice's voice was shaking. "There's a button on the bottom of that teddy to open the crotch."

"I know," Sandy said. "Would you like me to open it?"

"Please, God, yes," he muttered.

"Only if you open your pants first," Sandy demanded.

"Way ahead of you, babe. My jeans are already down around my ankles. My dick is so hard, I could use it to batter down doors."

Sandy laughed deep in her throat. She loved being able to affect him in the same way he affected her. "Are you sure you're watching this, Justice?"

"Yes, damn it. Now will you open that damn button?"

Sandy slid her right hand between her legs and unhooked the crotch closure. The thin silk was already soaked. "I'm so wet," she said.

"Ohhhh. Sandy, touch yourself for me."

"Are you touching yourself?"

"Baby, I'm making like an eggbeater."

Sandy giggled. She parted her nether lips to find her clit. Using a circular motion, she began to fondle her pleasure button. The tiny organ hardened, and she could feel it swelling. She thrust her hips forward.

"Touch your breasts, Sandy. Squeeze those pretty pink nipples."

Her left hand had been resting on her belly. Now she raised it and began to stroke her breast.

"That's it, baby. You look good enough to eat."

Yielding to impulse, Sandy removed her right hand from her clit and held up her fingers. They were slick with juice from her pussy. She held them out toward the camera and then slowly brought her hand toward her lips. Without saying a word, she began licking her fingers.

Despite the musky scent, her fingers tasted spicy. Her left hand remained on her breast, rubbing and squeezing the nipple.

"Oh, honey," he breathed.

She twisted her hand, inserted it into her mouth and began sucking her fingers. Justice's sudden gasp told her she had his attention. Tilting her head backward, she raised her hand so that she was simulating the act of sucking a man's penis. In this position, he'd have a clear view of her throat muscles moving as she mimicked swallowing a load of cum.

"Damn it, Sandy!" Justice groaned. "I'm about to explode."

"Not yet," she mumbled around her fingers. Removing her hand from her mouth, she sat up. "Not until we play with some of the toys Santa left me."

# Chapter Five

Sandy reached for the shallow box sitting on the coffee table and began digging through it. Glancing over her shoulder toward the camera, she asked, "Any special requests?"

Justice's voice was strained. "The nipple clamps." His obvious effort to sound casual amused her.

"You mean these?" She held up the nipple device, which consisted of two small, rubber-tipped alligator clips linked together by a length of silver chain.

"Yeah." For some reason, he didn't seem capable of constructing full sentences. She controlled her smile.

"Okay, that's your toy. Now we need to find something for me." Sandy was astounded at how easily she'd slipped into the dominant role in their sex play. She continued rooting around in the box before removing what looked like a silver egg attached by a cord to a control device. "A vibrating egg. This should do it." She held up the vibrator so that he could see it.

Sandy heard the whoosh of breath as he exhaled. She carried her toys to the overstuffed chair and sat back down.

"Let's see," she said, pretending to be confused. "How do these clamps work?"

"You're killing me," he muttered.

Sandy turned to the right, using her arm to block the camera's view of her breasts. She picked up the nipple device and squeezed one of the spring-loaded clamps. The rubber tips parted and the clip opened. She placed it over her left nipple and released. It snapped shut, seizing and gripping her tit.

"Owwww." Sandy hunched forward in an instinctive move to ease the biting pain. Her hands fluttered toward the clamp, on the verge of yanking it off. She hesitated, knowing that Justice was watching.

After another moment, she straightened, took a deep breath and waited for the discomfort to lessen.

In a couple of seconds, the pain was much less intense, and she turned her attention to the other clamp. This time, when putting it on, she released the spring-loaded device very slowly and was rewarded by only a slight twinge of pain.

"Sandy, let me see you." Justice's voice was urgent.

She turned sideways, giving him a view of her breasts. The ache on her left breast had diminished, giving way to a tingling warmth. Her tits felt unbelievably sensitive, as though a lover had been nibbling on them for hours.

"Well, what do you think?" she asked Justice.

"You look amazing." His voice was strangled, and Sandy decided the pain was worth it. She rubbed her thighs together, enjoying a new rush of arousal.

The vibrator was still beside her where she'd dropped it while examining the clamps. She picked it up and studied the control device. It appeared to be relatively simple with a toggle power switch and five speeds. She looked toward the camera lens.

"This is to stimulate my clit, right?"

He didn't immediately answer, and she called to him. "Justice."

"Sorry, babe. I was too busy looking to talk. I forgot you couldn't see me and just nodded."

"Well, then, let's get started." She leaned back against the cushions, spreading her legs wide and draping them over the arms of the chair. The movement tugged at the silver chain that connected her breasts. She gasped as waves of pain and pleasure swept her body.

When she could breathe evenly again, Sandy turned on the vibrator and set its speed on low. She picked up the egg and pressed it against the folds of her pussy.

She slid the vibrator up and down. The throbbing stimulation combined with the pressure of the clamps on her nipples was almost too much to bear. "My God," she whispered.

Using the fingers of her left hand, Sandy parted her nether lips to press the vibrator directly against her clit.

"Ohhhhhhh," she moaned.

"Move your hands out of the way," Justice begged. "I want to see."

Sandy ignored him. "It feels soooooo good." She shifted her weight to one hip so she could see the vibrator's control device. With her index finger, she moved the thumbwheel from its lowest setting to the middle setting.

The sensual jolt almost knocked her off the chair. Sandy writhed in ecstasy, her toes curling and her thighs pressing in an attempt to hold the egg even closer. Without thinking about it, she began moving her hips in a humping rhythm. The egg slipped slightly, deeper into her labial folds.

"Sweet mercy," she murmured. She pushed the egg back toward her clitoris.

"Sandy, open your legs," Justice wheezed. His voice sounded as though he'd been running a race.

Obediently, she spread her legs apart.

"Your pussssy'ssss so beautiful."

She wanted to answer, but had neither the breath nor the will. Her total concentration was fixed on that small flange of flesh at the apex of her sex.

Her release, when it came, was shattering. As she climaxed, Sandy gripped the chair cushions, trying to anchor herself in the real world. She felt as though she were flying, separated from her physical body, in danger of spinning off into space.

Forgotten, the egg fell to the floor, dragging its control device with it.

Zeke leaned forward, mesmerized by the sight of Sandy's orgasm. Her neck and breasts were stained with that same pink color he'd seen in Rubens' painting of Bathsheba. He wanted to reach out and touch that warm, pink skin, to feel the climax that made her tremble.

She seemed totally unaware of him, as though she were a million miles away. That wasn't what he wanted. He wanted her to cry out his name, to grip his arms instead of the damn seat cushions.

When they'd been setting up the camera, he'd thought of this as his very own interactive porn movie, one that he could direct and even play a starring role in.

Sandy's response stopped him dead. She was so honest and real. Nothing like those phony skin flicks. He couldn't explain it, but suddenly it didn't feel right to jerk off while he watched her on the screen. He didn't want to reduce the moment to her performing for him so he could get his rocks off.

*Who are you kidding, Prada? You just want to bury your cock up to the hilt inside her.*

There it was, the truth. Watching wasn't enough anymore. He wanted the whole enchilada. *But will she let me touch her? Taste her? Fuck her?*

He looked down at his penis. His guy was ready. A couple of strokes, and he could still get himself off. He tightened his hand and pumped his cock once.

*Nope. No good. I want the real thing.*

"Sandy." Justice's voice pierced the haze surrounding her.

She slowly resurfaced. Limp and damp, she was still draped over the chair.

Lifting her head, she looked toward the camera's eye. "What?"

"That was amazing. *You* were amazing," he said.

Something in his tone caught her attention. "What about you? Didn't you come?"

"No. I want to wait."

"Wait? For what?"

"For you."

Sandy sat up, ignoring the juice dripping from her pussy onto the upholstery. "What are you talking about?"

"Sandy, I want to touch you. I want to fuck you. For real."

Forget butterflies in her stomach. She had a flock of damn ravens flapping away down there. She pointed toward the camera's lens. "Justice, we just spent a freaking hour setting up this closed-circuit system." While she was thinking about it, she switched off the camera and removed her mask.

"Awwwww," he complained.

"Get to the point," she snapped, staring at the telephone speaker. "Are you saying you didn't like this?"

"No, baby. It was fantastic. But I can't stand it anymore. I want you, not a fucking TV screen."

She wasn't ready for this. Twenty-four hours ago, he was blackmailing her. Now he wanted inside her condo, inside her body. This was crazy.

"Sandy, I know you're scared, baby. I am, too, a little. I've never done anything like this before either. But I want you so bad. I want *us* so bad that I can't stand it."

The scary thing was that she wanted it, too. He already knew what she looked like. All she had was a shadowy image in her mind of what she *thought* he looked like.

But what if, after they slept together, he didn't want her anymore?

Hell, what was she thinking? What if he turned out to be a sexual predator?

She remembered Leah, who was always urging her to be more bold, to take more chances.

"I don't know," she said out loud. "I wouldn't feel safe having you come to my apartment, and I'm not going to yours."

"Fine. Let's meet out in public, where we can have a drink together and get to know each other."

She hadn't expected this. "You mean, like on a date?"

"If you want to call it that, fine. Yes, like a date."

"When?"

"Why not right now? It's still early. There are lots of bars open on McKinney. We can meet in one of them, have a drink and talk about our fantasies face-to-face."

"I'll need an hour," she heard herself saying.

"Aw, come on, Sandy. You don't need to primp for me. I already know what you look like. Thirty minutes."

"Not up close you don't. Forty-five minutes."

"Fine. Forty-five minutes. At Jerry's."

Jerry's was one of her favorite bars. She felt comfortable there. Sandy thought about asking if he had known that, and then decided she'd rather not know. If the answer scared her, she might back out.

"Jerry's. How will I recognize you?"

"Not to worry, sweetheart. I'll recognize you. I can't wait to touch that soft, perfect skin of yours."

She jumped up and hit the disconnect button on the phone.

After carefully unclipping the nipple clamps, she dropped them into the cardboard box. Walking quickly into the bathroom, she turned on the water and piled her hair into a plastic cap.

Sandy focused on her shower, refusing to examine the decision to meet Justice. If she allowed herself to think about what she was doing, she wouldn't be able to go through with it.

When she'd finished bathing, she wrapped a large bath sheet around her body and pondered her clothing choices. Jeans and a funky top were the usual picks, but she wanted something special tonight.

After a frustrating five minutes yanking things off hangers only to discard them, she pulled a short black dress out of the closet. Dora had talked her into buying it, but she'd never worn it. The dress had an off-the-shoulder neckline, a wide belt around the waist and a hem that was five inches above the knee. Sandy had very good legs and, in fuck-me black pumps without hose, hoped that Justice would concentrate on her legs instead of on her wide hips and tummy.

Without allowing any time to talk herself out of it, she pulled the dress on and adjusted its built-in bra. As she smoothed the material over her hips, she checked her appearance in the dresser mirror. The dress looked even better on than she remembered.

After a fruitless search of her lingerie for something sexy, she decided not to wear any panties at all. She smiled at herself in the mirror. Justice wouldn't complain.

Over the next fifteen minutes, while applying makeup, she questioned her sanity a dozen times. She remembered all the warnings she'd read, all the horror stories she'd watched on television. What if Justice was a serial killer who stalked women and then murdered them?

At the same time, it wasn't like getting into a car and driving off with a stranger. They'd be at Jerry's, her neighborhood hangout; nothing would happen to her in public. She'd watch her drink and make sure he didn't get a chance to slip a roofie or anything else into it.

As a kid, Sandy had engaged in rituals to help her feel safe. At night, she'd close the closet door tightly and check the bedroom window before climbing into bed—even though she knew there were no monsters hiding in the closet and that the window had not been opened that day. Her slippers had to be arranged in a precise pattern beside her bed, both pointing the same way, exactly even, but not touching each other.

Tonight, while she applied her mascara, Sandy wished there was something she could do to feel safer about meeting Justice.

During her early dating days, she and Leah went to clubs together, operating on the buddy system. Neither ever went home alone with a man she'd just met. They always introduced new guys to each other, both to show off their catch and as a subtle reminder to the man that he'd be remembered if he later chose to rape and pillage his new date. In her heart, Sandy always knew this was just another ritual meant to help her feel safe. She wished now that she could introduce Justice to Leah, but her friend was off with her latest boyfriend this evening.

While she fluffed her hair one last time, it occurred to Sandy that she could call and leave a message on Leah's answering machine. Pleased with the idea, she dialed her friend's apartment and said, "Hi, honey. It's about ten fifteen on Saturday night. I'm on my way to Jerry's to meet a guy I don't really know for drinks. I . . . uh . . . met him over the phone. In case he turns out to be Jack the Ripper, I thought I'd better tell *someone.* Hope you're having fun with Richard. Talk to you later."

She hung up, feeling much better. It was just another meaning-less ritual—she didn't even know Justice's name—but it helped to calm her nerves.

The phone rang. *Oh, God, don't let it be him canceling. I couldn't stand it.* She snatched the receiver off the cradle. "Hello?"

"Alexandra, it's your mother." Sandy's heart sank. "I'm calling to remind you that you still need to get fitted for your brides-maid's dress."

"Oh. Uh, thanks, Mom. I'll take care of it next week."

"Next week? You should have taken care of it at least two weeks ago. Although I can't say that I blame you. If I weighed as much as you do, I wouldn't want to try on dresses either."

For once, her mother's barbs bounced right off. "Okay, Mom, thanks for calling. I'll be sure to get a fitting next week."

"Wait a minute. Why are you in such a rush?"

"I've got a date waiting for me. Talk to you later." Sandy hung up the phone and moved toward the door. She'd pay for that later; her mother would extract a full cup of revenge. But for now Sandy could enjoy the picture of Victoria Davis sitting there staring at the telephone in complete shock.

A few minutes later, she walked into Jerry's and looked around.

The bar was a typical neighborhood joint: vinyl booths along two walls, and small tables crowded together in the center. There was a postage-stamp-sized dance floor and on the weekends, like tonight, there was usually a musical duo—local talent who played for drinks and tips.

At ten thirty on a Saturday night, the place was pretty busy.

Sandy had to take a table closer to the dance floor than she liked. She sat down and smiled at Pete, the bartender, who nodded and handed a Bud Light to Annie, the waitress, with a few words.

"Hi, Sandy," Annie said, putting a coaster and the bottle in front of her. "Where's Leah?"

"On a date. I'm waiting for my own date to get here now." She liked being able to say those words.

"Well, let me know if you need anything."

"I will. Thanks."

There was only one couple on the dance floor, and Sandy eyed them critically. They weren't so much dancing as groping each other.

"Would you like to dance?"

She looked up to find Dennis smirking down at her.

Dennis was another regular, a guy who came in most weekends, looking to hook up for the night. Sandy and Leah had often laughed about his determined pursuit of pussy. He got lucky more often than they would have expected. He wasn't bad looking, just single-minded.

"No, thanks, Dennis," she answered now.

"Why not? You're alone; I'm alone; it's Saturday night. We could keep each other company."

"No, thank you," she repeated.

"Come on. Dance with me and I'll buy you a drink."

"I believe the lady said no."

Both Sandy and Dennis jumped. The familiar voice made her eyes widen and her thighs clench.

"I'm sorry to keep you waiting, darling," Justice said, leaning down to kiss her cheek.

"That's all right," she stuttered.

Justice straightened and stared at Dennis. "Are you still here?" he asked.

Dennis held both palms out in front of his body in a calming gesture. "Sorry, man. Didn't mean to poach in your territory." He shambled off in search of new prey.

Justice pulled out the chair next to Sandy and sat down. He leaned forward to sniff her hair. "Delicious. I knew it would be." He sat back and grinned at her.

She was too busy staring at him to speak.

He'd told the truth about his hair being dark brown and curly. Although it was cut short, she could see where it was still trying to curl.

His face was clean-shaven and had a look of the Midwest: square-jawed and vaguely Nordic. He had blue eyes and a generous mouth. Sandy pictured that mouth sucking on her nipple and felt her vagina tighten.

Justice was wearing a blue dress shirt, jeans and a sports jacket. He held out a hand. "Let's dance, honey."

She let him lead her to the small dance floor. The musical duo was taking a break, and the speaker system was playing an old love ballad from the seventies.

Justice held her close with his lips touching the top of her head. His breath ruffled strands of her hair.

She was five foot six, and he was at least six feet tall. His cock pressed against her belly; she could tell it was happy to be there.

She rested her face against his right shoulder and wrapped her arms around his torso.

They danced in silence, content with the music and each other. Justice nuzzled her, but didn't use his hands to feel her up the way that guy on the dance floor had done to his partner earlier.

When the ballad ended, the pianist and guitar player returned from their break. Justice led Sandy back to their table and pulled out her chair for her.

"Do I pass muster?" he asked as he reseated himself.

"You'll do." She smiled. "When did you see me on my balcony?"

He shook his head. "No questions."

"That's not fair. You just asked me a question."

He grinned. "You're right. I should have said 'no nosy questions.' Let's just enjoy tonight and each other."

She didn't say anything. She wasn't sure what to say. He'd just squashed the usual first-date questions: Where do you live? What do you do? WHAT'S YOUR NAME?

Justice reached across the table to rest his hand on top of hers. "I know this feels strange, Sandy. It does for me, too. I was telling the truth when I said I've never done this kind of thing before either."

"Well, you're pretty damn good at it," she muttered.

Before he could answer, Annie came by to take his order. He asked for a Coors and another Bud Light for Sandy.

There was a moment of awkward silence after Annie left the table. Sandy searched for something to say, but her mind seemed to be operating in slow motion.

"Tell me something about yourself that no one else knows," he suggested.

She tilted her head to the side. "Something that no one else knows? I'd have to think for a second."

He shook his head. "No, don't think. Just tell me the first thing that popped into your head."

She smiled ruefully. "Well, after sitting here for the last few minutes trying to think of something to say, the first thing that popped into my head was that I've read the entire series of Zane Grey books."

"Zane Grey?" His eyebrows drew together in a thoughtful frown. "You mean the Western writer?"

She nodded, running her index finger around the rim of her beer glass. "When I was twelve, I had a huge crush on the boy next door, Tim Shores. He was a big fan of Zane Grey. So I started reading the books in order to have something to talk to him about."

He grinned. "Did it work?"

She laughed, shaking her head. "I'm afraid not. I just couldn't figure out how to work *Riders of the Purple Sage* into casual conversation."

Justice had a nice laugh, warm and friendly.

"Your turn," she said. "Tell me something about you that no one else knows."

He tilted his chair back so that only two legs were still connected to the floor. "Well, since we're talking about young love, I had a crush of my own when I was sixteen. She was a gorgeous blonde, and she lived next door."

Sandy struggled to keep the smile on her face. "Did she like you, too?"

He shook his head. "Nope. I was jailbait. She was almost thirty and a single mother with two kids. I used to hang around outside washing and polishing my car just so I could see her when she came home after work."

"So you never told her about your crush?"

"Not then. Later, when I got out of the service, I ran into her in the supermarket one day, and we went out for a drink."

Sandy arched her brow. "Did you consummate your passion?"

His smile was even sexier than his laugh. "We did. Turns out women over forty really like learning that they were the object of a teenage boy's lust."

They laughed together. "No fair," Sandy said. "You were supposed to tell me something no one else knew. Obviously, your Mrs. Robinson knows the whole story."

He shook his head for a second time. "Nope, not this part of the story. I used to babysit her kids. I wanted her to see me as a responsible adult, and . . ." He looked down at the table. "And I wanted her kids to get used to me so they wouldn't ruin our wedding plans later."

His words caught Sandy swallowing the last sip of her beer. Her startled laugh turned into a cough, and the cough turned into a choking fit. Justice pounded her on the back.

Annie arrived with their beers and asked if Sandy wanted a glass of water. She shook her head while tears streamed down her face.

When she finally had control over her breathing again, she looked at him with reproach. "You did that deliberately."

"I swear I didn't. I was just trying to share something no one else knows."

The exchange of secrets had broken the ice. Conversation was much less stilted now. They talked and danced again.

When they returned to the table from the dance floor, Justice leaned forward and whispered into her ear, "What are you wearing under that dress?"

His words sent a thrill of excitement like an electric shock running down her spine. She stared up at him.

"Nothing," she whispered, her mouth gone dry.

She saw the knowledge fill his eyes and watched the blaze ignite.

"Sandy, honey, how would you feel about going back to your place now?"

"But we haven't finished our drinks," she protested.

He yanked his wallet out and threw a twenty-dollar bill on the table. "There. That's covered. Let's go." He reached for her hand.

She let him lead her to the entrance. He opened the door, but before she could step through, a man entered.

"You," Sandy gasped, face-to-face with Mr. Dominant for the first time.

# Chapter Six

A slow smile spread over Dom's face as he looked her up and down. "I'm afraid you have me at a disadvantage. Have we met?" He stepped into the bar, followed by the girl Sandy had nicknamed Dolly.

Overcome with confusion, Sandy gaped at him.

Justice pulled her away from Dom. "No, she just has a thing for men in expensive suits. Come on, honey, we need to get home." Without giving her time to speak, he stepped past Dom through the entryway, dragging Sandy with him. As soon as the door slammed behind them, he began hustling her south down McKinney with a hand under her elbow.

It took four or five steps before she gathered her wits enough to yank her arm out of his. She stopped in the middle of the sidewalk. "I live in the other direction." Looking back the way they'd come, she saw Dom standing outside the bar, watching them walk away.

"I know. Just keep walking. Now!" he grated, grabbing her upper arm in a tight grip. "Don't look back, for God's sake."

Sandy didn't argue, just let him hurry her down the street. She was thoroughly confused, first by the sudden encounter with Dom, and then by the fact that her companion seemed to know him. A part of her was grateful to Justice for pulling her away from Dom before she made a complete fool of herself. Another part wanted to know what was going on.

When they were two blocks away, Justice turned left into a

gelato shop. There were four or five customers waiting for the Italian ice cream, and no one took any notice of them.

"Justice, what are you doing? What's wrong?"

"Zeke, my name's Zeke," he muttered. He moved to a corner of the shop by a window where he could watch the street they'd just left.

"Zeke," she tried the name out, and liked it. "What the hell is going on, Zeke?"

He shook his head, his gaze glued to the foot traffic outside.

She waited for him to turn around and face her again.

"Come on. Let's go," he said, reaching for her hand.

"I'm not going anywhere until you tell me what just happened." She kept her voice low but firm.

He glanced at the other patrons of the shop. "Let's go outside first."

When they were again standing on the sidewalk, he started south. "Zeke, my condo is in the other direction," she said in exasperation.

"I know, sweetheart. Let's go around the block and walk back on Oak Grove."

One block to the east, Oak Grove ran parallel to Sandy's street, McKinney Avenue. Unlike McKinney, Oak Grove was not well traveled. This was because an old cemetery, no longer in use, ran the length of the boulevard. When urban renewal hit the neighborhood, the developers had been unable to get permission to move the cemetery, which contained graves dating to the Civil War.

The suggestion that they walk along a deserted street raised alarms and made Sandy nervous again about being alone with him. "No, I'm going home the way we came. You can come along or not, as you please." She turned and started walking north toward her building.

"Sandy, please, this is important. If you won't take Oak Grove, let's walk up Cole."

Cole Avenue was on the other side of McKinney, one block to the west, and ran behind Dom's apartment building. It was a much busier street. She hesitated and then nodded.

They waited for a trolley car to go by before crossing McKinney. Together they walked to Cole and turned north.

She was first to break the silence between them. "Okay, bucko, what's the story?"

"Sandy, that is one very bad hombre. His name is Victor Cabrini, and he's the go-to man for the wiseguys in this part of the country. You don't want anything to do with him." His tone was serious.

She stared at him for a moment before asking, "How do you know?"

"I just know. Trust me on this. Please."

Her shoulders tensed. She stopped walking, forcing him to a halt.

"Zeke, you keep asking me to trust you, but you don't trust me enough to share anything. That has to stop."

"I know, honey, but just give me a little longer and I'll tell you everything. I promise."

Either he was sincere, or he was the best liar she'd ever met. Sandy started to walk north again.

They traveled in silence. She could feel the tension humming through his body. His gaze seemed to dart everywhere as though he was expecting to see someone he knew.

A pleasant September breeze fluttered leaves on the oak trees. Even though it was after eleven, Cole Avenue was wide-awake. Several people were walking dogs. Two couples, headed in the opposite direction, argued the merits of a film they'd seen at the art house theater.

Sandy thought about what he'd said. How would Zeke know Dom was a mobster? Ordinary citizens couldn't usually identify gangsters on sight. The two classes of people most likely to recognize a mafioso would be cops or other criminals.

If Zeke was a cop, he'd be able to show her a badge. If he couldn't produce one, the likelihood increased that he was a criminal—either that or a sleazebag lawyer who defended criminals. The thought that she might be running around the streets of Dallas at night with someone who hung out with crooks was not comforting.

They were passing Cabrini's building when Zeke pushed her toward the garage.

"What—"

"Sandy, listen to me. We're being followed." When she started to turn her head, he pulled her body against his. "No! Don't look back. Just keep walking."

"Zeke? What are you talking about? Why would someone—?"

He interrupted her again. "Because you stirred Cabrini's curiosity. He wants to know who we are. Let's go into the garage."

They went through the entrance for residents' cars, angling

around the lowered bar that blocked other traffic. The floor of the garage sloped upward. Although the building was well lit for a garage, shadows lurked between cars and in dark corners.

"Zeke," she said.

"Shhh." He was scanning the garage as he pulled her up the slope. Apparently satisfied the place was empty, he leaned down to look into her eyes.

"Sandy." His voice was urgent. "I need you to keep walking up this slope. You can't see them from here, but at the top is a pair of elevators. If you get there before I catch up with you, press the button for the lobby. Go upstairs and wait for me there." He hesitated and then kissed her cheek. "If I don't follow in five minutes, ask the doorman to call the police. Understand?"

"But, Zeke—"

"We don't have time to argue. Just do this. Okay?"

She jerked her head once, nodding agreement. He squeezed her shoulder before releasing her and melting into the shadows between two cars.

Sandy resisted the impulse to turn around and look to see if there really was someone following her. She took an unsteady step forward. *Let's get this over with.*

*I can't believe I did that to her.* Zeke crouched between a Cadillac and a Jaguar, listening to Sandy's retreating footsteps. He slipped his gun out from behind his waistband and checked the safety. *Are you sure you're doing the right thing?*

Hell, no, he wasn't sure. But what was he going to do? Let the guy track Sandy right to her door? If Cabrini was determined to find her, he would. This was just a delaying tactic.

He bent down to peer beneath the cars. One thousand. Two thousand. Three thousand. Four—

The elevator's chime sounded. Good. Sandy would be getting out of there.

The legs of the man who had been following them came into view. The guy was moving quickly, obviously trying to see what floor the elevator went to.

Zeke tensed. He forced himself to wait until the man was half a step beyond his hiding place. Springing forward, he leaped toward the man's back.

At the last minute, something alerted the guy. He started to turn just as Zeke reached him.

Zeke brought the butt of his automatic down on the side of the goon's head. The guy crumpled without a sound.

Zeke caught the man in an awkward hold before he hit the ground. He lowered the unconscious body to the cement. Shoving his gun back into his waistband, he knelt and checked the guy for a pulse.

It was there: strong and steady. No blood either.

Satisfied that the man was just out cold, Zeke glanced around quickly. The garage was still deserted. He shifted position so that he was standing behind the fellow's head.

Bending over, he shoved his hands under the prone body's shoulders and hauled him up.

A clanging sound announced the arrival of a car at the garage entrance. A tenant coming home. He needed to move fast.

Dragging the unconscious body between two cars, Zeke crouched, waiting for the car—an SUV—to drive past his hiding place on its way to an upper floor.

Once his level of the garage was quiet again, Zeke searched the wiseguy. He removed a gun, slipping it into his jacket pocket. After locating the man's wallet, he checked the ID and returned it.

*Hurry up, man. Otherwise, Sandy will be calling 911. Then there'll be hell to pay.*

Brushing his hands off on the unconscious man's jacket, Zeke stood and headed in the direction Sandy had gone. Ignoring the elevators, he entered the stairwell and raced up the steps.

He entered the lobby just in time to hear the security guard asking Sandy, "Which tenant are you visiting, ma'am?"

"I, um—"

"Sorry to keep you waiting, honey," Zeke interrupted. The look of relief on her face stabbed him with guilt. He looked at the guard. "This is Roanoke Place, right?"

The middle-aged man shook his head. "No, this is Thackeray Faire. Roanoke Place is up the street." He pointed to the north.

"Oh, sorry to bother you. Come on, honey." Zeke grabbed Sandy's arm and guided her toward the door. She made no protest.

Outside on the sidewalk, Zeke checked both ways for unfriendly eyes. Not seeing anyone, he hustled Sandy toward the north.

"Zeke? My condo is right across the street."

He grabbed her hand before she could gesture. "I know,

honey, but that security guard is watching. I don't want him to see where you live."

She sighed, but didn't complain. They walked north for almost a block before crossing the street.

Zeke was grateful that she didn't immediately begin to question him. He was busy enough keeping an eye on the street ahead and behind them.

Zeke insisted on walking a block beyond Dom's—or, rather, Cabrini's—building before crossing to her side of the street. Sandy could feel the tension in his arm and decided to humor him.

She kept sneaking covert glances at his face. He was too busy watching the street to notice.

This was like something out of a spy movie. A part of her enjoyed the intrigue and the feeling of being protected by a strong, good-looking man. The whole thing was making her feel like a sexy femme fatale.

When they finally crossed the street, she said, "If you're worried about being seen entering my building, we could cut through my parking garage and avoid the front door."

"Great idea," he agreed.

She led him to the garage entrance. They walked past two rows of cars to her building, and Sandy used her key to admit them through the side door on the ground floor.

Because he had her thinking defensively, instead of taking the back elevator, she brought him past the security desk and cameras in the lobby. He didn't protest. She made a point of saying hello to the man on the desk. She wanted the guard to get a good look at Zeke, and she wanted Zeke to know that he did.

Once they were safely in the elevator heading upstairs, Zeke relaxed. She felt the tension ooze out of his body. He turned to face her. "Thanks for humoring me out there."

She nodded. "Tell me. What happened in that parking garage?"

He stuck his hands in his jacket pockets. "I knocked our tail out. He's probably waking up right now with a headache."

"You . . . assaulted him?" Sandy could hardly speak the words.

"I discouraged him. He was carrying, Sandy." He pulled a small black gun out of his pocket. While she watched, he emptied the bullets into his hand and offered them to her.

She stared at the lethal-looking pieces of metal in her palm. *Okay, if he thinks emptying that gun is going to reassure me, he's crazy. You're not getting into my condo, much less my panties. Even if I were wearing pant-ies.* She dumped the bullets back into his hand and pushed the EMERGENCY STOP button on the elevator.

The car came to a sudden halt, and an alarm clanged loudly. She didn't pay any attention to the jarring sound.

"Show me some ID, Zeke, or we're heading right back down to the lobby. Now."

He reached into his jacket pocket and pulled out a leather case that he flipped open to reveal a badge.

The phone on the wall of the elevator rang. Sandy ignored it and leaned forward to read Zeke's ID aloud. "Detective Zeke Prada. You're a cop?"

"That's right," he said. "Shall I answer this now?" He pointed to the phone. At her nod, he lifted the receiver. "Sorry, man. We hit the wrong button by accident." He pressed the red button again, and the clanging alarm stopped. The elevator shuddered and began to move again. "Yeah, I know it's late. Sorry." He replaced the receiver. "It seems we've ticked off the security guard."

She shrugged. "He'll survive."

He leaned his shoulders against the side of the car. "Feel better now?"

She nodded. "I just needed to make certain you weren't some sleazebag crook."

He raised one eyebrow. "Satisfied?"

"For the moment."

He pushed off from the side of the car and put his hands on her waist. But instead of pulling her toward him, he waited. Asking permission.

Bringing him to her condo wasn't the smartest move she could make. But she'd spent two years sleeping alone, and right now, common sense didn't have its usual strong hold on her. Sandy missed sex. She missed the intimacy, the thrill, the comfort of being naked with a man. She remembered Leah's encouragement to take more chances, to be more spontaneous. Despite the unorthodox way they'd met, Zeke had been kind, and she wanted to feel his lips and hands on her body.

He was still waiting for her to make the first move. She stood on tiptoe and kissed him for the first time. As her lips touched his, she forgot everything—except the taste of him, the feel of him and the smell of him.

———

Zeke didn't speak during the walk from Cabrini's lobby to Sandy's building. He was too busy scanning the street for signs of Cabrini or the task force team. *Shit! The lieutenant will have my ass for mixing with a surveillance subject during a stakeout. What the hell am I going to tell him?*

No one had seen him knock Cabrini's goon out. He was sure of that. He was equally certain that the surveillance team following Cabrini had recognized him coming out of the pub. With any luck, that would be the only thing he'd have to explain. And it had clearly been an accidental meeting.

He'd been enormously relieved to arrive at Sandy's building without further incident. By the time they reached her elevator, he'd even managed to relax a little.

She stood beside him with a pinched, anxious look on her face. *Poor kid. She doesn't have a clue what's going on. I'm acting like fucking Clark Kent, trying to hide my Superman identity.*

When she pulled the alarm and stopped the elevator, he'd been shocked. He hadn't expected anything so aggressive from his sweet little social worker.

He could feel the tension in her body when he put his hands on her hips. It was her turn to make the first move.

To his delight, she reached up and touched her lips to his. Needing no further urging, he pulled her body against his. Her kiss was tentative, vulnerable. He wondered who and what had hurt her so badly.

Instead of deepening the kiss immediately, wanting to take her pain away, he touched his lips to her face, feathering kisses along her cheekbone, to the corner of her mouth and, finally, to her lips.

She held herself stiff for a second or two, but gradually melted into his embrace.

Zeke moved his hands up from her waist, cupping her breasts. He couldn't wait to get this damn dress off her. Just the memory of her naked image on that video monitor was enough to make him hard.

He pressed his lips along the seam of her mouth, and she opened up for him. Accepting the invitation, he slid his tongue inside. He teased her tongue, twining, twisting and then retreating until she followed his lead.

Shyly at first, but then with greater confidence, her lips and tongue stroked and provoked him.

He dimly heard the elevator pinging its arrival on the sixth floor. Unwilling to release her, Zeke used his hips to guide her off the car.

Sandy pulled her mouth from his to whisper, "I have to find my keys."

"I know," he said, bumping her against the wall, where he could press his body to hers. His erection pushed urgently against her belly.

He wanted to fill his hands with those round, white buttocks he had only seen on the monitor before. Grabbing the hem of her dress, he began to drag it up. He was thrilled when she made no attempt to stop him.

"Oh, baby. You really aren't wearing anything."

"I told you," she whispered.

"I know you did." He kneaded and squeezed her ass cheeks and she arched against him.

Desperate to crawl inside her body, he began to move her in the direction of her condo. Neither of them wanted to let go long enough to walk the twenty feet to her front door. They banged along the papered wall, a four-legged blind creature.

She fisted her hands in his hair; he licked her mouth.

About halfway down the hall, Zeke heard the sound of someone unlocking a door. He pulled back to see where the intruder was coming from, instinctively shielding Sandy with his body.

A door opened less than six feet away, and a scrawny old man in a ratty bathrobe poked his head out into the hall.

"What's going on out here?"

Zeke was reaching for his badge to tell the old guy to mind his own business when Sandy spoke up.

"Oh, Mr. Guzman, I'm so sorry we disturbed you."

"Sandy." A slow grin spread over the man's face as he surveyed the two of them. "Was that you playing with the elevator alarm?"

*Okay, it's her neighbor. Play nice, Prada.* "We're sorry, sir."

"That's all right. My wife thought it was burglars." The geezer called over his shoulder, "It's okay, honey. Sandy and her boyfriend were just coming home." He turned back to wink at them. "Better take it inside, kids."

"We will, Mr. Guzman. Thank you," Sandy replied.

Zeke listened to make sure the old dude turned the lock and put the chain on his door before he looked back at Sandy. He halfway expected her to go prudish on him again. To his delight, she giggled like a teenager. He held out a hand. "Give me the damn key."

She rummaged in her purse, pulled out her key chain and handed it to him. They walked to her condo with Sandy still trying to stifle her laughter. *This little social worker is just full of surprises.*

He unlocked the front door and pushed it open for her to walk through first.

She took her keys from him and flipped on the overhead light.

Before she had a chance to take more than a couple of steps inside, he grabbed her and pulled her back against his body.

"I want to bend you over a chair and take you from behind right now," he murmured. His hand moved down her belly and under the front hem of her dress.

She dropped her keys and purse and leaned back into his body.

He nudged her forward and kicked the door shut with his foot. His fingers probed her pussy, sliding between the folds.

"Ohhhhhh," she gasped.

His hand fondled her nether lips, seeking her clit. He felt her knees begin to buckle, and wrapping his left arm around her body, he pushed her deeper into the condo.

His right hand continued to massage her clitoris, his index finger moving in small, tight circles. She was warm and wet, and he was throbbing. *Damn. I hope I can last long enough to get inside her.*

He had three condoms in his wallet. Before things got too far, he stopped to retrieve one and put it on. Once he was safely sheathed, he began to rub her clit in earnest. Her pussy was already swollen and dripping. *God, I'd love to taste her. I want to feel her come against my mouth.*

She began moving her hips, rubbing them against his erection, and his legs almost folded under him. He staggered, moaning into her ear.

The sound seemed to energize her. She squeezed his left forearm and pressed down on his right index finger, grinding her clit against his hand.

He pushed her toward the back of the sofa, frantic to shove himself into her tight channel.

When he removed his hand from her clit, she cried out in protest, twisting her head to look over her shoulder at him. "Zeke!"

He put one hand on the nape of her neck and pressed her down over the back of the couch. She tensed and started to push up, but then she seemed to figure out what he was doing and relaxed.

Seconds later, he was rubbing his cock against her damp pussy.

She wriggled, making it harder for him to get the head of his cock into her vagina. He steadied her with one hand and pushed himself into her body. *Dear Lord, she's tight.*

Not wanting to hurt her, he inched his way inside. *Oh, God! She feels incredible.*

The minute he was sheathed, she began moving her hips back and forth.

They quickly found a rhythm: Zeke pounded into her and she

thrust back. Their rapid breathing was interspersed with small cries of pleasure.

Her dress was rolled up around her waist, and he was bent over her body, his hands clutching her naked hips. He pulled nearly all the way out and then slammed back into her, his balls slapping against her.

He knew he was close to coming, but he didn't want to climax until she'd had her orgasm. Trying to distract himself, he began counting in his head. *One, two, three. Damn it, Sandy, come! Four, five—*

"Now, Zeke, now," she moaned.

Panting like a long-distance runner, he emptied himself into her body. She arched against him and then sagged forward. He pulled her hips toward his, wanting to feel every last tremor as her vagina milked him dry. Her muscles continued to contract around his cock long after her hips stopped moving.

At last, drained and exhausted, he rested against her limp body. Long minutes passed before he could catch his breath.

For some reason—even in this ridiculous position, draped over the back of the couch—he didn't want to separate his body from hers. His head rested on her right shoulder. He could see the tendrils of damp hair clinging to her temple. Lifting a hand, he brushed the wet curls back from her face.

Although he'd had sex with dozens of women over the years, he couldn't remember when it had been better. *I hope it was as good for her.*

The thought surprised him. He wasn't the type of guy who needed reassurance about his skills in bed. Women were always complimenting him for being a sensitive lover, concerned for his partner's pleasure. *Why does Sandy's good opinion matter so much?*

For some reason, she moved him. He didn't know if it was her gutsiness, her vulnerability or her innate honesty. All he knew was that he wanted more of her.

# Chapter Seven

When she recovered, Sandy found herself draped over the back of the couch with Zeke's body on top of hers. The heavy perfume of sex surrounded them. She felt breathless; whether from the force of her orgasm or the pressure of his heavy body across hers, she wasn't sure.

She pushed backward, and he immediately stood.

"Are you okay?" he asked.

"I think so." After-tremors rippled through her womb. "Help me up."

He slid his hands under her armpits and pulled her to him.

"I need to go to the bathroom," she said without looking at him.

"Wait." He grabbed for her hand.

She evaded him and ran for the bathroom.

Once inside, Sandy closed the door and sat on the toilet.

After unbuckling her belt, she threw it onto a nearby counter and pulled her dress off over her head.

What on earth had she done? She'd just had sex with a stranger. Sweet mercy!

A tap on the bathroom door interrupted her train of thought. "Sandy? Are you okay?"

"Yes, yes. I'm fine. I'll . . . I'll be out in a minute." She flushed the toilet to lend credence to her story.

The door suddenly opened, and Zeke walked into the bathroom.

"What are you doing?" she shrieked, bending over to cover her breasts and genitals. "Get out!"

"Nope." He took two steps into the long, narrow bathroom with his limp penis still hanging out of his pants.

Ignoring her, he walked to the sink. Grabbing a hand towel, he dampened it under the faucet and began to wash his dick.

"Get out," she ordered again. Her robe was hanging on the back of the door, and she eyed it longingly. She'd have to walk past him to reach it.

He looked up to watch her in the mirror. "I'm not leaving. We're not having a repeat of that first time."

"What are you talking about?"

"You've got a short memory, honey. Remember last night when we had phone sex? We're not doing that again." He reached for the robe and handed it to her. "Here. Take it."

Relieved, Sandy stood, turned her back to him and slipped into the robe. She belted it tightly around her waist.

He dried himself with a second hand towel. "Happy?"

"Thank you," she said stiffly.

"Whose voice is it you hear?" He didn't look at her, concentrating instead on tucking his penis back into his jeans.

She didn't understand. "What?"

"When you start to feel shamed. Whose voice is it talking to you?"

"No one . . ." She stopped to think. "My mother."

"Is she the one who made you ashamed of your body?"

She didn't even pretend to misunderstand. "Yes. She complains about my weight all the time. But she's right."

He dropped the towel on the counter and took two steps toward her. She looked down at her feet, embarrassed.

Zeke put a finger under her chin and raised her face. "Your mother doesn't know what she's talking about. You have a beautiful body with wonderfully lush curves. I could spend weeks exploring all your lovely white skin. I love the way you respond when I touch you."

"You're not just saying that to be kind?"

He smiled. "I'm not a kind person, honey. I calls 'em like I sees 'em." His hands went to the robe's belt. "I've been dreaming about your breasts. I want to see them for real."

Her stomach clenched, but a wave of heat flowed over her. He still wanted her. She watched—trembling with equal parts nervousness and excitement—as he untied her belt.

When he spread open her robe, his smile grew wider. "God, they're beautiful." He pushed the robe off her shoulders and placed both palms underneath her breasts.

Sandy relaxed, savoring the feel of his hands on her body. His thumbs rubbed back and forth across the tips of her nipples. "That feels so good," she murmured.

"I want to suck them." In a sudden move, he shifted his hands to her waist and lifted her.

"Zeke," she cried in alarm.

He swiveled on the balls of his feet and set her down on the tiled counter. "Relax, honey. I just wanted to get you where I could reach these gorgeous melons of yours." Lowering his head, he licked her nipple.

Her muscles tensed and a spear of lightning raced through

her body from breast to pubis. She could have sworn she heard the crackle of energy searing her internal organs.

His lips encircled her areola, and he gently sucked the tip of the breast into his mouth. As her cool skin met his heat, she shivered and her nipples hardened.

He stroked her naked thigh with calming fingers, his hand warm and reassuring.

She cradled his head against her chest, resting her chin on top of his crisp brown hair while he continued to suckle.

His mouth was an instrument of exquisite torture, making her thrum with need. Sandy began to rock back and forth, her sensory circuits on overdrive. She was keenly aware of everything: Zeke's sandalwood and soap scent; his big hand on her knee; the rough denim of his jeans chafing her open thighs; the cold, hard tiles against her bottom.

She'd just leaned forward in unconscious surrender when, without warning, he bit down on her breast. The light pressure on her already-sensitized nipple made her convulse, and she yanked away from him.

"I'm sorry, honey. Did I hurt you?" He raised his eyes to look into hers.

"No," she gasped. "It was a good hurt. I just wasn't expecting it."

He kissed her lips and then leaned down to plant a kiss on the swell of her breast. "I asked you last night if you'd ever had an orgasm just from having your breasts sucked. Remember?"

She felt the blush that swept her neck and face. "Yes."

"Will you let me try, honey?"

Sandy was incapable of answering; she just nodded. His smile was her payoff.

"Lean back, baby, and enjoy." His mouth went to her left breast. He began the same way he'd done on the right side, licking and sucking the tip. This time, he used his fingers on the other breast. He squeezed and tugged on the nipple.

Zeke went back and forth between her breasts, lavishing attention on each. She gave herself up to the pain/pleasure of sensation, thighs clenched in response. Her vaginal muscles tightened, hungry for a hard penis.

"Please, Zeke," she whimpered.

"That's what I'm trying to do: please you, Sandy."

Her breasts were so sensitive that she had to bite down on her lower lip to keep from crying out as his teeth and hands continued their tender torment.

Her orgasm erupted with a sudden force that took them both by surprise. Sandy rose off the countertop, straining forward. As she reached her peak, she cried, "Zeke!" and jerked backward.

Her breast popped out of his mouth, making him jump and bump his head on her chin. He shifted his grip to seize her shoulders and anchor her against the tremors that shook her frame.

Cream gushed from her pussy while spasms ripped through her body. She collapsed against him in a boneless heap and rested her cheek on his shoulder.

Zeke held her tenderly, stroking her hair over and over with one large palm. She snuggled against him.

It was some minutes before she could whisper, "Thank you."

"Thank *you*," he said. "It's a pleasure to pleasure you."

She giggled sleepily. "We're being awfully polite, aren't we?" Lifting her chin, she nuzzled his ear. "That was fabulous, Zeke, but I'm feeling a little guilty. You didn't come."

"We still have time, honey." He pulled back so he could look into her face. "Unless you want me to leave right now?"

She shook her head. "No, but I do need a break. I need to clean up a bit and maybe have a drink." Despite the words, she made no move to leave his embrace. She rubbed her cheek back and forth on his shoulder.

He slid one hand between their bodies and began to softly rub her left thigh. As his fingers moved higher and higher, she pushed him away.

"About that break . . ."

He grinned. "Okay, why don't you wash up while I make us something to drink? What do you want?"

"Vodka and orange juice with lots of ice. There's a serving cart in the living room with booze."

"Coming up." He gave her a light kiss before moving toward the bathroom door.

This time, when the door closed, Sandy locked it. In addition to a shower, she wanted some privacy. So much had happened so quickly, she needed time to decompress. To get used to the idea of having a lover and being desired. It was hard to get her mind around the idea.

Zeke dropped ice cubes into a glass and poured a shot of vodka on top of them. He filled a second glass with scotch, no ice, and started toward the kitchen.

The sight of Sandy's keys and purse lying forgotten on the floor where she'd dropped them made him smile. She'd been as on fire for sex as he had. And she'd been amazingly responsive. If he could just get her past that postcoital shame . . .

His cell phone rang, and he put the drinks down. He fished around in his jacket pocket for it.

"Hello."

"Prada, what the hell are you doing?" Jenkins, the task force supervisor, growled in his ear.

Zeke's heart sank. The surveillance team monitoring Cabrini must have reported the incident at Jerry's.

"Hey, Lieutenant, how are you doing?" he said, stalling for time.

"I'm sitting here wondering why one of the men working on my case is socializing with the goddamn suspect—that's how I'm doing. What the hell were you thinking?" The lieutenant's voice climbed higher in register.

"It wasn't like that, Lieu," Zeke protested. "My girlfriend and I went out for drinks at Jerry's. We were getting ready to leave when Cabrini . . . put the make on her."

There was a silence while Jenkins digested what Zeke had said. Everyone on the task force knew what a pussy hound Cabrini was, and Zeke's explanation would ring true.

"Was that it?" the lieutenant asked in a tone that was a shade milder than before.

"Yes, sir. I'm sure the surveillance team reported that I got Sandy out of there and down the street as fast as I could."

"All right. I guess it couldn't be helped," Jenkins said. "Just keep your girlfriend away from Cabrini. I don't want that scum-bag claiming entrapment and the federal prosecutor stomping all over my balls."

"Yes, sir. I understand, sir."

Jenkins hung up without saying good-bye.

Zeke picked up the scotch and drained it in a single gulp.

Sandy finished washing her breasts and moved to her genitals. As she touched her labia with soapy fingers, she sighed at the plea-sure and the tiny bit of pain. Her body felt like one big exposed nerve. Even the gentlest of pressures brought her close to orgasm again. She was tempted to stroke herself and finish the job.

At the same moment her index finger found the little pleasure button, she heard Zeke's voice at the door. "The ice is melting in that drink of yours." He rattled the doorknob.

"I'll be right there," she called, and returned her attention to the business of bathing.

Turning off the water, she climbed out of the tub and wrapped a large fluffy bath sheet around her body. She unlocked the door to find Zeke standing there, waiting. He handed her a tumbler and picked up a fresh drink for himself.

"Here you go. Feel better?"

"Mmmmmmm," she murmured, sipping the vodka and juice.

They walked together to the living room. Cool air caressed her still-damp body and she shivered. Zeke had opened the glass door to the balcony, although he'd left the draperies closed.

Yielding to impulse, she lifted a panel of the drape and

stepped out on the balcony in her bare feet and bath sheet. The solid wall and deep shadows hid most of her body from view.

Zeke followed. Together, holding their drinks, they rested their forearms on the brick ledge and looked down.

Despite the fact that it was now after midnight, six stories below, McKinney Avenue was still hopping. A soft breeze carried the sounds of laughter and the strains of music to Sandy's condo. The M-Line trolley had stopped running at ten p.m., but cars still lined the street, heading for the bar at the Hard Rock Cafe, which remained open until two.

While the street was brightly lit, the balcony was steeped in velvet shadows, the rustling of the ficus leaves a gentle counterpoint to the loud gaiety below.

The night air raised goose bumps on her wet skin. She shivered and Zeke flung an arm around her shoulders, pulling her close. They cuddled together.

Sandy's gaze zeroed in on Mr. Dom's penthouse across the way. The living room was lit, but she couldn't see anyone moving around in the apartment.

"What did you think the first time you saw Cabrini flogging a woman?" Zeke's quiet voice startled her, and the memory of that night came flooding back.

That first time, Sandy had freaked. The red welts Dom had raised on his submissive's back terrified her. She'd left her condo, raced downstairs and found a public phone a block away, from which she'd called the police. Pretending to be a neighbor in Dom's building, she reported screams coming from his apartment and then hung up without giving her name.

By the time the police arrived, Sandy was back on her balcony. She watched Dom open his front door to admit two cops while the submissive—a tall, thin blonde—scrambled to collect her clothes off the floor.

The cops insisted on interviewing the blonde, who—although appearing embarrassed—obviously assured them that she had participated willingly in Dom's sex play.

The cops waved toward the walls, cautioning against disturbing the neighbors, and left.

Since that incident, Dom had experimented with various methods for keeping his submissives from screaming during floggings. The device he'd finally settled on never failed to creep Sandy out: a cloth hood attached to a red rubber ball.

Dom kept the hood in a convenient drawer. Before a flogging, he would shove the ball into his playmate's mouth, lower the hood over her head and buckle the straps around her neck. From watching, Sandy had learned that the hood and ball rendered the submissive blind and dumb, but still able to hear orders. The device permitted Mr. Dominant to use his cane without fear of disturbing his neighbors.

When Sandy finished relating the story to Zeke, he tightened his left arm around her. "Does it excite you to see him with his women?"

"I'm not sure," she said in a thoughtful voice. "I mean, the Kinkys two floors below spank each other sometimes and that's really exciting to me. But they're . . . sharing, having fun together. What Dom . . . I mean, Cabrini . . . does isn't about being a couple or sharing. It's about controlling and degrading his partners. Something has to be very wrong with those poor girls for them to let him do what he does."

Zeke reached over and plucked the tumbler from her hand. Since it was mostly melted ice by now, she didn't protest. He placed it with his drink on the brick ledge and then wrapped both his arms around her. She leaned into the embrace, resting her head against his chest.

"I suspect most of 'those poor girls' are hookers."

She lifted her face. "Really? But they look so young."

He laughed without a trace of humor in his voice. "There isn't a big market for old hookers, Sandy."

She hesitated, but then asked what she was thinking, "Have you ever been with a hooker, Zeke?"

He shook his head. "No, paying for sex doesn't turn me on. And I've seen what that business does to kids."

Sandy inhaled a deep breath and asked quietly, "As a cop, you mean?"

He nodded, keeping his voice to an almost whisper. "I'm with Vice. Six months in that detail is enough to destroy anyone's illusions." He glanced down at her. "I'm on loan to a task force doing surveillance on Cabrini. That's how I first saw you."

"How?" she whispered.

"I was checking to see if our surveillance post could be seen from Cabrini's penthouse. I looked down and saw you on your balcony . . . with your telescope."

She felt a cold finger of fear touch her spine. "Did you tell anyone else?"

"No. No one."

Her shoulders sagged in relief. "Thank God."

"Listen, Sandy, you know you can't spy on the neighbors anymore, don't you?"

"Oh, Zeke, I won't. Ever again. I promise."

He stroked her hair. "Okay, then it's all over. We don't need to talk about it again." His hand moved downward, past her shoulders to the top of the bath sheet. He began tugging at the edge she'd tucked under to hold the towel in place.

Sandy slapped at his hand. "What are you doing?"

"I just want to see what's under that towel." His voice was light and teasing.

"You know very well that there's nothing under this towel." She pulled away from him, but stopped as a thought occurred to her.

Keeping her eyes fixed on his, Sandy knelt in front of him.

"What are you doing?"

Below the railing of the balcony wall and out of sight of the nearby apartments, she slowly unwrapped her bath sheet.

# Chapter Eight

"What the hell . . . ?" Zeke gaped down at her.

She smiled at him. "I'm just returning the favor. I owe you one orgasm." Rolling the terry cloth into an impromptu cushion, she slipped it under her knees. Without the towel, she was completely naked at his feet.

"Oh, baby," he breathed, starting to bend toward her.

Sandy stopped him with a gesture. "No, it's my turn to pleasure you." She reached up and stroked the swelling in his jeans. The bulge immediately grew larger, and his frozen expression made her giggle.

"Like that, do you?" she teased. Her fingers found his zipper, and she carefully maneuvered it open.

Freed, Zeke's penis jutted out at an aggressive angle from his body, gleaming like Carrara marble in the dim light of the balcony. Pale white with darker veins running along its length, the cock looked huge. His erection had prompted the foreskin to retract, exposing his glans. She could see a single drop of pre-cum clinging to the mushroom-shaped tip, and she captured the lonely bead with a lick of her tongue. It tasted salty and viscous.

"Jesus," Zeke swore.

She giggled and leaned forward. Opening her lips wide, she sucked the head of his penis into her mouth. She ran her tongue up and down the slit in the tip and was rewarded with another drop of pre-cum. After swirling her tongue over the surface to lubricate it, she popped the tip out and licked the notched underside.

Zeke trembled and swayed above her. Remembering the pleasure he'd given her thirty minutes before, Sandy delighted in being able to return the favor. While she had gone down on boyfriends in the past, she had never enjoyed the experience. This was different. Zeke was so exciting and so generous in his lovemaking that she wanted to please him. She alternated the licking and sucking motions, concentrating on the engorged head of his penis.

He grabbed handfuls of her hair, trying to pull her closer and shove his cock in deeper. She resisted and yanked her face away, popping the head out of her mouth.

"Not yet, bucko. You're not nearly ready enough."

Determined that this would be the best blow job he'd ever had, she lifted his cock and ran her tongue along its underside—from the head to the base. He tensed, and she could feel his muscles contracting.

"Honey, you're killing me," he muttered.

Pleased to have him feeling off base for once, she continued her tender torment. With the head of his penis pointing toward the night sky, she had access to his testicles. Bending forward and tilting her head, she nudged the hairy sacs with her nose, inhaling their musky, slightly sour scent. She took one of his balls into her mouth and rolled it around gently before grazing it with her teeth.

"God, Sandy, be careful." His voice was hoarse.

She opened her mouth wider and waggled her tongue over

the testicle to soothe him. She committed it to memory: its odd, cushiony feel, wiry hair and distinctive taste. At the same time, she lightly scraped the insides of his thighs with the nails of her left hand.

His breath was coming in short, staccato bursts. "Honey, suck me, please," he begged.

Releasing the testicle, she raised her head to find his penis waving frantically at her. She smiled and seized the bobbing dick. The time for games was over.

Spreading her lips, she took him deep into her mouth.

He groaned as if in agony. "Yesssssss."

She kept her right hand at the base of the rod to keep him from shoving the whole thing into her throat. He was so long and wide, she was afraid she would choke if she took him too fast.

Slowly at first and then more rapidly, she moved her mouth back and forth on his shaft, taking a bit more penis each time. Above her, she could hear Zeke's labored breath and strangled moans. His hips thrust forward, trying to speed things up. She refused to be rushed, setting her own pace and stretching his torment out.

His hard knob rained pre-cum, and she swallowed greedily. She shifted position to take him as deeply as she could. His cock hit the back of her throat. Knowing that she was at her limit, she loosened the pressure on the base of his rod to free him to finish.

He pushed forward eagerly, increasing his pace. Back and forth he rocked, faster and faster with each thrust. He was panting now, completely beyond words.

Sandy concentrated on breathing through her nose, catching a quick breath on every alternate stroke. She knew he was on the verge of coming, and she focused on being ready when he exploded.

His orgasm was sudden and violent. He stiffened, gave an inarticulate shout and released his seed. She gulped as the spurting ejaculate flooded her mouth and dripped out the sides. Pulling back a bit, she tried to give the hot cum more room inside her mouth. She wanted to swallow every precious drop.

Above her, Zeke groaned and swayed. His fists, still balled in her hair, tightened as he stretched with the final tremors of his orgasm.

Sandy felt the cock shrink in her mouth. She released it and licked her lips. Sitting back on her heels, she looked up at him. His eyes were closed, and he panted like an overheated dog.

"Hey, guy. Are you okay?"

Zeke opened his eyes and smiled dreamily at her. "Never been better, baby." He shook his head. "God, where did you learn to do that?"

She giggled. "I just wanted to please you. Sounds like I succeeded."

He staggered two steps backward to lean against the balcony wall. "I'll say. At least now I know I'm in good health."

"What?"

"If I wasn't, I'd be dead right now. You almost blew the top of my head off."

She pulled the bath sheet out from under her knees and wrapped it around her body. Holding a hand up, she let him help her stand. Once she was on her feet, she smoothed the terry cloth over her hips and leaned forward to touch his lips with hers.

"Now we're even."

He grinned. "So it's like that, is it?"

She leaned her head against his shoulder. "Uh-huh. Turnabout is fair play."

He directed her toward the glass door. "Let's go inside. You're shivering again."

"Don't forget our drinks. I don't want them to fall down and kill someone on the street," she said.

Zeke turned to pick up the two tumblers from the balcony ledge. He followed Sandy into her condo.

Once the two of them were inside, she closed and locked the sliding glass door.

He carried the glasses into the kitchen and rinsed them out.

"Can you stay tonight?" she asked, concentrating hard on keeping any hint of desperation out of her voice.

"Absolutely," he said, smiling sideways at her. "We haven't had sex in a bed yet. I'm looking forward to it."

Her relief was so enormous she had to close her eyes to keep him from seeing the emotion. He wasn't in a rush to leave. He wanted to sleep in a bed with her—like a real boyfriend, not a one-night stand.

When she opened her eyes, Zeke was walking toward the refrigerator. "Do you have anything to eat? I didn't have dinner." He opened the door and bent to rummage around.

"Why did you miss dinner?"

He stopped rooting among her vegetables and lifted his head to grin at her. "I was too nervous to eat. You could say I was suffering a crisis of conscience."

"A what?"

"I was going out of my mind, trying to convince myself that we'd both be better off if I didn't call you again."

"Why?" She remembered all the pain she'd experienced in the forty minutes before he'd finally telephoned.

He straightened up and shrugged. "I knew what I was doing was wrong, but I couldn't stay away from you."

Sandy felt as though a rainbow had touched her—she could almost feel the bright colors dancing in her heart. She opened her mouth to speak, but nothing came out. When she tried the second time, she was able to say, "How do you like your eggs?"

He fixed fresh drinks while she cooked. They ate the ham-and-cheese omelets with rye toast in her small dining area with Sandy still in her bath sheet, barefoot.

Conversation seemed to flow. There was so much she wanted to know, and for the first time, he seemed willing to talk. She learned about his childhood in New Jersey, his parents and two sisters. He talked about going into the service, becoming a military cop and then, later, a civilian cop.

Zeke wouldn't let her keep the focus solely on him. With gentle questions, he learned that her boyfriend Josh had morphed into her future brother-in-law. She explained how she had started peeping on her neighbors.

"The night I came home from Josh and Tricia's engagement party three months ago was the first time I ever spied on anyone."

"Where did you get the telescope?"

"Oh, I've had it since I was a teenager. It was stored in the closet." She looked down at her empty plate. "I was driving home and the car radio said stargazers would be able to see three planets that night. I was so depressed, I got the telescope out, hoping for a distraction. I was setting it up when I caught sight of Dom—I mean, Cabrini—having sex with one of his submissives. It was an accident. That was the start of my career as a Peeping Tom."

He grinned. "Don't you mean Thomasina?"

She shook her head. For some reason, it was important that he understand. "I wasn't just spying on people having sex. There were other people, too. Like Mrs. Blue Hair, Mr. Hudson and Miss Skinny-Minnie. It got to where I was checking on them to make sure they were all right."

Zeke leaned forward. "Mrs. Blue Hair, I can understand. She must be an old woman. Tell me about Mr. Hudson and Miss Skinny-Minnie."

Sandy stood, picking up her dirty plate and utensils. "Mr. Hudson is this handsome, elderly gay man who reminded me of Rock Hudson. Once or twice he brought young guys home, but mostly he was by himself. He looked so lonely." She started to reach for Zeke's plate.

Zeke picked up his own dirty dish and stood. "And Miss Skinny-Minnie?" He moved toward the kitchen.

"Oh, she's a model." Sandy followed him to the sink. "Her

whole apartment is decorated with these giant black-and-white blow-up photos of her. She's bulimic. I've watched her scarf down food, like a half gallon of ice cream, in one sitting. Then she stuck her fingers down her throat and bolted for the bathroom."

He turned on the water. "So, you've been keeping an eye on them?"

She nodded, bringing him the frying pan and spatula from the stove. "It sounds stupid, but I felt like their guardian angel, just making sure they were all okay."

Zeke looked down, his gaze meeting hers. "It doesn't sound stupid. It's kind of sweet. But you still need to stop."

"I know and I promise I'll never do it again."

"Good. Now why don't you go get ready for bed, and I'll take care of these dishes." His smile was teasing. "No pajamas, okay?"

Sandy felt a warm tingling between her legs. Without another word, she headed toward the bedroom.

It was one twenty a.m., and she didn't feel tired at all. He'd said no pj's, but she wasn't about to greet him naked. She went to her closet and pulled out the long, sexy black nightgown Dora had given her for Christmas. Removing the bath sheet, she slipped the gown over her head and studied the reflection in the mirror. Not bad.

She washed her face and brushed her teeth. By the time Zeke came looking for her, she was pulling down the spread and plumping up the pillows on her queen-sized bed.

He gave a long, low whistle at the sight of her nightgown. "Very nice. Did you buy that for Josh?"

She held a pillow in front of her body and shook her head, suddenly shy. "No, it was a gift."

He came toward her and took the pillow away. "Well, it's a gift for me—that's for sure." Leaning forward, he kissed her gently.

When she reached to pull him toward her, he stepped back. "Let me take a quick shower, baby. You're all nice and clean and I want to be, too."

She released him. "There's a new toothbrush in the medicine cabinet."

"Thanks. I'll be right back."

Sandy climbed into bed and drifted into a pleasant reverie while she listened to the water running. She could hardly believe all that had happened in the last twenty-four hours. Here she was, dating—okay, well, maybe she was fucking, not dating—a vice cop who could have busted her, but didn't. And he didn't just screw and run. He was hanging around, eating her food, bathing in her tub and sleeping in her bed. It was like a gift from God.

She heard the shower stop in the bathroom. Zeke would be coming to bed any minute now. Her heart was pounding so hard that her rib cage was reverberating. Her mouth had gone dry. She sat up in bed and checked her reflection in the mirror over the dresser. Her face was flushed and she was breathing fast. Should she turn the bedside lamp off or leave it on? Sweet mercy! She felt like a twenty-year-old virgin.

Zeke was brushing his teeth; she could hear him at the sink.

Throwing back the covers, Sandy jumped out of bed and ran to her vanity. She began fluffing her hair, trying to get the dark waves to lie straight. Reaching for the hairbrush, she bent over, then combed her hair forward from the nape of her neck over her face. Suddenly the bathroom door opened.

"Hi," Zeke said.

Sandy jumped and bumped her head on the front of the vanity. "Ow!" she yelped, dropping the brush.

"Are you okay?" he asked.

"Yeah, I'm fine." She pushed her hair back from her face. It took a second before she could see again. The first thing she saw was the naked man standing in front of her. She gasped and staggered back a step.

He grinned. "I didn't bring any pj's with me. Is that a problem?"

She stared at his body, unable to take in all of him at once.

Despite the fact that he was nude, Zeke conveyed an image of strength and power. His torso was long and lean, his shoulders broad and his hips narrow. Wiry hair covered his muscular forearms and legs. Jutting out from its own nest of hair, his semierect penis waved at her. The sight made her smile, and she relaxed a fraction.

"Do I pass?" he asked as he'd done earlier at the pub.

"You're gorgeous and you know it," she said, shaking her head. "I feel like a hippo next to you."

"None of that, baby." He came forward and cupped her elbows with his hands. He leaned down to kiss her mouth. "You're my beautiful, bodacious lover, and I won't have anyone insulting you. Not even you."

She pressed her forehead against his. "You're good at perking up my ego."

"I hope so because you're good at perking up something of mine, too." He slid his right hand inside the bodice of her night-gown. His fingernails lightly scraped across the top of her breast, almost but not touching the nipple. "In fact, I think it would be hard for me to perk up any more."

Sandy giggled and reached between their bodies for his cock. She began to pump her hand up and down, sliding his foreskin back and forth over the glans. He responded immediately, his penis lengthening and hardening.

Zeke closed his eyes and tilted his head to one side. His breathing became audible. "Oh, baby, that feels so good."

Still pumping, she leaned forward to nibble on his bare shoulder. She worked her way along his collarbone, licking and biting the clean, taut skin.

He began to fondle her breasts, teasing her nipples.

"Mmmmmm," she moaned as he rolled the already sensitive tips between his thumbs and forefingers.

He nudged her backward until the backs of her legs hit the bed.

"Is this a hint?" she teased.

"Baby, I'll say it straight out: I want you on your back so I can fill you with my cock."

Her lungs tightened. She let him help her onto the bed, where she scooted along the mattress to make room for him. For a moment he lay on top of her, his cock rubbing against the thin silk of her nightgown. Then he propped himself up on his elbows, creating a space between their upper bodies.

Sandy reached up to lightly kiss his lips. "Hi."

"Hello, yourself." He deepened the kiss, stroking her tongue with his.

This time, there was none of the frantic desperation that had characterized their first joining. By unspoken agreement, they kept their pace slow and easy.

Her nightgown was soon discarded beside the bed.

Zeke touched her everywhere, asking again and again, "Do you like this?" and "What about this?" He moved his lips and fingers along her jawline, inside her wrist and behind her knees.

When he licked behind her right knee, Sandy almost flew off the bed in shock. She hadn't realized there was an erogenous zone behind her knee. Or in the hollow behind her ear. Or inside her belly button. It astounded her that he could know things about her body that she didn't know.

She had never had a lover who was so attentive to her needs. He made her feel like a cherished treasure. She found herself responding in kind, trying to maximize his satisfaction.

Time after time, they brought each other to the brink of climax and then backed off, opting to prolong their foreplay rather than culminate the act.

When Sandy finally whispered to him, "Now, please," both of them were trembling on the edge of excitement and exhaustion. Zeke shifted his hips and increased his tempo, sending them over the precipice and flying off into space.

Her vagina and womb seemed to expand into one large flaming ball. Fire raced along her spine to her brain, overloading its circuits. Sandy caught a glimpse of a bright smattering of lights, and then everything went dark. She slipped from wakefulness to sleep without even being aware that the boundary had been crossed.

For his part, Zeke stayed conscious just long enough to shift his weight off her body and to her side. He reached over to switch off the bedside light before wrapping his arm around her waist and snuggling his head in the warm curve between her neck and shoulder.

# Chapter Nine

S andy slowly roused from sleep, aware of two things: Her right leg was draped over a man's hairy leg, and she needed to pee.

Opening her eyes, she found herself staring into Zeke's blue eyes. The sight of him reminded her of the previous night and filled her with contentment.

"Good morning," she murmured.

"Back at ya," he responded. "Now that you're awake, I can go to the bathroom."

She grinned. "Have you been waiting for me to wake up? I'm sorry."

He shook his head. "Don't be. I like watching you sleep and didn't want to disturb you." He dropped a kiss on her forehead before untangling his limbs from hers to sit up. "But now that you are awake, I need to go see a man about a dog."

Sandy ignored the pressure from her own bladder in order to enjoy the sight of him crossing the room naked. He had one of the finest asses she had ever seen.

Once he'd closed the bathroom door behind his excellent ass, she checked the clock—nine thirty—and bounded out of bed to heed nature's call herself.

The hall bathroom was not as tidy as usual. Her silk bathrobe was on the floor along with her black dress and the hand towels that Zeke had used the night before. Sandy stepped over the discarded items to reach the commode.

The shock of the messy bathroom was nothing compared to the shock of seeing her reflection in the mirror. Sandy gaped in amazement at the nude, sexy creature staring back at her. The woman in the mirror had disheveled hair, puffy lips and several hickeys on her neck and breasts. But more importantly, her reflection had a satisfied, happy expression.

For the first time in two years, Sandy felt beautiful.

She could hear Zeke moving around in the condo and hurried to finish. After washing her hands and face, she picked up her robe and went to find him.

He was in the kitchen, making a fresh pot of coffee. As she rounded the corner, she saw he was in jeans, his feet and chest bare.

"Hey, babe, what have you got to eat?"

"I can slice up some fresh fruit and make toast," she offered.

"That will work. I just want to take the edge off now. Later we can go out for brunch." He reached into the cupboard for a couple of mugs.

Sandy almost sighed with joy. He was staying! She opened the refrigerator, looking for the grapes, oranges and apples, hoping they hadn't gone bad.

While she was slicing the fruit, the phone rang. Sandy reached for it and then hesitated, her hand above the receiver.

"What's wrong?" Zeke asked.

"It might be my mother. I'm going to let the machine pick up first."

After the fourth ring and her message, a female voice spoke. "Sandy, it's Annie from the bar."

She grabbed the receiver. "Hi, Annie. What's up?"

"Pete told me to call you. I told him he was being silly, but he insisted I tell you. . . ." Her voice trailed off.

"Tell me what?" Sandy cradled the phone against her shoulder and continued slicing the apple.

"There was this rich older guy in here last night, asking about you. You probably saw him; he came in just as you were leaving."

Sandy dropped the knife.

Zeke, who was setting the table, looked up. "What's the matter?"

"What did you tell him?" Her voice fell to a whisper; fear made her throat tight. Zeke moved to stand beside her. He was frowning.

"I didn't tell him anything, of course. It was that stupid Dennis who shot his mouth off."

Sandy closed her eyes and waited. She knew Annie wasn't finished yet.

"Dennis told him your first name and that you lived in the neighborhood. Pete heard him and stepped in to stop him from flapping his gums."

"Thank God. Did Cabrini say why he wanted to know?"

"Is that his name? Pete said he looked like bad news and that—"

Sandy interrupted her. "Annie, did he say anything?" She was being rude, but she needed to know.

"He said you were a hottie, and he wanted to give you a call."

*Yeah, right. Like I believe that.*

Annie continued speaking. "Anyway, Pete didn't like the look of him and told me to call you. Okay?"

"Yeah, thanks, Annie. And thank Pete for me, would you?"

"Sure. Talk to you soon." The phone went dead.

Sandy handed the receiver to Zeke, who hung it up for her. "What was that all about?" he asked.

"Cabrini was asking questions about me in the bar. Dennis, the guy you blew off, told him my name and that I lived nearby."

She could tell from the look on his face that he was as unhappy as she was.

"Shit." He slammed a palm down on the counter. The sudden noise made her jump. "Maybe you should come stay at my apartment for a while."

The words comforted her, but . . . "I can't do that, Zeke. You said your apartment is on the other side of White Rock Lake. It would add an hour to my commute in the morning." She shook her head. "He won't go looking for me. And even if he did and found me, I'll just say that he reminded me of my ex-father-in-law or my psychiatrist or something weird like that." She patted his hand. "Nothing is going to happen." *Am I trying to convince him or me?*

He frowned. "Fine. I'll move in here. I'm not leaving you alone in this condo with Cabrini right across the street."

She smiled. "And that reduces your commute to the time it takes to ride the elevator upstairs to your surveillance post."

His expression cleared. "Yeah, think of all the gas I'll save."

The phone rang again. For the second time, Sandy waited to see who was on the line.

"Alexandra, it's your mother. Pick up. I know you're there. You don't go to church on Sunday mornings."

Zeke raised his eyebrows, and Sandy shook her head. She wasn't ready to try to explain Victoria Davis to him.

"You hung up on me last night. I expect an apology and an explanation. Call me." Her mother slammed the phone down.

"Wow." Zeke recoiled from the answering machine. "You said your mom was difficult. You didn't say she was a dragon."

Sandy sighed. "You should hear her when she's really angry."

They'd both lost interest in sitting down at the table to eat. Instead, Sandy carried their plates to the living room, where they sat in front of the television and watched the Sunday morning news shows.

Over the next hour, they slowly relaxed. The discovery that Sandy was a Democrat appalled Zeke, a typical conservative cop. They argued amicably about politics, and the specter of Cabrini gradually faded.

At eleven a.m., as *The McLaughlin Group*'s closing credits rolled, he began to nuzzle Sandy's ear. "Hey, sweetheart, are you hungry?" He picked up her hand and put it on the fly of his jeans.

She twisted her head to look at him. "I thought you were going to take me out to brunch."

"And I will. Later. Right now, I was thinking we could satisfy another hunger." He pressed her hand against his hardening cock.

Sandy started to giggle. "You're a mess." She let him push her back against the sofa cushions.

He stood and peeled off his pants before kneeling on the floor beside her. Leaning forward over her, he parted the folds of her robe. He kissed her belly button before moving upward to lick her breasts.

"Ohhhh," she moaned. "More."

He lifted his head so that he could see her face. "Tell me about your fantasies."

"Whaaatttt?" She didn't want to think; she wanted to feel.

He nibbled on one nipple for a second and then let it pop out of his mouth. "I said, tell me about your fantasies."

"This is one." She squirmed, trying to maneuver her breast back into his mouth. "Come on, Zeke. You started this."

"And I'll finish it. Once you've told me about your fantasies." He rolled the nipple between his fingers.

"What fantasies?"

"The ones you think about when you're alone in bed at night, masturbating." He slipped his other hand between her legs and massaged her nether lips. "Come on, baby. Tell me what you dream about."

"I . . . think about the things I've never done before."

"Like what?" His voice was lower, rougher.

"Like bondage. I've never been tied up and I'd like to know what that's like."

"What else?" He parted her folds and slipped a finger into her vagina.

Sandy arched, pressing herself against his hand.

"You're getting wet, baby. You like talking about this stuff." He added a second finger to the first.

"I like what you're doing," she groaned. "Oh, God, more, more!"

"Answer my question." Three fingers now. He rubbed his thumb against her clit. Sandy started a rocking motion to match the in-and-out slide of his fingers in her vagina.

"What other things do you dream about your lover doing to you?" he asked. His breathing was audible now.

Sandy threw her arms over her head and lifted her hips toward him. His hands stopped moving, and she gasped her dismay. "Zeke!"

"Answer my question."

Desperate for his touch, she responded. "I've wondered what discipline would be like. I mean, if someone else . . . a man was in control of my body."

"Mmmmmm," he murmured encouragingly.

"Not flogging or anything like that. Just teasing. You know. Touch me. Please."

He rewarded her by moving his hands again. For several minutes, the only sounds were Sandy's sighs and moans. Her pussy was weeping now, bathing Zeke's fingers with her juices.

"Tell me when you're ready to come," he rasped.

"Now," she begged. "Please!"

There was a pause while he ripped open a condom. Once he had it on, he climbed on the couch to cover her body. He pushed his penis against her folds, probing for the vaginal opening. She wriggled and scooted, helping him. As his cock slid into her wetness, they both groaned their pleasure.

She ran her hands down his muscled back, lightly caressing him. When she reached his ass, she cupped his cheeks with her palms, squeezing the twin globes.

His response was immediate. He pulled partway out of her body and then slammed back in, setting the pace. The rhythmic wet slap of their bodies was audible.

Sandy could feel the sweat running down her hips and thighs. The scent of their passion was everywhere.

She thrust her hips back and forth against his, seeking release.

Zeke panted above her, a look of intense concentration on his face. He groaned, "Sandy. Oh, baby. You feel so good." With his every thrust, she felt the thwack of his balls against her body.

One minute Sandy was straining to reach the precipice; the next, she had tumbled over the edge. She was dimly aware of Zeke's body stiffening as he poured himself into her. Her vaginal muscles clamped down on him, trying to squeeze every precious drop from his penis.

They collapsed into a boneless heap, huffing and panting as they recovered.

For several minutes, they were content to lie side by side. Sandy lifted a hand to softly brush the damp curls back from his forehead.

He opened his eyes and smiled. "A penny for your thoughts."

She smiled back. "I'm just thinking how fast things changed.

Two days ago, we didn't even know each other. Now look at us."

"Oh, I knew you. I'd been following you, watching you, thinking about you for a couple of weeks."

"You were?" She propped herself up on one elbow, surprised. It had never occurred to her that he had been watching for that long.

"Yeah. Every night, I'd lie in bed, wondering about you. I wanted to know who you were and what you were thinking."

She stroked his cheek. "I was wishing for someone like you."

He turned his head to kiss her palm. "Now that you've got me, what do you want to do with me?"

"Everything."

Zeke grinned, his eyes dancing. " 'Everything' is a tall order. I figured we'd start with your fantasies and work from there."

Sandy outlined his lips with her index finger. "What about *your* fantasies? You keep asking about mine, but you haven't shared yours."

He grinned lazily. "You got a start on my fantasies last night on that balcony."

She tilted her head and looked quizzically at him. "You mean my going down on you?"

He shook his head. "No, going down on me in public."

As the meaning of his words sank in, Sandy sat upright. "Let me get this straight. You fantasize about having sex in public places?"

"Sick, isn't it?" he agreed.

She giggled. "Really sick. What's that about?"

He shrugged. "I've always been an adrenaline junkie. It's why I joined the military and then, after I got out, why I became a cop. Most of the guys in Vice are like me."

"But those are legal ways to get a rush. Having sex in public will get you arrested."

He shook his head a second time. "No way. No cop is going to arrest a brother officer for diddling his girl." He reached up to stroke her right breast.

Hearing herself described as "his girl," Sandy felt as though he'd just hugged her. She watched his hand caress her body. "You had a nerve, judging me for peeping at people—a perv like you."

He shrugged. "I agree. Maybe that's what attracted me to you in the first place."

"So where have you had sex in public before?"

"Your balcony was the closest I've ever come."

"Ever come?" she repeated in an arch tone.

They laughed together.

"I'm really interested," Sandy insisted, looking down at him. "Where do you dream about having sex?"

"I don't know." He shook his head. "Just somewhere that I might get caught. Like in an office on a desk or in my car or on a plane."

"The Mile High Club."

"Yeah, like that."

Sandy slid her hand along his bare shoulder and squeezed his bicep. "Well, maybe we can make some of our fantasies come true."

Instead of answering her, he glanced at his watch. "It's close to noon. Why don't you shower, and then I'll take you out to brunch?"

"Okay." She stood and looked down at him. Lying there naked on her sofa, he was sex on a stick—so gorgeous he took her breath away.

"Go on," he said. "Use your bathroom. I'll shower in the other one."

Sandy headed toward the bedroom. Going out to eat with Zeke was another milestone. He was so hot, she'd be proud to have her friends and neighbors see them together.

His clothes were hanging in her bathroom. She liked seeing them there. The sight was both intimate and reassuring.

She left the bathroom door to her room standing open because she hated coming out of the shower to a room full of steam. After turning the water on, she removed her robe. Pushing the shower curtain aside, she climbed into the tub and reached for the soap.

Her nipples and pussy were pleasantly sore; in less than forty-eight hours, they'd had quite a workout. She lathered her body while fantasizing about bringing Zeke to meet her family. Her brothers, Matt and Tony, would like him immediately and Tricia would be thrilled just to see Sandy dating again. The problem, as always, would be her mother.

Victoria Davis was a formidable woman. Nothing was ever good enough for her—including her children. Sandy had spent her entire childhood being told she was too fat, too lazy and too stupid. Her father had acted as a buffer between his wife and his children; things had been much worse since Richard Davis' death.

Sandy's mother had been furious to find that her husband had left a specific monetary bequest to each of his four children in his will. Richard had known that Victoria would use his money as a weapon to control their children and had taken action to prevent her from doing so. His generous bequests allowed Matt to start medical school, Tony to move to L.A. to pursue an acting career, Sandy to upgrade from an apartment to a condominium with security staff, and Tricia to begin her own small business binding and repairing books. Sandy smiled through the cascade of water. Her father would have been pleased. *I miss you, Daddy. You'd like Zeke.*

As she soaped her legs, she tried to imagine Victoria's reaction to Zeke. Knowing her mother as she did, Sandy suspected that an introduction would be followed by an interrogation. The questions would start out pleasant and innocuous-sounding, but would soon become condescending and harsh. Zeke didn't seem like the kind of man to be easily intimidated and that would bring out the worst in her mother. Sandy resolved to keep the two of them apart as long as possible.

After rinsing the shampoo out of her hair, she reached down to turn off the faucets. *No family is perfect.*

Getting ready to climb out of the bathtub, she pushed the shower curtain out of the way and almost had a heart attack.

Zeke was standing just outside the bathtub.

Before she could gather her wits enough to ask what the hell he was doing there, he'd grabbed one wrist and pulled it over her head.

"Zeke," she exclaimed.

Ignoring her, he snapped a handcuff over her wrist and secured the other end to the shower-curtain rod.

While Sandy was still staring at her bound wrist and tugging ineffectually at it, he captured her other wrist. Quickly and with an economy of motion, he handcuffed that one to the rod as well. He took two steps backward, away from the tub, and grinned at her.

Sandy stared in shock at her reflection in the mirror. She was hanging, dripping wet and bound by her wrists, from the shower-curtain rod. Her bare feet were still inside the bathtub, where droplets of water ran down her body.

"What are you doing?" she cried.

"Helping to fulfill one of your fantasies." For the first time, she realized that he was stark naked. His cock was at full mast, jutting aggressively toward her unprotected body. He reached out one hand to brush her wet locks off her face.

As the meaning of his words sank in, Sandy felt a hot thrill course through her body. She was naked and helpless in her own bathroom.

"But I was thinking about being tied to the bed," she protested.

"Sorry. You didn't specify that. I was forced to improvise." His expression was smug. "Baby, I've got to tell you. You look fantastic hanging there."

She stared at her reflection. He was right. With her arms stretched over her head, her full breasts were uplifted and pulled taut. The contrast between her dark hair and pale white skin was unbelievably erotic. She looked like a pagan goddess being offered in sacrifice to appease an angry god. As she watched, her nipples hardened and jutted proudly forward. She felt a flood of warmth between her legs.

"What now?" she asked.

"Now we play."

# Chapter Ten

Zeke stared at Sandy, mesmerized by the sight of her hanging there, helpless. He had to restrain himself from grabbing her legs and wrapping them around his waist while he shoved his cock inside her.

She looked so incredible—like a slave on display in an auction. He was free to do whatever he wanted to her.

When she had first mentioned the bondage thing, he hadn't been excited by it. As a cop, he'd seen too many women who had been raped to get turned on by a woman being forced into sex— even as a game. He'd worked too many scenes where hookers—or their johns—had been restrained to a bed or a chair in a motel room. Tying a woman to a bed held no appeal for him. But this . . .

"I'll be right back," he told her.

"Wait, Zeke! Don't leave me like this."

"I'm not. I'll be right back." He wanted to give her a few minutes to think about being chained and completely helpless.

In the living room, he headed for the items he'd retrieved from the box of sex toys. His old nickel-plated handcuffs had come from that box. The DPD no longer used metal handcuffs, instead employing the newer plastic restraints to secure suspects. When he'd put together the collection of sex toys to scare Sandy, he'd thrown two pairs of the old metal cuffs into the box.

He collected the nipple clamps, a blindfold and a long purple feather. There was also an item in the shape of a blue butterfly, but that was for later.

From the living room, he went to the kitchen, where he filled a small bowl with ice cubes.

"Zeke!" Sandy hollered.

*Good. She's getting anxious.* "I'll be right there," he answered.

By the time he returned to the bathroom, Sandy was looking agitated. She had scrambled out of the tub and her bare feet were now resting on the bath mat.

"Where were you?" she asked in an aggrieved voice.

"Finding the accessories we'll need." He began setting the items he'd collected on the tiled counter.

Trying to see what he was doing, she slid her handcuffs to the right along the shower rod to get a better view.

He picked up an ice cube and turned to face her.

"What are you going to do with that?" she asked.

"Whatever I want."

Her eyes widened, and she drew away from him, bumping into the side of the bathtub. "No, Zeke."

"Yes, Sandy. If I remember your exact words, they were 'I've wondered what it would be like if a man was in control of my body.' Well, baby, here I am. Sometimes you do get what you ask for."

As his words sank in, she began worrying her upper lip between her teeth.

He reached out an arm and snaked it around her waist. Pulling her naked body toward him, he pressed the ice cube against the curve of her right breast.

She gasped and then shivered, but Zeke didn't think it was wholly because of the cube's temperature.

He continued around her breast, making tighter and tighter circles on every circuit as he approached the center. The nipple lengthened and its color darkened to a pale purple. He could feel the tension in her body and hear the hitch in her breathing.

Zeke tossed the ice cube into the bathtub and seized her rosy nub, rolling the nipple between his thumb and index finger.

"Mmmmmm," Sandy sighed.

He lowered his head and took her other nipple into his mouth. He began to nibble, gently at first and then a little more roughly.

Sandy's murmurs escalated to full-fledged moans. She was also rocking back and forth, bumping his erection with her stomach and hip. "Please, Zeke," she groaned, her eyes closed.

He released the nipple and looked up at her face. "Please what?" he asked.

"Please more," she begged.

He reached across the room and grabbed the blindfold off the counter.

Sandy's arms were beginning to ache from being held above her head for so long. That strain was counterbalanced by the pleasure of Zeke's mouth and hands. Despite the icy cube, her breasts were burning, and her pussy was on fire.

When he removed his mouth from her nipple, she pleaded with him for more. Instead, she felt him shift away from her. As she opened her eyes, he slipped a black mask over her head.

"Zeke! What are you doing?"

"Relax, baby. It's all right."

The blindfold was really a set of nylon eye patches with two straps that he adjusted to fit her head.

"What are you going to do?"

"Just trust me."

Without pausing to think, Sandy responded, "I do trust you, Zeke. More than any man I know."

She felt him freeze, and her heart clenched. *I shouldn't have said that. I'm such an idiot.*

His hand gently stroked her cheek. "Thank you."

She turned her face away from him. "I'm sorry. I shouldn't have said anything."

He captured her face between both his hands. "Don't, Sandy. I know exactly how you're feeling because I'm feeling it, too." His lips lightly touched hers. "It's as though I've known you forever. I'd trust you with my life." He hesitated and then added, "And my heart."

Sandy's heart swelled. "I wish I could see your face."

He kissed her again. "It's a good thing you can't. I probably wouldn't have had the courage to say that if I was looking into your eyes." His voice changed. "Now stop distracting me. I have work to do here."

She waited nervously, reminding herself that she had been the one who'd introduced the subject of bondage into their conversation.

There was an odd noise, like the clinking of a chain. Sandy felt something brush her breast and realized that Zeke was attaching one of the nipple clips to her right breast. He released it slowly so that while she felt the pinch, it did not snap closed. The pressure on her tender nipple made her squirm.

"Is that good?" he asked as he put the second clip on her other breast.

"Yes," she whispered.

"Great. I want you to spread your legs as wide as you can."

She tried to obey, but found that the handcuffs limited her range of motion.

"That's all right," he said, stroking her hip. "This is fine."

Fine for what? What was he planning to do?

The first touch of the ice cube on her right breast made her jump. Once she realized what it was, she relaxed again.

Then he angled the cube against her nipple where it could touch both her skin and the alligator clip. The metal quickly became painfully cold. She wiggled, trying to escape the frigid grip of the clip.

"Zeke," she whimpered.

He didn't answer her, but he did remove the ice. She felt a featherlight touch across the surface of her right nipple. The gentle caress took away the pain of the cold.

All the physical sensations on her tender flesh at one time were overwhelming: pressure from the clip, the cold metal and now the brush of what felt like a feather across her skin.

Zeke continued to skim the feather over her body: armpits, lower belly, behind the knees.

"You look like a pagan queen," he told her. "All that smooth, white skin. You should never cover your body, Sandy. Everyone should be able to see you as I see you right now."

Despite the ice, a wave of heat spread from her core to her belly and breasts. Her limbs felt weak and alien, as though they were no longer under her control. Even though she trusted Zeke, being exposed in this way was a little frightening. If he walked out of the condo, she'd be left here until . . . until her job sent someone to check and find out why she didn't show up at work on time tomorrow morning. Or until they called her emergency contact. Whose name had she put on her employment application as the emergency contact? *Oh, God. Mother.*

The idea of being discovered by her mother bound and naked like this was too horrible to contemplate. She pushed the thought away and concentrated on listening. What was Zeke doing now?

A change in air current warned that he had knelt down in front of her. Putting his hands on the insides of her thighs, he spread them wider. He parted her nether lips with his fingers. She waited for him to begin stroking her clitoris.

Sandy felt his warm lips touch her clit.

"Ohhhhhh," she moaned with pleasure. And then: "AHHH!" The shock of an ice cube against her clit made her leap away from him.

He was ready for her reaction. One hand cupped her ass and pulled her back toward him while the other found her pleasure button again. She felt the warm touch of his lips once more.

Alert now, she remained tense, waiting for his mouth to open and press that damn ice cube against her pussy. She didn't have long to wait. His lips parted and the dripping cube touched her flesh.

This time, since she was expecting it, Sandy didn't jump. Zeke held the cube against her clit for a count of three before closing his mouth and pressing his lips to her skin again.

She now understood the pattern and relaxed. Warm-then-cold. Cold-then-warm. The contrast was . . . stimulating. Warm-then-cold. Cold-then-warm. She began to rock back and forth in counterpoint to his mouth. The heat in her pussy intensified. Zeke seemed to sense this, because she heard him spit the ice cube out into the bathtub. He returned to licking and sucking her clit in earnest. His big hands cradled the globes of her ass while his tongue teased the tiny flange at the top of her labia.

Sandy panted now, grinding her mons into his face. Her clit was fully erect, protruding like a tiny penis into his mouth. She pulled on the handcuffs.

"Zeke," she groaned as an orgasm overtook her.

He tightened his arms around her hips just as her legs gave way. Between his grip and her restrained wrists, she couldn't collapse if she'd wanted to. As the firestorm swept through her body, she strained in his embrace. Stars danced across her vision, and her head fell forward limply.

She was dimly aware when Zeke unclipped the nipple clamps and unlocked the handcuffs. He caught her body as she sagged forward into his arms. Shifting her weight, he toted her to the bedroom in a fireman's carry. After laying her on the bed, he lifted her head to remove the blindfold.

She opened her eyes. "Hi."

"Hi, yourself," he said, brushing her hair back from her forehead. "How are you?"

"Great."

"Did we fulfill your fantasy?" He smiled down at her.

"I'll say." She let her eyes drift closed again.

"Hey, don't go out on me," he said, tapping her cheek with a gentle hand. "We still haven't had brunch."

"Brunch? What time is it?"

"After one. Where would you like to eat?"

She thought about it for a minute. "What about Gemima's? It's right down the block and they have a courtyard where we could eat outside."

"Gemima's it is." He grabbed her hands to pull her into a sitting position.

"Owwww," she complained. "My wrists and arms are still sore."

"I'm sorry, baby. I didn't think. Do you need something for the pain?"

She shook her head. "No, I'll be all right. Just don't yank on my arms."

"Okay, baby." He patted her naked shoulder. "I'm going to go get dressed. How about you?"

"I can get dressed if that's what you really want." She nodded toward his penis, which—while not fully erect—was still flying at half-mast.

He grinned. "For once, I'm more hungry for food than sex. I'm used to a more substantial breakfast than you serve."

She smiled at him. "Okay, okay. I get the message. I'll get dressed."

"Wear a skirt."

She frowned at his commanding tone. "Why?"

"Because I like your legs." He turned and headed back toward her bathroom.

Pleased by the compliment, Sandy stared after him, but the sight of his bare buttocks distracted her. *God, he's gorgeous.*

When he shut the bathroom door, she stood up and went to her closet. She was glad that he'd noticed her legs. They were one of her best features.

When Zeke returned, he was fully dressed in jeans, shirt and jacket. She was wearing a white peasant blouse—off the shoulders and billowy—and a multicolored skirt.

"Very, very nice," he approved.

"You shaved," she said.

"Yeah. Hope you don't mind my borrowing your razor and cream."

"Don't be silly. I did sort of like your gangsta five o'clock shadow."

"Tell me that tonight when I start scratching you with my beard." He studied her appearance with a critical eye. "Are you wearing anything under that getup?"

She smiled flirtatiously. "Not a thing. You like?"

The corners of his mouth quirked up. "Yeah, I like. And it will go perfectly with your gift."

"Another gift?" she asked.

He looked around the room and then retrieved the nylon blindfold off the bed. When he approached her, she began backing up.

"No way, Zeke. I've had enough."

"It's just a gift. I promise you'll like it."

Against her better judgment, she let him slip the blindfold over her head and eyes.

"Now stand there. I'll be right back."

She heard him leave the room. *He's heading back to that box of sex toys.* Then she realized he was in her bathroom.

In a moment, he returned. He bent over and touched one of her calves.

"Lift up your leg, honey," he ordered.

She picked up her right leg and felt him slip something over it.

"Okay, now pick up the other one."

He slid two straps up over her thighs, raising her skirt at the same time. "Hold this up, please." He tucked the gathered skirt into her hands to keep it out of the way.

"What are you doing, Zeke?"

"Something nice, I promise." He hugged her as he pulled the straps up to rest on her bare hips. The device seemed to be some kind of harness with a thong that went between her legs. His hands separated her thighs and then he positioned what felt like a piece of plastic against her pussy, parting her lips to nestle the alien object inside, against her clit and vaginal opening.

"Zeke, what on earth . . ."

"Just trust me, Sandy. You'll like it." He pulled the blindfold off her head. "All done. Take a look."

Still holding her skirt in the air, Sandy looked down.

There seemed to be a piece of blue plastic resting against her mons, covering her pubic hair. She turned to look at herself in the dresser mirror. The blue plastic was in the shape of a butterfly. Together with the blue straps, it looked almost like a bikini bottom. She reached below the butterfly to touch the bullet-shaped object he'd tucked within her labial folds.

"Is it a vibrator?"

He smiled and nodded.

She frowned at him. "Where's the control?"

His smile widened to a grin. "Here." He patted his jacket pocket.

"It's remote controlled?" As the implications of that dawned on her, Sandy's mouth dropped open. "You mean you can switch the vibrator on while we're out to lunch?"

"Yup." He looked absurdly pleased.

She glanced from him to the reflection of the blue butterfly in the mirror and back again. A tiny fire began to burn inside her at the thought of the vibrator buzzing while they were out in public.

"Ready to go?" he asked, holding a hand out to her.

She smoothed her skirt down over her hips and took his hand, and they left the condo together, stopping long enough for Sandy to collect her purse.

After she locked her door, they started down the hallway. Mr. and Mrs. Guzman were standing at the elevator, waiting. Their toy poodles, Sasha and Gigi, danced at their feet. Jacob Guzman smiled at Sandy and Zeke.

"Look, Lois. It's Sandy and her new boyfriend."

Sandy felt a flutter of excitement at hearing Zeke referred to as her boyfriend.

Zeke took her hand and squeezed it.

Sandy smiled and began the introductions. "Mr. and Mrs. Guzman, I'd like you to meet Zeke . . ." She stumbled, suddenly realizing she didn't know his last name. Lois Guzman's gaze sharpened as she stared at the couple.

"Zeke Prada." Zeke rescued her by reaching his hand out to Mr. Guzman. "I'm really sorry that we woke you up last night."

Jacob Guzman took the proffered hand and shook it. "That's all right. Lois and I, we were young once, too." He elbowed his wife. "Weren't we, honey?"

Mrs. Guzman was still staring at Zeke the way a judge eyes a murder defendant. Sandy stabbed at the DOWN button, wishing the elevator would hurry up and arrive.

"What do you do, Mr. Prada?" Lois asked.

Zeke offered a winning smile. "I'm a cop, Mrs. Guzman."

"Really." The old woman's voice warmed several degrees.

The elevator doors slid open and Sandy breathed an inaudible sigh of relief. The two couples and the dogs got on board, and the doors closed soundlessly.

Sandy desperately searched her mind for an innocuous comment that might distract Lois from her interrogation. Before she could open her mouth, she jumped in surprise. The silver cylinder nestled against her vagina had suddenly started to vibrate.

# Chapter Eleven

The vibrator humming against her clit chased every other thought out of Sandy's head. She was vaguely aware of Zeke making idle conversation with the Guzmans on the way to the lobby, but her focus was on the wonderful sensations she was experiencing. She tightened her buttocks in order to bear down on the cylinder. In seconds, her pussy was wet and aching.

The elevator arrived at the lobby and Mr. and Mrs. Guzman stepped out, tugging the poodles behind them. With a hand on her elbow, Zeke guided Sandy out of the car.

"It was very nice meeting you, Zeke," Mrs. Guzman purred.

"And you, too, Lois. I hope I'll see you both again."

Sandy mumbled some sort of good-bye as Zeke led her across the lobby and out onto the street.

It was a beautiful afternoon, mild and sunny. The M-Line trolley clattered past them.

"How are you doing?" he whispered in her ear.

"You bastard. I'll get you for this," she threatened. "Turn it off now before I lose control right here on this damn sidewalk."

Instantly, the vibrator shut off. Sandy wasn't sure whether she wanted to celebrate or grieve the loss of the throbbing bullet.

"Better?" he asked.

"Yes, no thanks to you."

"Come on, how did it feel?"

"Like heaven."

"That's my girl." He dropped a kiss on the top of her head. "Now, come along, and I'll feed you."

They crossed the street and walked the two blocks south to Gemima's. Sandy calmed down while Zeke entertained her with a line of silly chatter about the shops they were passing. When they arrived at the corner, he bypassed the outdoor seating and held the door open for Sandy to enter the restaurant.

A hostess greeted them, asking where they would like to sit. Sandy asked for the courtyard, and the woman led them across the hall.

The courtyard was paved with uneven red bricks and furnished with wrought iron tables and chairs, surrounded by luxuriant trees and plants in large earthenware pots. Since it was now almost two p.m., there were no other diners in the outdoor room.

The hostess waved a hand, offering them their choice of tables. Zeke pointed to a corner, one partially screened by a huge dracaena plant. He leaned over and whispered to the hostess, slipping her a bill before he pulled Sandy's chair out. After Sandy was seated, he took the opposite chair. The hostess handed them each a menu and then departed.

"What did you say to her?" she asked.

"I told her we wanted a waiter with some discretion, not one who was going to interrupt us every five minutes. I'm here to talk to you, not the help."

Sandy giggled and placed her hand over his on the table.

"What shall we do after lunch?" she asked.

"Well, we need to stop by my apartment and pick up some

clothes. I have to be at a meeting at the station at nine in the morning. If you want me to spend the night, I'll need to pack a bag." He turned the hand that was under hers over and squeezed her palm.

Trying to act cool despite being thrilled by his words, Sandy asked, "You said your apartment was east of White Rock Lake. Where?"

"On Garland Road, near the Arboretum. It's convenient to the station and I've lived there since I got out of the service."

"I love the Arboretum. My father was a big gardener, and he used to be on their board."

Zeke shrugged. "I don't really know the place. I've been there a couple of times for weddings, and I took my nephews one year for the Easter egg hunt, but that's all."

A germ of an idea took hold in Sandy's brain, but they were interrupted before she could fully explore it. The waiter brought a tray with water and a bread basket.

They ordered lunch: eggs Benedict for Zeke and a seafood salad for Sandy. Zeke asked that their drinks be brought with the meal. As soon as their waiter departed, Zeke slipped his hand into his jacket pocket and activated the vibrator again.

Sitting down, with the silver cylinder wedged firmly against her pussy, Sandy could feel the hum of the vibrator all the way to her toes. Her nipples hardened, her belly began to ache and she started to perspire.

"Nice?" he asked.

"Yes," she gasped, moistening dry lips with her tongue.

He lifted her hand to his mouth and began licking the inside of her wrist.

She clenched her thighs together and felt the familiar wave of heat beginning to spread over her body.

"Zeke! I can't do this in a restaurant."

"Of course, you can, baby. We're all alone out here. No one can see you." He shifted his chair slightly to the left. "That plant and I block all view of you from the doorway." Nibbling on the fingers of her right hand, he smiled sexily. His other hand slipped into his jacket pocket and he raised the setting of the vibrator.

"Sweet mercy," she breathed as the humming of the silver cylinder increased. "Ohhhhh," she moaned.

"Let it happen, baby. Give in to it."

She pulled her hand out of Zeke's and put both of her palms down flat on the table in front of her. She leaned forward, bearing down on the vibrator and allowing the waves emanating from it to overtake her. Chewing on her lower lip, she began to pant.

"That's my girl. Just let go." He raised the vibrator setting yet again.

Tears leaked out of her eyes and she strained to maintain her composure. "Please, Zeke," she whispered. The effort of holding it together was giving her a stomachache.

"Come on, Sandy. Just let go," he repeated.

Without warning, she fell off the cliff. She leaned forward and then sagged backward into her chair as the orgasm racked her frame.

For several seconds, she could do no more than tremble as wave after wave of ecstasy rolled through her body. It was a struggle to remain in her chair and not slide down onto the paved bricks like a puddle of water. The courtyard, Zeke, everything else, faded into the background as her nerve endings sang.

She slowly regained control. Sweat beaded her forehead and she could feel more droplets running down between her breasts. The vibrator was still humming against her sensitive clit. What had been intense pleasure before was now nearly unbearable pain. She snapped, "Turn that thing off."

Zeke obeyed instantly. "Are you okay, honey?" he asked anxiously.

She picked up a linen napkin and dabbed her face and neck with it, but didn't answer.

"Sandy, you told me this morning that you wanted to know what it was like to have your body under a man's control."

He was right; she had said that. And he'd done exactly what she'd asked: provided experiences in bondage and in losing control over her own body. The orgasms had been mind-blowing. A reluctant smile tugged at her lips.

Seeing the smile, he visibly relaxed. "Thank God. You scared me."

Her mouth twisted wryly. "Just keep in mind that I trusted you and went along with your plan. When I ask you to return the favor, you *will* do the same."

He raised both hands in a peace gesture. "Absolutely. Just say when."

Their waiter chose that moment to appear with the food and drinks. They concentrated on casual conversation for the rest of the meal.

———

By three fifteen, Sandy stood in the middle of Zeke's living room, looking around his small apartment, while he packed a change of clothes in the bedroom.

It was a typically male place, furnished with what was obviously secondhand furniture. The only exception was the electronic equipment. There was a big flat-screen television, DVD and VCR players and a state-of-the-art stereo system.

A photograph on a nearby table caught her attention and she picked it up. It was a studio photo of five people: Zeke in military uniform and what were evidently his parents and two sisters.

"Zeke, when was this photo of your family taken?"

He came to the doorway, carrying a garment bag. "Right before my older sister got married, about eight years ago. I was home on leave and my mother insisted we have a professional portrait done."

"You have a very attractive family."

"Thanks." He threw the garment bag on the couch and came up behind her. Sliding his arms around her waist, he nuzzled the side of her neck. "What do you want to do now?"

She felt his cock beginning to harden against her ass. Time to put her plan into action. She swiveled around and wrapped her arms around his neck.

"You know what I'd really like to do? Take a walk through the Arboretum. They close at five, so it wouldn't take long."

Sandy saw the look of disappointment on Zeke's face. "You want to look at flowers?" His voice was filled with disbelief.

Looking down shyly—careful to hide her eyes from him—she said, "I'm still a little sore from everything we've done in the last couple of days. I think my body needs a little break."

"Oh." He tried a sexy smile. "I just grabbed some new condoms."

She peeked up from under her lashes to watch him but didn't respond.

"Sure. I understand. A walk in a garden would be nice." He was obviously trying hard to swallow his disappointment.

Sandy felt the thrill of triumph. "I have a membership so we won't even have to pay," she said brightly.

She kept up the chatter as they left the apartment, hung his garment bag in the back of his Explorer and drove the half-dozen blocks to the Arboretum entrance.

Sandy showed her membership card for admission, and the docent at the gate reminded them that the gardens would close in less than ninety minutes.

The Dallas Arboretum sat on sixty-six acres on the southeastern bank of White Rock Lake. Lush green lawns, stately trees and fragrant flower beds provided a stunning setting from which to view the thousand-acre lake.

"Let's go to the Jonsson Color Garden," Sandy suggested.

She was delighted that Zeke showed no signs of sulking about the unexpected detour to visit a garden, unlike Josh, who had a nasty habit of pouting when asked to do something he didn't find appealing.

As she had anticipated, there was practically no one still on the grounds. They passed one or two elderly couples and several people in tennis shoes, there for a daily walk or run. But the farther into the property they went, the fewer people they encountered.

White Rock Lake was a hundred yards to their left. Half a dozen sailboats skimmed across the surface of the calm waters. Afternoon sunlight glittered, creating a mirror effect.

"Did you know that the Jonsson Garden has over two thousand varieties of azaleas?" Sandy asked.

Zeke grinned and took her hand. "No, Sandy. I'll have to admit that I didn't know that."

She bumped his shoulder with hers. "Smart aleck."

The sidewalk ahead of them began to curve. Sandy had chosen the azalea garden because it was laid out in the form of a loop that turned back on itself. There were nearly a dozen paths that intersected with the loop at various points, but she knew that at the southernmost tip, they would be standing on a slight rise, able to see anyone approaching from any connecting path.

"Oh, look," she said with genuine pleasure. "The chrysanthemums and fall azaleas are in bloom."

Bushes bright with the golds and purples of autumn greeted them. Caladiums and dwarf crape myrtles provided contrast.

"Very nice," Zeke responded agreeably.

They had reached the hill Sandy remembered. There was a wood and wrought iron bench from which guests could get a vista of both the gardens and the lake. She turned casually around to survey the area. Although she could see people in the distance, there was no one in the immediate vicinity.

"This will do," she said.

"For what?" he asked as he touched the petal of a violet-colored flower.

"To fulfill your fantasy."

He snapped his head to stare at her. "What are you talking about?"

Sandy waved toward the bench. "Unzip your jeans and have a seat."

He stared at her incredulously. "Are you out of your mind? Anyone can see us here."

She grinned. "Not before we see them. Those bushes on the other side of the sidewalk will conceal our lower bodies and you'll be able to see anyone approaching."

He licked his lips. She could tell that the idea excited him. The bulge in his jeans was apparent. He glanced toward the lake.

"Do you think those sailboats have binoculars?"

"Probably." She nodded. "But what if they do? They're too far away to do anything but enjoy watching us."

Her words and cool demeanor obviously convinced him. He began unbuckling his belt and undoing the top of his jeans. "We'll need to make this quick."

"Why don't you just slide them down to your knees?" she suggested, gesturing to his jeans. "That way they won't get in the way, and we won't get them messy."

Completely committed now, he pushed the jeans off his hips, sat on the bench and pulled his cock out of his boxers. He dug a condom out of his pocket.

While they'd been at his apartment, Sandy had taken the opportunity to remove the blue butterfly vibrator and put it in her handbag. Unencumbered, her pussy was twitching in anticipation. She climbed on the bench and straddled Zeke's hips with her knees. Putting a hand between her thighs, she helped guide his penis toward her vaginal entrance.

His cock slid into her wetness like a key into a lock. Both of them groaned with pleasure.

Sandy perched on his lap, enjoying the full sensation. Zeke put his hands on her waist. "Come on, baby. Ride me. I'm your big stallion. Ride me fast and hard."

She took control of the rhythm, moving up and down in an ever-increasing tempo, holding her hands on his shoulders to steady herself. "Are you watching the path?" she asked.

His chin was on her shoulder and he panted a reply, "Yeah."

Without a bra, her large breasts bounced all over the place. Sandy took one hand off Zeke's shoulder to pull down the top of the peasant blouse and expose her left breast. "Bite me," she said.

On her next upward movement, he swiveled his head and nipped at her nipple. He wasn't at all gentle, but Sandy didn't care. She wanted wild and untamed. As her breast jiggled out from between his lips, he turned his head to watch the garden again.

They were both so excited that within a minute or two, he was asking, "Are you ready?"

She answered breathlessly, "Yes."

Zeke grunted and muttered and banged his hips hard against hers. He shouted, "Ahhhhh!" as he came.

Sandy had time to think, *Someone is going to hear us,* but then her orgasm overtook her and she forgot everything, including her own name.

The bench rattled from the force of their convulsions.

When it was finally over, the two of them collapsed against each other like a pair of rag dolls.

Sandy found herself wondering, for the first time, if it was possible for a heart to simply explode during sex. Hers was pounding like a jackhammer, and the question seemed legitimate.

Suddenly, Zeke whispered urgently, "Someone's coming."

She leaped backward off his lap so fast that she stumbled and nearly fell into an azalea bush. Glancing around, she spotted the elderly couple slowly making their way through the garden.

When she looked back at Zeke, his cock was no longer in sight. He'd raised his hips off the bench and was yanking his jeans back up to his waist.

She stepped toward him. "Go ahead and stand up. I'll block any view of you."

He zipped up his jeans while she stood in front of him.

By the time the old man and his wife reached the hilltop, Zeke and Sandy were standing, innocently admiring the scenery. The only trace of their recent coupling was the heavy odor of sex in the air. Even the fragrant flowers could not mask that unmistakable scent. Sandy prayed that the newcomers either wouldn't notice or wouldn't recognize it.

The visitors were dressed in their Sunday best: He wore a black suit and matching vest, while she was dressed in a pink sweater set and alpaca knit skirt.

"Good afternoon," the old man said.

"Good afternoon," Zeke and Sandy said in unison.

The couple hobbled past. Sandy had just started to relax when the old woman looked over her shoulder and winked at them.

Sandy's jaw dropped. She stared after the pair in consternation. When, at last, she turned to look at Zeke, he was grinning from ear to ear. The sight of him made her begin to giggle, and before they could stop themselves, they were both laughing out loud.

When they finally regained their composure, Zeke leaned forward to kiss her lips tenderly.

"Thank you," he said.

"Thank *you*," she answered.

He shook his head. "No, I mean it. That was one of the nicest gifts anyone has ever given me. I just wanted you to know it." He kissed her again. "I'll never forget it."

Sandy felt a warm glow of happiness in her chest. "You're welcome."

He took her arm. "Let's go home."

Together, they walked arm in arm out of the gardens.

# Chapter Twelve

Sandy woke at five thirty on Monday morning, her limbs tangled with Zeke's. He was sound asleep and didn't budge as she scooted out from under him. For a moment, she stood, looking down at him.

In the dim morning light, he looked younger. She wanted to reach out and stroke his forehead.

Yesterday, she'd thought she might be falling in love with him. Today, she knew. *I love him and we're going to make the most of whatever time we have together.*

Resisting the impulse to touch and risk waking him, she headed down the hall to the second bathroom.

The night before, she'd made spaghetti and meatballs, but hadn't eaten much of it. All the sex seemed to have taken away her appetite for anything else.

After dinner, they'd gone for a ride in Zeke's car—no special destination, just an opportunity to sit and talk. He'd told her about his dream of opening his own private security company one day. He could retire from the DPD in another twelve years. By then, he'd be forty-six and he anticipated he'd have enough in savings to get the business off the ground.

His honesty prompted Sandy to share her dream of writing fiction. She had completed several short stories, using fairy-tale themes in a contemporary setting. Zeke asked to read one of the stories, but didn't push when she hesitated to share her work.

They talked about everything from favorite movies to how many children each wanted.

This morning, reflecting on their conversation, Sandy realized what an unusual man Zeke was. He seemed as comfortable talking about his feelings as he was talking about the things that mattered to him.

She glanced at the clock on the bathroom counter. Five forty. She was due at work at eight fifteen; Zeke had his meeting at nine. As she showered, she mentally reviewed their options for breakfast. Eggs and toast were all she had to offer. She'd need to go grocery shopping after work.

While she showered, Sandy began a mental shopping list of everything she wanted to buy. After she finished bathing, she wrapped a towel around her damp body and did her hair and makeup. When she was finished, she opened the bathroom door.

The flavorful scent of coffee met her. She peeked around the doorjamb.

Zeke was standing in the breakfast nook, sipping a cup of coffee and glancing at the headlines of the paper. His hair was wet, he wasn't wearing a shirt and he was in his bare feet.

Sandy's heart skipped a beat. He looked so damn sexy standing there, so . . . at home.

He must have felt her gaze on him because he glanced up.

"Good morning. Ready for your coffee?"

Feeling unaccountably shy, she nodded.

He disappeared into the kitchen and returned with a mug of steaming coffee that he handed to her. "I'm going to make some eggs. How do you want yours?"

"I can do that," she protested, accepting the cup.

"I'm almost dressed. You're not. By the time you get your clothes on, breakfast will be ready. Scrambled okay?"

Sandy didn't argue. This felt so natural, so ordinary, so nice. She headed for her bedroom, a small flame warming her heart.

At five forty that afternoon, Sandy entered her building's lobby and checked her mailbox. There was a yellow slip inside, indicating a package.

The guard on duty was Frampton. She approached the desk, holding the yellow piece of paper out. "Do you have something for me?"

"Yes, ma'am, Ms. Davis. I've got it right here." He lifted a huge vase of colorful flowers and put them in front of her.

"Oh, they're beautiful," she said.

"Yes, ma'am. There's a card, too."

Sandy did not want to open her card in front of the security guard. "I'll read it when I get upstairs." She picked up the vase and carried it to the elevator.

On the way upstairs, she buried her face among the fragrant blooms. The bouquet was gorgeous, all yellow, orange and rust for fall. *Could that man be any sweeter?*

She reached her floor and juggled the huge arrangement in one arm while she unlocked her front door. Carrying the flowers across the room, she set the vase down on the breakfast table.

The card was in a small white envelope. She opened it and stared in shock at the message:

*I'm sorry we didn't get a chance to talk Saturday night. Let's meet.*
*Here's my number. . . . VC*

*Oh, God! He found me.* Her throat constricted, and for a moment, she couldn't catch a breath. *What do I do?*

She glanced toward the sliding glass door. The draperies were closed, blocking view of Cabrini's penthouse. *Okay, he can't see me. Thank God.*

*Should I call Zeke?* He'd given her his cell phone number that morning. *No, there's no point in upsetting him while he's still stuck at work.*

The scent of the flowers permeated the room. Suddenly she couldn't bear either the sight or the smell of the bouquet. She picked up the vase and headed for the door to the hallway.

Each floor had a trash chute. Her plan was to dump the flowers—vase and all—down it.

As Sandy turned the corner that led to the chute, she saw Lois Guzman pushing a white plastic bag through the small swinging door. The old woman looked over her shoulder and smiled.

"What gorgeous flowers," she exclaimed. "Those rust-colored chrysanthemums are spectacular."

On impulse, Sandy held the bouquet toward her neighbor. "Would you like to have them?"

"Oh, no, dear. They were sent to you."

"I have serious sinus issues, and the mums would put me in my grave," Sandy improvised. "I was going to discard them. I'd love for you to take them."

Mrs. Guzman hesitated, but when Sandy pushed the flowers

into her arms, the elderly matron buried her face in the blossoms. "Oh, they're wonderful. Thank you so much."

Sandy shook her head. "No, thank *you.*"

She chatted with Mrs. Guzman for two or three minutes. Predictably, her neighbor, who had married off three daughters and a son, wanted to know how serious Zeke's intentions were. After dodging half a dozen questions, Sandy slipped away with the excuse that she needed to get to the grocery store.

Back inside her condo, Sandy congratulated herself on not getting hysterical over the flowers. There was no point in calling Zeke at work; there was nothing he could do. She'd wait until after dinner tonight to tell him about the delivery and the card.

She'd just picked up her purse and was on the way to the door when the telephone rang. Thinking it might be Zeke, she dropped the handbag on the kitchen counter and grabbed the receiver off the wall unit.

"Hello," she said.

"Did you like my flowers?" a smooth, confident voice asked.

Sandy was so startled, she couldn't speak.

"I thought you might like them, being as your father used to be on the board of the Arboretum," Cabrini continued.

*Oh, God. He had me investigated. What do I say?*

"Cat got your tongue?"

"How did you get my phone number?" Her number was un-listed.

"Oh, you'd be surprised what a thousand dollars spread around a neighborhood will buy these days." He sounded smug.

"What do you want?" Her voice came out in a squeak, and

she bit her lower lip in aggravation. *He's going to think I'm afraid of him.* A voice in her brain responded: *Well, you are, aren't you?*

"I want for us to talk. I thought you and I could go get some dinner together. Someplace nice and private."

*Is he nuts?* "We have nothing to discuss. Do not call me again." She hung up the phone with more force than necessary and winced at the banging sound.

Thirty minutes later, Sandy pushed a grocery cart through the nearby supermarket.

After hanging up on Cabrini, she had paced her condo for a quarter of an hour. The temptation to call Zeke had been strong, but she'd repeated her earlier arguments to herself. There was nothing he could do. Better wait and tell him later tonight.

It was a good thing she'd written a grocery list during lunch today. She was so rattled she couldn't concentrate on anything. Walking through the store on automatic pilot, she filled her cart with items from the list.

When she reached the meat department, the butcher and his assistant were both waiting on other customers, and there were at least two more customers ahead of her. She parked her cart to one side where it would be out of the way of busy shoppers rushing to pick something up for dinner before heading home.

She took a number from the dispenser on the counter and tried to occupy her mind by scanning the price notices. Shrimp was on sale. Maybe she'd pick up a pound in addition to the two steaks she'd planned to buy.

It was nearly fifteen minutes before she could carry the two butcher-wrapped bundles back to her shopping cart. As she reached into the basket to put the meat and shrimp down, she noticed an article that wasn't hers. Thinking she had the wrong cart, she checked the other items. *No, this is my cart. What is this?*

The object was black, about five inches long and four inches wide with a thin tip, a wider middle and a flared base.

Curious, she had already picked up the odd-shaped piece of latex before her brain caught up with her hand. *Oh, my God! It's a butt plug.*

She dropped the sex toy into the cart as though it were on fire, and glanced around in embarrassment.

Standing about five feet from her was Victor Cabrini with a satisfied smirk on his face. He was wearing an expensive black suit, complete with a vest. Two of his men stood off to the left of him, seemingly oblivious of the shoppers forced to walk around them.

Rage overtook her fear. She stalked across the space between them.

"How dare you?" she hissed.

"I wanted to meet you. Since you hung up on me without even saying thank you for the flowers, I thought you might prefer something a little more practical."

"If you come anywhere near me again, I'll call the police on you." She heard her voice tremble, which only made her angrier. "You're disgusting."

He raised one eyebrow. "Is that why you called the police on me the first time?"

Although she tried not to react, she knew her face must have given her away. She hadn't expected him to put things together so quickly.

Cabrini nodded as though she had answered his question. "I thought so. It really bothered me not to know who'd sicced the boys in blue on me." He reached out and ran his fingers over her forearm. "You've been watching me from your balcony, haven't you, Alexandra?"

"I . . . I don't know what you're talking about," she stammered. She wanted to pull her hand away, but her body seemed paralyzed, unable to respond.

"Now, now. Let's not start our relationship with lies. You and I both know that you've been spying on me. I should be angry with you, but I'm not." He leered, his white teeth flashing against his olive complexion. "I sort of like the idea of a woman like you watching me fuck one of my whores."

His obscenities broke the stupor that held her frozen. She started to yank her hand away, but he caught her wrist in an iron grip.

"Not yet, Sandy. I didn't give you permission to pull away from me. I can see you have a lot to learn." His gaze left her face to travel insolently along her body. "I'll bet that wide white ass of yours turns a nice shade of red when you're disciplined."

His words reminded her that she wasn't Dolly alone with him in his apartment. "Mr. Cabrini, if you don't let me go right now, I'll scream. You can be charged with assault for laying hands on me. What's it going to be?"

He blinked as though surprised by her response. Releasing

her hand, he turned to the men waiting beside him. "Hey, Augie, my fatty has a temper."

"You'll trim her claws, Vic," the taller of the two heavies responded. "She'll be eating out of your hand before long."

Sandy spun on her heel and headed back toward her grocery cart. When she got there, she picked up the butt plug and threw it at Cabrini.

His hand moved as fast as a snake, neatly snatching the projectile out of the air. He tossed it casually toward his men. The shorter of the two caught it and shoved it into a pocket. "I'll save this for you, boss, so you can use it on her later."

"I'll be seeing you, Alexandra." Cabrini gestured to his men to follow him. The three walked down the frozen-food aisle toward the front of the store.

Sandy glanced around to see if anyone had noticed their interaction, but the shoppers all seemed to be intent on their own business. She maneuvered her cart around a display of cereal boxes and turned down a different aisle from that taken by Cabrini and his men.

She was shaking all over. The incongruity of being confronted by three gangsters in the middle of a supermarket was somehow far more terrifying than meeting them on the street. The sheer brazenness of it took her breath away.

Ignoring the bright lights and shelves crowded with cans and boxes, she rushed toward the entrance. Her only thought was to get home as quickly as possible, where she could bolt the front door and wait for Zeke.

Had a register not been open, Sandy would have walked out

of the market, abandoning her cart filled with goods. However, the cashier beckoned to her.

Too overwhelmed to argue, Sandy obediently steered her basket into the line and began piling groceries on the conveyor belt. In a few minutes, she was standing just inside the entrance, looking out at the parking lot.

Although she knew her fear was probably irrational, Sandy was afraid that Cabrini or his men might be waiting at her car for her to leave the market. She could see her Buick through the plate glass window, but there were a dozen places nearby where a stalker could hide.

She could call Zeke. He'd come to get her right away. But then he might go after Cabrini. He could be killed.

"Do you need help with those bags, ma'am?" A teenage bag boy interrupted her train of thought.

Would Cabrini risk hurting this kid to get to her? Yeah, he would, but he probably wouldn't risk a scene with all these witnesses milling around.

"Yes, please," she told the boy, making a mental note to give him an enormous tip as though that might make up for putting him in jeopardy.

Together, she and the teenager walked out into the parking lot.

# Chapter Thirteen

B y nine p.m., with the help of a couple of calming shots of scotch, Sandy was able to think again, although she was still jittery. Every unexpected noise, no matter how small, made her jump in fear.

Even though Zeke was due home at any moment, she still hadn't decided whether to tell him about Cabrini. While she longed to share the frightening incident in the market, her logical side leaned toward keeping quiet.

Although they'd known each other for only four days, Sandy was confident that if she told Zeke what had happened, he'd want to take action to keep her safe. His doing so might have disastrous consequences for both of them.

If he confronted Cabrini directly, the mobster's bodyguards might harm him. On the other hand, if Zeke pushed Sandy to file assault charges against Cabrini for grabbing and threatening her, the crime boss was sure to defend himself by saying he was only confronting the person who'd been peeping on him. Her career would be over.

And Zeke's.

His lieutenant was already furious over the accidental encounter at Jerry's. He would be even angrier if Zeke or she did anything to compromise the surveillance. Worse yet, if he found out Zeke had known about, but hadn't reported, her peeping, his job could be in real jeopardy. She wasn't willing to take any chance that might hurt his career.

A small voice inside asked, *But what if Cabrini is serious about harming me?*

She told herself Cabrini enjoyed mind games and domination, but he knew enough to confine his play to hookers. She was a respectable, hardworking professional. Surely Cabrini wouldn't risk everything just to get revenge on her.

A quick rat-a-tat on the front door startled her and interrupted the gloomy train of thought. She'd expected the doorman to call up and announce Zeke's arrival. But, of course, Zeke was inside the building already at the surveillance post.

She checked the peephole, to be sure. Her lover's smiling face banished all thoughts of Cabrini. Unlocking the door, she threw herself at him.

His arms enfolded her. "Wow! If this is the way you're going to greet me every night, I won't be stopping off with the boys for drinks anymore," he joked.

"I'm so glad to see you," she responded, pressing her head to his chest. For the first time in hours, she felt protected.

"Sandy, are you all right?" He loosened her hold on him and pulled free. "What's wrong, baby?" He stared into her face, concern in his voice.

If she was going to tell him, now was the time. She could see his tired eyes and the lines of weariness around his mouth. He'd just come off a twelve-hour shift.

"Nothing," she said. "I just missed you."

His look of worry vanished and was replaced by a grin. "I missed you, too, sweetheart." He pressed his mouth to hers.

Sandy leaned into the kiss with a sigh. He felt so warm, so

familiar, so safe. Her eyes drifted shut, and she let the awful thoughts slide to the back of her consciousness. She'd forget about Cabrini for tonight.

Zeke gripped her hips with his big hands. "What's for dinner?" he asked.

It took a moment for the words to penetrate. She pulled her head back. "What's for *dinner*?" she repeated.

"Sandy, Ben's kid got sick, his wife couldn't get away to pick him up at school, and I covered for him by running a surveillance post alone while he took his son to the doctor. I peed in a soda bottle, and I munched on stale peanuts. I haven't had anything real to eat for ten hours. I'm starved. I don't have the strength for anything else."

"Really?" She slid her hand between their bodies and groped the front of his jeans. His cock immediately hardened. "Your little friend here has a different opinion."

"Trust me, Sandy. He doesn't know what he's talking about. Feed us both now, and I promise we'll take care of you later."

She giggled. "Men. How do shrimp cocktail, a nice thick steak, salad and garlic bread sound?"

"Like heaven. If you have a grill, I'll even cook the steaks."

"Good. I've been marinating them." She hesitated. There was a tabletop gas grill in the closet off the balcony, but she didn't want Cabrini watching them from his penthouse.

"There's a charcoal grill upstairs on the roof," she told him. "One of the tenants bought it for everyone to share. There's a table and chairs up there, too."

"Great. Do you have charcoal?"

"In the pantry along with starter fluid." She led the way to the kitchen.

He grabbed her around the waist and turned her to face him. "Would you do something for me?"

She looked up at him with a tiny smile. "Depends on what it is."

"Don't wear any underwear."

Sandy pulled a grimace. "You're a pervert. You know that, don't you?"

He dropped a kiss on her forehead. "Yeah, but I'm YOUR pervert, sweetheart." He released her. "I'll get the fire started."

Sandy was still staring after him when she realized she was smiling. Shaking her head, she left the kitchen. In her bedroom, she quickly stripped and removed the teddy Zeke had given her.

She surveyed her reflection in the mirror and marveled at how different she felt from just days before. The body she looked at was the same rounded, fleshy one the mirror had captured four days ago. However, now secure in her sexiness, she found that the extra pounds didn't bother her.

*Okay, they still bother me, just not as much as before. I can be plump and sexy, too.* She winked at her reflection.

For the next hour, Sandy and Zeke worked together to prepare dinner. While waiting for him to arrive home, she'd made the shrimp cocktails and Caesar salad. Now she put together a picnic basket containing a tablecloth, food and dinnerware. She carried the basket upstairs to the roof, where Zeke had the fire going and was grilling the steaks. It was after ten by the time they sat down to eat.

"Wine"—Zeke lifted his goblet and gestured toward the twinkling lights of downtown Dallas—"a gorgeous setting and"—he saluted her—"a beautiful woman. What more could a man ask?"

"Thank you." She looked around. "It is a nice night, isn't it?" The temperature was in the midseventies with a cloudless sky. A full moon lit the roof, and music drifted up from the street.

"How was your day?" she asked as she speared a piece of lettuce.

"Frustrating. The team tailing Cabrini lost him this evening." He ignored the shrimp cocktail and salad to concentrate on the beef.

Her heart stuttered. "How did they lose him?"

His voice was filled with disgust. "By being lazy. I saw Cabrini getting ready to leave the penthouse and radioed the team on the ground. The two of them waited for him to come out of the garage, but he went out the front entrance instead." He hesitated before putting his fork in his mouth. "It was a total rookie mistake. We're trained to cover all the entrances of a building. The ground team just got lazy." He popped the fork into his mouth.

"Do you think Cabrini knows you're watching him?" Sandy had to struggle to keep her face calm and her breathing even.

He shook his head and finished chewing. "No, we don't think so. Our guys simply missed Cabrini's departure. The doorman said a car picked him up out front."

Afraid to meet his eyes, she kept her gaze on her salad. "Did you find him again later?"

Zeke trimmed a bit of fat off his steak. "Yeah, about an hour later, the car brought him back. We don't know where he went, but it couldn't have been very far."

*That's right. He just stopped in at the grocery store to terrorize me.* Unable to think of something to say to Zeke, Sandy prayed he'd drop the subject. She chewed with fervor on a shrimp tail.

"You look wonderful, honey."

She lifted her eyes to look at him. "What?"

"I said, 'You look wonderful.' "

Sandy shook her head. "You're crazy."

"Crazy about you. Do you know how hot that sweater makes me?"

She looked down at the black pullover sweater and frowned. "Why?"

"Because that's what you were wearing the first time I ever saw you. In the dark alone, peeping."

She put down her fork. "It made you hot to see me that way?"

"Oh, yeah. I wanted to touch you so bad."

Her appetite disappeared. She leaned back in the chair, cupping her breasts. "Like this, you mean."

He dropped his knife and fork. "Exactly like that."

Still holding her breasts, she lifted them and brushed her thumbs over the nipples. "You liked seeing me touch myself?"

He shifted his chair so that they were facing each other, separated by three feet. "Take off that sweater, Sandy."

She glanced around. Her building was the highest point for several blocks in all directions, and downtown Dallas was nearly three miles away. It was late. If a member of a cleaning crew or an overworked lawyer was watching them from a distant skyscraper, she couldn't tell and didn't care. She wet her lips. "Make sure the door to the roof is locked first."

"Come on, baby, don't worry about that," he pleaded. He rubbed his palms along the top of his jeans in a drying gesture.

*He's sweating. I've really made him hot.* She realized that because the unlocked door increased their odds of being caught, it escalated his excitement. "I'll be cold," she said, more to prolong the moment than to argue.

"I'll keep you warm, baby, I promise."

Sliding her hands to the hem of her sweater, she grabbed the bottom edge and pulled the top over her head.

"Awwwww," he groaned when he saw her naked breasts. He stretched his long legs, and Sandy could see his leg muscles tightening under the formfitting jeans. His growing erection pressed against his pants.

"Your turn, cowboy. Open that zipper for me." She tossed her sweater on the table. The cool evening air made her bare nipples pucker and harden.

He fumbled with the fly to his jeans.

Sandy unbuttoned the top of her own black slacks. "Tell me what you're feeling," she said.

"I'm feeling like you ought to spread your legs, baby."

"No, that's what you're thinking," she chided. "Tell me what you're feeling." To encourage him, she parted her legs.

"I'm feeling that I'd like to see you touch yourself," he said, raising his hips off the chair as he tried to free his shaft from the confines of its cloth prison. His cock sprang forward, pointing toward Sandy.

She laughed. "No, you're THINKING you'd like to see me touch myself. What are you FEELING?"

"Damn it, Sandy. Will you stop with that social work crap and rub your pussy for me?" he growled.

His aggrieved tone amused her. She slid her hand into the opening of her slacks. She stroked her mons and was rewarded by a rush of warmth from her belly button to her vagina.

Although she'd heard Zeke masturbate during their phone sex, this was the first time she'd ever seen him holding his cock and lazily pumping it. The sight of his hand wrapped around the hard length aroused her even more.

"What are *you* feeling, Sandy?" he asked.

"I'm feeling warm and sexy and happy I packed that can of whipped cream in the picnic basket," she responded. Her fingers found her clitoris. The tiny organ was already erect.

"Whipped cream?" His eyes gleamed. "You really are a bad girl, aren't you, baby?" The hand on his cock moved faster.

"Yeah, but I'm *your* bad girl."

He swiped his tongue around his lips. "I'd like to see your tits covered in whipped cream."

"Only if you lick the cream off."

"I can guarantee that. Are you rubbing your clit?"

"Uh-huh," she said dreamily. "It feels so good."

"Can you make yourself come while I watch?" he asked.

"I don't know. Maybe." Seeing the heat in his eyes, she felt her own excitement heighten and moved her fingers with greater urgency.

They did that to each other, created hunger and wanting. She wasn't sure what it was about Zeke, but this man, this cop, moved her like no one else she had ever known. Her eyelids drifted closed, and she floated off on a wave of sensation.

"That's it, baby," he encouraged. "Come for me. I want to see you come for me."

And—just that easily—she did.

# Chapter Fourteen

Tuesday afternoon, Sandy stood at the entrance to an apartment in South Dallas talking to an elderly black woman. "Thank you, Miss Prudie," she said. "I'll see you again on November fourteenth."

"Thank *you*, Sandy. I'll be here, waiting." Prudie Collins was tall and lean, with a face tempered by years of hard work in minimum wage jobs.

Prudie was among Sandy's favorite clients: a woman who had outlived two husbands and successfully raised five children, using an iron hand. She was now the matriarch of an extended family that included thirteen grandchildren, forty-two great-grandchildren and two great-great-grandchildren. Even at eighty, with her organs being slowly devoured by cancer, the old woman continued to care for her family. She'd assumed custody over three of her great-grandchildren after their mother was murdered in an armed robbery of the convenience store in which she worked.

Prudie Collins didn't have time to whine about her pain or her bad luck. She was too busy putting her affairs in order so that the three grandbabies would be provided for after her death. The cancer had neither bowed her nor taken away the quiet dignity that Sandy so admired.

The two women stood in the middle of the South Dallas projects on Hatcher Street. Two- and three-story brick apartment buildings lined both sides of the boulevard east of the Texas State Fairgrounds.

When Sandy had first come to Hatcher Street three years earlier, she'd stopped by the nearby Dallas Police storefront. The cop she'd spoken to had suggested she get in the habit of checking in at the storefront before entering the projects so that the police could keep an eye on her while she was working. Although she'd followed the recommendation on her first few visits, Sandy had quickly learned how to spot signs of trouble and how to avoid becoming a crime victim. She never carried a purse or wore jewelry when she visited Hatcher Street, and her cell phone was always near at hand with the storefront's number programmed into the speed dial.

After Sandy bade Prudie good-bye, she started down the sidewalk toward her Buick Park Avenue. She hadn't taken many steps when she realized something was wrong.

The small children who had been playing on the patch of weeds between the street and the brick apartment building when she'd arrived had disappeared. In fact, there were no children within sight, an unusual occurrence on a mild, beautiful October afternoon. Kids in the projects had a sixth sense for trouble. When anything went down, they made themselves scarce.

The hair between her shoulder blades prickled. Something was very wrong. She resisted the impulse to run toward her car and, instead, scanned the street and buildings with a careful eye.

There. Parked on the crowded street behind her Buick was a late-model black Cadillac. The car was spotlessly clean with dark tinted windows. From her position, she couldn't tell whether anyone was inside the vehicle, but that car did not belong in this neighborhood. Cabrini.

Sandy swung on her heel and started back toward Prudie's apartment. She'd call the cops from there.

She'd gotten only a few feet when two men grabbed her—one on either side. Her clipboard fell to the ground.

"Come on, Miss Davis. Someone wants to talk to you." The duo gripped her upper arms and propelled her in the direction of their vehicle.

Sandy screamed as loud as she could. One meaty hand slapped across her mouth, and the two men hustled her toward the Cadillac.

"Yo, man! What do you think you're doing there?" The gravelly voice came out of nowhere.

The men holding Sandy hesitated. The taller of the two shoved her toward the other, who picked her up by her shoulders and pushed her through the open door of the Cadillac.

Sandy stuck her legs straight out so the soles of her feet landed flat against the side of the passenger seat. She locked her knees.

The man trying to cram her into the car cursed out loud, but he couldn't get the leverage to budge her. He shifted his left hand to the top of her shoulder while he tried to maneuver her into the car.

Sandy swiveled her head and bit down on his hand. Her teeth pierced the skin, and she bit off a chunk of his flesh.

He let out a cry of pain and dropped her.

She fell against the curb, banging her tailbone. Scrambling to her knees, she attempted to crawl around him. The taste of his blood filled her mouth.

Still clutching his wrist, he blocked her with his legs. "You bitch, I'll kill you for this."

Sandy made a fist and swung upward as hard as she could. She connected with a solid punch to his privates.

He screamed and slouched forward, cupping his genitals and gagging.

She staggered to her feet and blinked in disbelief at the scene in front of her.

The second thug faced a group of perhaps seven African-American boys. Sandy recognized a face or two from the Hatcher Street families she regularly visited.

The boys sported the droopy pants and hooded sweatshirts common in this neighborhood. Some wore gimme caps, while others had do-rags tied around their heads. Sandy guessed the kids were somewhere between thirteen and sixteen.

The boy at the front of the pack, obviously the leader, took several steps toward the thug. He wore a Nike fleece hoodie loosely covering his cornrowed hair. "What you messing with Miss Social Worker for? She ain't done nothing to you."

Sandy edged closer to the boys and fished for the cell phone in her pocket.

The thug, who looked like an ex-marine dressed in a too-small brown suit, glanced at her and then back at the boys. "You kids stay outta this, and you won't get hurt."

The boys laughed in unison, poking one another. "Hear that?" "Hear the man?" "We stay outta this, and we don't get hurt."

Sandy could see no signs of fear on their young faces. She

flipped her cell phone open and hit the button to speed-dial the storefront.

The guy she'd punched vomited on the sidewalk.

One of the boys, about fourteen years old, his hair shaved close to the head, took a step forward to stand beside his leader. "Miss Social Worker there, she take care of my granny when the food stamp people were being bitches. You ain't taking her nowhere."

Ex-Marine slipped a hand inside his jacket in what was obviously a threatening gesture. "You boys get moving now, or I'll put a hole through one of you."

Her cell phone chirped a busy signal. *Sweet Jesus, don't let these kids get shot because of me.* She hit disconnect and redial.

"Who you calling 'boy'?" The lead teen's hands turned into fists. "You heard my man Binks." He gestured toward the kid with the shaved head. "Get your ass back where you come from before we hurt *you*."

The storefront telephone was still busy. Sandy wanted to sob in frustration. She disconnected and redialed again, at the same time moving closer to the boys, ready to step between them and the thug's gun. No kid was going to die because of her.

Ex-Marine started to pull the weapon from inside his jacket. Before he could do so, four automatics were pointing at his head.

In the silence that followed, Sandy gaped at the teenage boys brandishing the guns. The laughter had stopped. They suddenly looked as serious as death.

"Mister," the lead teen drawled in a hard voice, "you pick up your friend there and get the hell off Hatcher Street. You don't, and you ain't going nowhere else never again."

The thug froze. A breathless quiet hung heavy over the block.

A familiar voice cut across the silence. "You, mister. I already called the police. You better get moving now before they get here."

God bless her. It was Prudie standing on her front stoop.

For the first time, Sandy realized there were half a dozen other women in their doorways, too. Another shouted, "I got your license number, Mr. Man. You better listen to Miss Prudie and get gone now before I decides to hand this number over to the po-lice when they arrive."

Ex-Marine held his left hand in the air in the time-honored gesture of surrender. He withdrew his empty hand from inside his jacket and turned away from the teenagers. His angry gaze raked Sandy.

She shivered at the cold malice in his eyes.

He went to his companion, who was now dry retching. Grabbing the guy's upper arm, Ex-Marine guided him toward the open car door. He shoved the helpless man onto the front seat, slammed the door behind him and then moved quickly around the car to the driver's side.

Before he climbed into the Cadillac, Ex-Marine stared one last time at Sandy. "We'll catch you later, honey," he said, a smirk on his face.

Her limbs went liquid with fear. It took all her willpower not to crumple to the ground while he was watching her. The slamming of the Cadillac door was muffled by the rapid pulsebeats in her ears.

As the car pulled away, a siren sounded in the distance, snapping Sandy out of her stupor. She did not want to explain to the police why someone had tried to snatch her off the street.

Bending to pick up her clipboard from where it had fallen, she swayed and almost collapsed to the ground. A pair of strong hands caught her.

"Miss Social Worker, you okay?" It was the teenager with the shaved head.

"Yes, thank you. I just need to get out of here before . . ."

"Before the police get here. Yeah, I know about that. Here, come on. I'll help you to your car."

He guided her to the driver's door of the Buick and waited while she fumbled with her keys. When she dropped the key ring, he picked it up, opened the lock and assisted her into the front seat.

"I don't know how to thank you . . . and your friends," Sandy said as she took the keys from him.

"You don't need to be thanking me. You helped my granny. That's enough. Now get outta here." He closed the door and slapped his palm on the roof of the car, urging her forward.

Sandy glanced toward the apartments. The other teenagers and women were nowhere to be seen. Hatcher Street looked empty. It was time for her to leave, too.

After turning the ignition, she lifted her left hand to wave to her new friend, but he was already gone.

She pulled away from the curb. In her rearview mirror, she saw a police cruiser coming into view at the end of Prudie's street. Taking the first available turn, she pressed hard on the accelerator to put more distance between her and the authorities.

# Chapter Fifteen

Sandy made another right turn and headed for Spring Avenue. Operating on automatic pilot, she took the route that would lead her back to downtown Dallas. Fearful of being followed by either the police or Cabrini's men, she kept checking her mirrors.

*Okay, I need to think this through. Cabrini tried to have me snatched right off a street in broad daylight. If he did it once, he'll do it again. I can't go back to my condo.*

She was having trouble wrapping her mind around Cabrini's brazen disregard of the law. *I knew he was a narcissist, but this . . . ? There's no telling what he'll do next. I have to tell Zeke. I don't have a choice.*

She glanced at the dashboard clock. Two thirty. Cabrini's men must have followed her to Prudie's. That meant, in addition to knowing where Sandy lived, they knew where she worked. She couldn't go back to the condo or to her office. *What am I going to do?*

*Don't panic, Alexandra. Think.* She pulled up to a stoplight. *First things first. Call the office and tell them you don't feel well, and you're going home.* She located her cell phone and made the call.

*Now what?* The light changed, but she had no idea where to go. *Do I call Zeke next? And do what? Tell him all this at work? No, I can't do that, not while he's on the job.*

The driver behind her honked his horn. She accelerated, taking the ramp back to Dallas. *I have to find somewhere to hide out,*

*someplace where I can ask Zeke to meet me so I can tell him everything.* She
merged onto I-30, approaching downtown.

Like most residents, Sandy usually viewed the gleaming Dallas skyscrapers with a sense of well-being and pride. This afternoon, however, her agitation made it impossible to appreciate the
imposing architecture.

*I can't go home; I can't go to the office. I don't dare go to my mother's. What
if Cabrini knows where she lives? Maybe I should check in at a hotel.*

A road sign pointing to Oak Cliff caught her attention. *Oak
Cliff! I can stay at Leah's.*

When Leah Reece first started her online magazine, *Heat*'s
executive office existed in virtual reality, not in real life. Her staff
was scattered across the city, which meant that meetings were
held online or over the phone.

After the magazine finished its first year in the black, Leah
asked Dora to find a building to which she could move the entire operation. Although *Heat* was an online magazine, Leah
wanted the synergy that emerges when creative types get together
to brainstorm.

Dora found a four-story brick building in Oak Cliff, a depressed area south of downtown undergoing gentrification. Leah
got the property for next to nothing, but spent a small fortune
renovating it.

Among the changes in the building's new design were a dozen
bedroom suites on the third floor where staff working against
deadlines could spend the night. The suites were supported by a
fully stocked kitchen and maid service.

When the building was dedicated, the *Dallas Morning News* ran an article about *Heat* and its staff of young Trojans. The story devoted a lot of space to what it called the "Workplace Playspace," implying that the staff used the third-floor bedrooms to hook up. When asked for a quote, Leah—aware of the value of publicity—said, "As long as *Heat* is produced, I'm not going to worry about brush fires along the way."

The article and the uproar it caused snagged Leah several interviews on national television, and gave her zine tremendous attention.

Sandy dialed *Heat's* executive office and waited while a secretary located her friend.

"Hey, girl," Leah greeted her. "What's up?"

"I'm in trouble, Leah, and I need a place to stay. Can I stay in one of the bedrooms on the third floor for a couple of days?"

"Of course you can. What's wrong?"

Sandy's relief whooshed out in a sigh. "I'm on my way to you now. I'll tell you when I get there. Where should I park?"

"When you get to the garage, press on the intercom. They'll let you in. Come to the second floor. I'll be in my office."

"Thanks, hon. I should arrive in about ten minutes."

"See you then." Leah hung up.

Relieved to have a safe place to hide out, Sandy next called Zeke's cell.

He must have recognized her number on his phone's display. "Hi, sweetheart, how's your day going?"

"Not so good, Zeke. I had a bit of trouble."

His voice changed. "Are you okay? What happened?"

"I'm okay, but I don't want to talk about it over the phone. How late are you working tonight?"

"Until eight, but Ben and I are due to take a meal break soon. Do you want to meet?"

"That would be great. Can you come to Leah's place in Oak Cliff?" She gave him directions.

Zeke promised to get there by three thirty, but he wouldn't hang up until she assured him for a second time that she was all right.

Sandy dropped her cell phone into her jacket pocket. At least now she had a plan, although she wasn't looking forward to telling Zeke she'd withheld information from him. Something told her their conversation wasn't going to be a happy one.

Zeke and his partner arrived at *Heat*'s offices thirty minutes after Sandy. She'd had time to brief Leah, who'd kept her questions to a minimum, opting instead to listen. Sandy described how she'd met Zeke and how scared she was that Cabrini was going to destroy their relationship. By the time the receptionist showed the two cops in, Sandy was pressed into a corner of a sofa with her legs curled underneath her body.

Zeke went directly to her, leaning over to kiss her forehead. "What's up, babe?" When he saw her gaze fixed on the man standing near the door, he waved for him to come closer. "Sandy, this is Ben Forrester. We've been partners for eighteen months. Ben, this is Sandy."

Ben was a good six inches shorter than Zeke and at least forty pounds heavier. Like Zeke, he was dressed in faded jeans and a T-shirt. His wire-rimmed glasses and crew cut made him look like a high school coach. Although his face was stern, Sandy thought he had kind eyes.

She reached a hand out toward him. "Hi, Ben. Thanks for coming with Zeke."

"No problem." The vice cop shook her hand and then took a step backward. His gaze swept the office. Sandy wondered what he thought of the framed layouts from previous issues of *Heat* that decorated the walls. Some of those layouts were pretty risqué.

She suddenly realized Leah was standing alone behind her desk. "Oh, I'm so sorry. Leah, this is Zeke and his partner, Ben."

"So I gathered." Leah smiled, coming around her desk to shake hands with the two men. "Can I get you gentlemen something to drink?"

"No, thanks, Leah. We don't have much time." Zeke turned back to Sandy. "What's up, honey?" He crouched beside the couch and took her hands in his.

She wasn't sure how much to say with Ben standing there, listening. Glancing back and forth from him to Zeke, she must have telegraphed her difficulty to Zeke.

"Sandy, I trust Ben with my life. You can say whatever you want in front of him."

Ben moved toward the door. "I can wait downstairs if you'd rather I leave. . . ." He left the question open.

"No." Sandy shook her head. "If Zeke trusts you, that's good enough for me."

He gave a small nod and took a seat in a straight-backed chair near the wall.

Everyone had fixed their attention on Sandy, waiting for her.

After a few seconds, she gathered her scattered thoughts and began to talk. She started with the previous afternoon when she'd come home to find the bouquet of flowers. She described hanging up on Cabrini's phone call and running into him in the supermarket.

No one interrupted her narrative, although Zeke's face flushed red when she recounted the incident in the grocery aisle. He squeezed her hand so hard, she winced and tried to pull away. When he realized he was hurting her, he released the hand, but didn't say anything.

Ben's presence embarrassed her, but—now that she was sharing the story with Zeke—Sandy was afraid to leave anything out. She lowered her gaze to her lap while she repeated Cabrini's comments about needing to discipline her "wide, white ass."

Zeke leaped to his feet. "Damn it, Sandy! Why the hell didn't you tell me all this last night?" His tall form vibrated with anger.

"I didn't know what to do," she said in a pleading voice. "I was afraid you'd do something crazy and get hurt, or get fired. And it would have been my fault. I didn't want something to happen to you because of me."

"So you decided to wait a day and then tell me?" He stomped across the room, as though his rage were too enormous to be contained in one place.

Sandy began to tremble. Everything that had happened in the past twenty-four hours slammed into her like a tsunami. When she thought she was protecting Zeke, she'd been able to hold the fear at bay. Now, seeing him in such a fury, she was without a defense. He frightened her more than Cabrini and all his men put together.

A quiet voice interrupted. "I think something else happened that's made it necessary for Sandy to tell you about yesterday," Ben said.

Zeke swung around to stare at his partner.

"Am I right, Sandy?" Ben asked.

With her gaze locked on Zeke, Sandy slowly nodded. "Yes," she said.

"Sit down, Zeke. You're scaring her, and she's not finished with the story yet." Ben stood and walked over to the wet bar in the corner. After locating a bottle of scotch, he found a glass and poured a generous slug. He carried the glass across the room and offered it to Sandy. "Here. You look like you need this."

Her hands were trembling so hard, she was afraid to accept the drink from him. She didn't want to spill alcohol all over Leah's sofa and carpet. Shaking her head no, Sandy knotted her fingers together in her lap.

Zeke sat on the sofa beside her. He reached for the glass from Ben and held it out to her. "Here, sweetheart. He's right. You're as pale as a ghost."

When she made no move to take the scotch, Zeke held it to her lips. "Come on, baby. Drink this. I promise I won't yell at you any more."

She took a sip and swallowed. "It's okay. Ben's right. There's more. I need to tell you the rest of it."

Ben withdrew to his chair. Zeke remained where he was, on the couch next to her.

Sandy didn't linger on the details of her encounter on Hatcher Street. She told the story in as matter-of-fact a fashion as she could.

Zeke grew more and more tense beside her. She could feel the tautness of his thigh muscle against her leg. Still, he rubbed her hands, which had grown icy cold despite the warmth of the room.

When she'd finished, she waited in tense silence for his re-action.

"I'm gonna kill that bastard. I'll start at the knees and work my way up. I'll blow a hole the size of Manhattan through his dick."

"No, you won't," Ben countered. "We're going to file an assault-and-attempted-kidnapping report against his men. With any luck, they'll break down during questioning and implicate him. We'll nail his ass on conspiracy charges."

"You can't," Sandy protested. "The police will find out about . . ." Her voice trailed off.

Zeke wrapped an arm around her shoulders. "No, they won't, baby. All Cabrini can say is that he suspects you of reporting him for abuse. You can't be charged for that. You were out on your balcony, saw him beating up a woman and called it in. There's nothing for you to be ashamed of."

Ben checked his watch. "You need to take Sandy down to the station. I'll go back to the post and call the lieutenant."

Zeke winced. "Thanks, but I need to call him myself. You take the vehicle. We'll use Sandy's car."

His partner nodded. Standing, he came back to the couch and extended a hand toward Sandy. "I'm proud to know you, Sandy. You're a brave woman. I can understand why Zeke is head over heels about you."

She gave him an uncertain smile. "Thanks for coming, Ben. I appreciate it."

"Hang in there. This will all be over soon."

# *Chapter Sixteen*

The next few hours flew by in a blur of activity. Zeke and Sandy drove to police headquarters at 1400 South Lamar. On the way, he coached her. "Tell the truth, but leave out the peeping."

Once at headquarters, Zeke brought her to the CAP unit—Crimes Against Persons—to file a report. He stayed at her side while she told her story. She followed his suggestion, telling the men interviewing her about everything except her nocturnal activities.

The officers pulled up the computer file on Cabrini's known associates and had her view photos. None of the mug shots she saw matched Ex-Marine and his companion. She then met with a sketch artist and described the two thugs to him.

It was after nine p.m. by the time Sandy and Zeke met with an assistant DA and the supervisor of the CAP unit. The news wasn't good.

"Miss Davis, you're sure that the two men never mentioned Victor Cabrini by name?" the CAP captain, a woman named Torres, asked.

She shook her head. "No, but they didn't have to. I knew who'd sent them."

ADA Jackson Green, a heavyset African-American, shook his head. "I'm afraid that's not enough. We don't have anything linking Mr. Cabrini directly to the attack."

"What the hell are you talking about?" Zeke asked. "The

man threatened her yesterday and sent two goons after her today."

"So you say," Green countered. Seeing the violence in Zeke's expression, he quickly added, "And I'm sure you're right. The problem is, there just isn't sufficient cause to arrest Cabrini."

"But it sure as hell is enough cause to pick him up for questioning," Zeke said, looking at Captain Torres for support.

"Yes, it is, and we can do that, can't we?" Torres looked to the ADA.

"Certainly. Just understand that Cabrini is no fool. He'll lawyer up and walk within an hour." Green stood, pushing his chair back against the wall.

Torres jumped in before Zeke could say anything. "I'll call Lieutenant Jenkins and get the film footage your team has gathered on Cabrini, Zeke. Maybe Sandy will be able to identify our perps that way."

Sandy spoke quickly. "Thank you, Captain, and you, too, Mr. Green. I appreciate your time."

Captain Torres smiled at her. "You look worn out. Take this boyfriend of yours and go get something to eat. We'll be in touch after we talk to Cabrini."

Zeke drove; the car ride north was quiet. He seemed to be lost in thought. Sandy was torn between her anxiety to know what he was thinking and her fear that he was still angry with her.

When they crossed the Trinity River, leaving Oak Cliff, she had to ask. "Where are we going?"

Obviously startled by her voice, he jerked and then looked

around. "I don't know. I guess I was operating on autopilot." He checked his watch. "It's pretty late. Where do you want to eat?"

"What about the Café Brazil on Cedar Springs?" she asked.

"Good idea. I could go for some chorizo." He turned in the direction of northbound I-35.

"Zeke, are you angry with me?"

He made a sound halfway between a sigh and a grunt. She waited through an uneasy silence.

"No, Sandy, I'm not mad at you. I'm mad at me." He took his eyes off the road to look at her. "When I saw you last night, I *knew* something was the matter, but I didn't push it. And I should have." He looked back at the road.

She rested a hand on his forearm. "This isn't your fault, Zeke. I chose not to tell you."

"And you were wrong, Sandy. You should have said something." He pulled up to a stoplight and turned to gaze intently at her. "Look, I don't exactly have a terrific record when it comes to relationships. I don't know whether we'll be together a year from now." He stared past her at a homeless man pushing a grocery cart along the service road. "One of the things about you that first attracted me was your honesty. If you stop being honest with me, we'll never make it." He looked straight at her.

She withdrew her hand from his arm, but met his gaze without flinching. "You're right. I was wrong. I made a decision that involved both of us without giving you a chance to cast a vote. I won't do it again."

The driver behind them honked his horn. The light had

changed to green. Zeke turned his attention back to the road and pressed the accelerator. The Buick leaped forward.

They didn't talk the rest of the way to the restaurant, but the quality of the silence was different now. It was comfortable, companionable. For the first time in hours, Sandy felt her shoulders relax.

Even though it was almost ten p.m. by the time they walked into the Café Brazil on Cedar Springs, the coffeehouse was crowded. Free Wi-Fi service attracted customers to the place twenty-four hours a day. While a few scattered tables held couples, most of the room was filled with single customers typing away on laptops while sipping cups of strong Brazilian coffee.

Sandy and Zeke found seats, and a friendly waitress took their orders. Zeke ordered chorizo tacos with scrambled eggs and flour tortillas covered in melted feta cheese. Sandy ordered spinach crepes with spicy cheese sauce. Their food had just arrived when Zeke's cell phone rang.

He dug it out of his jacket pocket and barked, "Prada." After listening for a moment, he mouthed *Ben* to Sandy.

She didn't have to hear both sides of the conversation to know that Zeke wasn't happy. He asked a half a dozen questions and then growled good-bye. She waited while he folded the phone and put it back in his jacket.

"What happened?"

"Ben finagled his way into Cabrini's penthouse with the guys from CAP. He says Cabrini was expecting them. They asked about you, and he said pretty much what we expected—that you had called the police on him, and he just wanted to talk." He frowned and tapped his fork on the table in what she recognized as an unusually nervous gesture for him.

"Did he demand a lawyer?" she asked.

"Nah, he isn't worried; he knows we don't have anything on him. In fact, Ben said he was packing up to go gambling in Shreveport. He and that hooker of his walked out with the CAP guys." Zeke speared a bit of scrambled egg.

"Will your team follow him to Louisiana?"

He finished chewing before answering. "No. We're not authorized to do surveillance in another jurisdiction, and besides, gas is too expensive these days. We don't have the budget dollars. Our guys made sure he left the city, heading east. Cabrini told the doorman they'd be back Thursday night."

"Thursday night? But that means I don't have to stay with Leah or at your apartment. I can go back to my condo tonight."

He leaned across the table. "Sandy, honey, you haven't been paying attention. We haven't caught the two bastards who tried to kidnap you yet."

"But with Cabrini out of the city, they're probably not going to try again. Besides"—she touched his cheek—"you'll be with me, right?"

He stared at her with an expression somewhere between amusement and annoyance. "Yeah, I'm not letting you out of my sight." The fork continued to tap. "I suppose we could stay there tonight and give you time to pack a bag. But you'll need to call your boss tomorrow. Until we put Cabrini behind bars, there's no way you can keep running around town seeing clients the way you have been."

She opened her mouth to protest, remembered the look on Ex-Marine's face before he got into the car, and nodded. "I understand. I'll talk to Julie about letting me do intake interviews in the office until this thing is resolved."

"Good." He looked relieved, and she realized he'd been afraid she was going to argue with him.

"I still can't believe he's so brazen," she gave voice to the thought that had been bothering her since Monday. "It's like he doesn't think the authorities can touch him."

"He's a psychopath, Sandy. He believes rules are made for other people, not him."

"He scared me, Zeke." Saying the words was a burden off her shoulders. She'd been avoiding thinking about what Cabrini might do if he got his hands on her.

"He scares *me*, Sandy. He's a stone-cold killer. But I promise, I won't let him touch you."

Her eyes welled with unexpected tears. "Thank you."

# Chapter Seventeen

Sandy woke a few minutes before the alarm went off at five thirty on Wednesday morning. She lay there, enjoying the warmth of Zeke's body beside her.

Turning carefully so as not to disturb him, she glanced at him.

He was still asleep, his mouth hanging open an inch. He'd been so tired the night before, it was no surprise he was still asleep. They'd fallen into bed and into sleep within minutes of their return from Café Brazil.

With his hair uncombed and the morning stubble of beard, he might have looked dangerous. But now that she knew him, he no longer frightened her.

She edged her way off the mattress, moving slowly. He didn't need to get up as early as she did. Closing the bedroom door behind her, she headed toward the hall bathroom.

While she showered, Sandy thought about the day before. Both Leah and Ben had been wonderful. While Leah was a friend of many years, Ben's thoughtfulness had been unexpected. She'd asked Zeke if there was anything she could do to repay his partner's kindness. Zeke grinned. "Don't you know that all cops love doughnuts? Ben really likes those little sprinkles."

Thinking about that comment, she remembered the German bakery two blocks north of her building. It opened at six a.m. She could run down there, buy a dozen doughnuts and be back before Zeke awoke. He could take the fresh doughnuts with him to work.

She hesitated. Zeke wouldn't be happy about her going outside alone. But Cabrini was in Louisiana until tonight. She doubted Ex-Marine and his companion would be standing outside at five fifty in the morning.

Satisfied with her plan, Sandy finished bathing and sneaked back into the bedroom to collect fresh clothes.

Twenty minutes later, she was walking along the deserted street, returning from Naugle's Bakery with a paper bag containing a dozen warm doughnuts, half with sprinkles.

The morning was cool, but not cold, a sign that fall was only weeks away. The rich buttery fragrance of the doughnuts made her mouth water. She wished she'd bought a couple for herself.

A long black limousine with dark-tinted windows was coming north on McKinney toward her. *Talk about partying the night away. They're getting home just in time to go to work.*

As the vehicle drew near, it slowed and a rear passenger window slid down. Sandy looked curiously toward the car, expecting to find someone who needed directions. Instead, she found herself looking into Victor Cabrini's face. She stared at him in shock.

Cabrini was smiling. "Ms. Davis, what a pleasant surprise. I've been thinking about you, and here you are."

*Run!* It took a moment for the brain's message to reach her paralyzed legs. She bolted. *Just get away.*

She heard a car door open and glanced over her shoulder. Ex-

Marine and Mr. Queasy were coming at her fast. She stumbled, and they were on top of her.

She opened her mouth to scream, but Mr. Queasy was ready for her. He shoved a leather-gloved hand across her face. "Try to bite me now, bitch," he snarled.

The men frog-marched her back to the limousine. Ex-Marine slid across the backseat and reached out to help Queasy maneuver her inside. She was sandwiched between the two of them. They slammed the doors shut, and the limo pulled away from the curb, accelerating.

Sandy struggled to free herself. Cabrini sat on the opposite bench seat with Dolly beside him. He gestured to Queasy to release Sandy, and the man instantly obeyed.

"Stop this car right now," Sandy yelled.

Cabrini held a hand out, and Ex-Marine pulled the bakery bag she was still clutching away from her and handed it across to his boss.

Opening the white bag, Cabrini peered in and selected a doughnut. One without sprinkles.

"Out to pick up breakfast, were you?" He broke off a piece and offered it to Sandy. "Want some? It's still warm."

"This is kidnapping. Turn this car around and take me back right now, and I won't press charges."

He ignored her and took a tiny taste of the glazed doughnut. After chewing it carefully, he said, "Not bad. Of course, too many of these and those rather large hips of yours will soon qualify as gargantuan."

*He's trying to intimidate me. I need to stay calm. He doesn't really want to hurt me. You can't just kidnap someone off a Dallas street. Stay calm. Stay. Calm.*

Taking a deep breath, she said, "Mr. Cabrini. You're making a big mistake." She was trembling so much that her teeth chattered, and the sentence didn't come out quite as firmly as she would have liked.

He quirked one eyebrow. "Ready to talk to me now, are you? Well, we'll need a quiet place for our conversation. Augie"— the driver turned his head sideways—"let's head for the fishing cabin."

"Yes, sir," the chauffeur replied. He was one of the two heavies that had been with Cabrini in the supermarket.

"Don't do this." Sandy realized she was pleading and shut her mouth with a snap. *That's just what he wants.*

"Let's see what's in that purse of yours." Cabrini gestured toward her shoulder bag with his chin. Queasy yanked the purse from her and handed it to him.

The mobster hummed a small tune as he rifled through her things. She realized it was the theme from *Gilligan's Island*.

*I must be dreaming. In a minute, I'll wake up and all this will have been a bad dream.*

The limousine suddenly accelerated in a violent burst of speed. Sandy stole a glance out the window. They were entering U.S. 75, a major north-south freeway. It was still too early for morning rush hour. The big car sped southbound. *There's no one to signal for help. Think, Sandy, think!*

Cabrini began to chuckle. He pulled something out of her purse and held it up. It was the blue butterfly vibrator.

Despite the danger she was in, Sandy wanted to crawl under the seat in embarrassment. She felt the heat of the blush that colored her neck and cheeks.

"Well, isn't this interesting?" He held the silver cylinder to his nose. "Ummmm. Pussy cream. Very nice." He smiled at Sandy; it wasn't a pleasant smile. "Maybe later today I'll smell the real thing."

Her stomach clenched and she could taste the acid that suddenly flooded her mouth. *Oh, sweet mercy! I'm in real trouble here. What the hell do I do?*

Zeke woke alone in bed. He stretched his arms above his head and glanced toward the alarm. Six a.m. *I've got plenty of time.*

Then he remembered that Sandy needed to be at work at eight. *Get your ass out of bed and go eat breakfast with her, numb nuts.*

He sat up and looked around. No sign of her. He couldn't hear her either. *Maybe she's in the kitchen, making coffee.* Smiling, he pushed himself out of bed.

After a quick stop in the master bathroom, Zeke crawled into his jeans and ambled toward the living room, slowing to glance into the hall bathroom. She wasn't in there, but he could see a wet towel hung over the shower rod. The room still smelled of her bath gel.

There was no sign of her in the living room or kitchen.

Zeke looked around in surprise. *It's six in the damn morning. Where the hell is she?*

He'd just begun searching for some clue as to where she'd gone when he saw the piece of yellow paper sitting on the little dining table. A note: *Ran down to the German bakery for doughnuts with sprinkles. Back in ten minutes.*

He frowned. *Damn it! Why couldn't that girl pay attention—just once?*

There was no way to tell how long she'd been gone. He checked his watch and looked around for his jacket. It was draped over the back of one of the chairs, where he'd left it the night before when they'd arrived home.

*Home? I'm already thinking of this place as home? Whoa.*

He didn't have time to examine the thought. Sandy. He had to find Sandy. Retrieving his cell phone from the jacket, he flipped it open and punched in her number. After four rings, the voice mail kicked in. *Damn. Damn. Damn.* Without leaving a message, he snapped the phone shut and ran toward the bedroom. He'd retrace her steps to the bakery and intercept her along the way.

Zeke snatched up his shirt and slipped into it. He'd button it in the elevator. His shoulder holster and gun were sitting on top of the nightstand, where he'd left them within easy reach of the bed.

After stuffing his socks into his pockets, he shoved his bare feet into the pair of shoes beside the bed. And checked his watch again. Six fifteen. She'd said she'd be back in ten minutes. He'd been awake fifteen already.

Sandy. Sandy. *Sandy!*

When the cell phone began to ring, Cabrini retrieved Sandy's purse from the floor. He opened the bag and fished around inside until he found the small silver phone. Squinting at the display, he read out loud, "Zeke Prada."

Sandy's heart leaped, and hope flooded her limbs. Zeke was looking for her. He'd find her. He wouldn't stop until he found her.

"Who is Zeke Prada?" Cabrini asked.

She met his gaze, but did not speak.

"Is he the man you were with Saturday night? Is he your lover, Alexandra?"

She remained stubbornly silent.

"To call before seven in the morning, he must be your lover. Does he make you come, Alexandra? Do you scream when you come? You'll scream for me." Reaching into his pocket, he pulled out a handkerchief. He used it to wipe off the surface of the cell phone.

Sandy fought to remain calm, despite the mind-chilling terror gripping her. *He wants to frighten me. This is nothing but a game to him, a game he wants to win. The longer I can hold out, the more time Zeke will have to find me. The police can use my cell's signal to track us.*

Cabrini leaned to his right, pushed the automatic window button and waited for it to slide open. He tossed the cell phone and the handkerchief out the window toward the shoulder of the road.

Sandy leaned forward to watch the flashing arc of the thrown phone until it was lost to sight. Her eyelids slid shut; despair threatened to overwhelm her. *Open your eyes. Don't let him see how scared you are.*

She opened her eyes and found herself looking at Dolly, who

sat stiffly beside Cabrini, her face expressionless. She looked like her namesake, a beautiful and empty doll. Sandy stared at her, willing the girl to meet her eyes. It was pointless. Dolly gazed into space, seemingly oblivious to the tension in the limo.

"She won't help you," Cabrini's voice intruded. "She's too well trained, aren't you, Lena?"

"Yes, sir," the girl responded.

Sandy pressed her arms against her sides in an effort to suppress the shudder rippling across her body. *Well trained, like a dog. That's what he wants from me.*

Cabrini grinned. "That's it, Alexandra. Shove those big breasts toward me. You're learning already."

Sandy looked at him in disbelief and then down at her chest. When she'd squeezed her arms against her body, she'd inadvertently pushed her breasts forward. She immediately shifted position to wrap her arms over her breasts.

He laughed. "I'm going to enjoy training you. Teaching you to display yourself whenever I tell you to. For anyone I tell you to." He leered at her.

She felt faint, nearly overwhelmed by his crudeness. Only one thought kept repeating in her mind. *Zeke, please find me. Please, please find me.*

# Chapter Eighteen

Zeke stood on the corner outside the bakery and tried Sandy's cell phone again. No answer.

The doorman had seen her leave around five fifty. She hadn't returned.

The bakery clerk recognized Sandy from Zeke's description. She'd said Sandy had come in, bought a dozen doughnuts and left nearly fifteen minutes earlier.

*Could she be in Cabrini's penthouse? If he had her snatched, would he be stupid enough to have her taken to his apartment? No, not stupid enough. Arrogant enough.* He cut across McKinney Avenue, running toward Cabrini's building.

The doorman sat on a tall stool at the front desk, reading the morning paper.

Zeke shoved his badge in the man's face. "Is Cabrini in?"

The man—whose name tag read GUY—squinted at the badge, folded his newspaper and reached for a clipboard.

Zeke bounced on the balls of his feet while the older man laboriously read the log sheets.

"Says here Mr. Cabrini left last night at nine forty. He won't be back until tomorrow."

"I know he left last night, but have you seen him since?"

The guard shook his head. "No, but he could have come in through the garage and gone straight upstairs. Residents have an elevator key that lets them bypass this desk. Visitors have to come here first."

"Let's go," Zeke said, gesturing toward the elevators. "We need to check his apartment."

"I don't know about that." Guy licked his lips nervously. "Don't you need a warrant?"

"Not if I believe someone may be in danger. Move it." Zeke knew he probably looked and sounded like a madman. He didn't care.

In the elevator on the way up, he remembered the surveillance team for the first time. They'd see him entering Cabrini's apartment. *Shit, what's wrong with me? Damnation. Well, if Sandy's not there, I'll call the lieutenant myself. If he wants to fire me, fine. But we've got to find Sandy.*

When the elevator came to a halt, Zeke rushed the guard to Cabrini's door.

"Go ahead, man. Open it."

Guy pulled his key ring from his pocket. He selected a key, but then stood there, looking undecided. "Maybe I oughta call my manager."

Zeke yanked the key out of his hand and inserted it into the door.

"Hey," the guard cried. "You can't—"

Zeke pulled his gun out of his holster, and Guy ran for the elevator.

After taking a deep breath, Zeke shoved the door open, holding his automatic at the ready.

The penthouse was empty.

He quickly searched the entire apartment, but it was obvious that no one was there.

"Shit!" he swore, looking around the master bedroom. It was time to report Sandy's absence to his lieutenant and Captain Torres. He reached into his jacket and retrieved his cell phone to begin making the calls.

The black limo was now traveling south on I-45. Sandy sneaked a glance at her watch. They'd been traveling for well over an hour. Cabrini had mentioned a fishing cabin, but where? I-45 was the highway connecting Dallas and Houston. Houston and nearby Galveston both sat practically on top of the Gulf. Was Cabrini referring to a fishing cabin along the Gulf of Mexico?

She looked at Cabrini, who hadn't spoken for miles, but who never took his eyes off her.

"Where are we going? Are you taking me to Houston?"

He smiled. "Should I tell her, Lena, or make it a surprise?"

Lena didn't speak, clearly understanding he was addressing her in the manner one does a child . . . or a pet.

"Alexandra, we need a quiet place to develop our relationship, a place where we won't be disturbed."

His words made her stomach flip over. It was a good thing she hadn't eaten breakfast yet.

The limo suddenly exited the highway, and Sandy looked out the window to see where they were going. The signs read U.S. 84 eastbound. *We're driving toward the Piney Woods.*

She turned to look back at Cabrini, who chuckled at her expression.

"That's right. It will be you and me and several hundred thousand acres of pine trees."

*Sweet mercy. He can do anything he wants to me, and no one will ever know. I have to get away.*

"Can we stop for a break?" she asked. "I need a bathroom."

His smile turned into a wolfish grin. "No, you need to learn discipline. Holding your water is good practice. We'll be there in another forty minutes. Sit back and relax."

Zeke waited on the street in front of Sandy's building for Ben to pick him up. He'd checked to be sure Sandy's car was in her garage. The car was still parked where they'd left it the night before. Whatever had happened, she had not been driving when it occurred.

He turned at a noise behind him. Mr. and Mrs. Guzman stepped out onto the street. Their faces hardened at the sight of him. He didn't care; he approached them anyway.

"Excuse me, Mr. Guzman. Have you seen Sandy this morning?"

Jacob Guzman placed his body between Zeke and his wife. "No, we haven't. Maybe she got smart and decided to break up with you?"

Zeke was too worried to waste time figuring out who had shoved a stick up the old man's ass. "Sandy may be in danger. I need to find her."

Mrs. Guzman pushed her husband aside. "You should be ashamed of yourself. Giving a nice girl like Sandy something like that."

"Something like what? What are you talking about? Sandy is missing and I need to find her."

Jacob seized the conversational ball back from his wife. "Just because we're old, that doesn't mean we don't know a thing or two about the world. I know a flogger when I see one."

"A flogger?" Zeke took a step closer to the elderly couple. "Where did you see a flogger?"

"Don't pretend you don't know," Lois Guzman cried. "Sandy gave me the flowers you sent her. When I took them out of the vase to change the water and cut the stems, I found that . . . that awful sex toy of yours."

Understanding hit Zeke. "Cabrini. Cabrini sent Sandy flowers with a flogger hidden in the arrangement."

"Cabrini?" Jacob Guzman repeated. "Who's Cabrini?"

"The stalker who's been following Sandy. Have you seen her this morning? It would have been between six and six fifteen."

Guzman shook his head. "No. I was walking Sasha and Gigi then, but I didn't see Sandy. What stalker?"

Zeke looked down McKinney and checked his watch again. No sign of Ben yet. "A guy who lives in the penthouse across the street."

Lois interrupted. "The freak? Jacob, you know who he means."

"That's a bad man, Zeke," Jacob chimed in. "My nephew works in that building. He tells us things."

Zeke waved away their comments. "Tell me about when you were walking your dogs. Did you see anything? Anything at all?"

The elderly man squinted his eyes in thought. "Let's see. We were late getting out because Gigi didn't want me to put on her leash. Usually we're on the street by six oh five, but it was almost six fifteen before we were—"

Zeke saw Ben's unmarked vehicle coming up the street. "Please, Mr. Guzman, did you see anything?"

"Only a black limousine pulling away from the curb. It accelerated too fast and left rubber on the pavement. Not good for the tires."

*Cabrini has a black limo.* "Could you see who was in the vehicle or its license number?"

Jacob shook his head. "No, sorry. The windows were tinted, and I had no reason to check the plate number."

The unmarked Plymouth pulled alongside them and stopped.

"Thank you, Mr. and Mrs. Guzman. You've been a help."

"You'll find her, won't you, Zeke?" Lois asked.

"I'll find her. I promise." He opened the car door and slid into the passenger seat. Ben accelerated before Zeke had the door closed.

"Did you find out anything?" Zeke asked, buckling his seat belt.

"There was some big rock concert at the American Airlines Center last night." Ben turned right toward Central Expressway. "Since Cabrini was supposed to be gone anyway, they pulled the guys on surveillance detail to help contain the mob at the concert. The post was scheduled to be uncovered until we came on at nine this morning."

206 / Maya Reynolds

"Damn it, Ben! The bastard snatched Sandy right off the street. Her neighbor saw a black limo speed away at about the right time this morning."

"We'll find her, Zeke. You know we will." Ben glanced sideways to meet his partner's eyes.

"I know we'll find her, Ben. It's *how* we'll find her that worries me." He pulled out his cell phone to call Captain Torres. If they knew Cabrini was in his limo, they'd be able to put a be-on-the-lookout report on the airwaves and use traffic cameras to track him.

In the month the task force had been observing him, Cabrini had led a remarkably constrained existence. He spent his time in a dozen regular haunts: his apartment, his office, a couple of clubs in Deep Ellum, a house in the suburb of Oak Cliff that was reported to host some wild parties, and the casinos in Shreveport. Cabrini might have taken Sandy to the South Dallas house. They could be there in twenty minutes.

Ben interrupted him. "We're coming up on U.S. 75. Which way?"

"South," Zeke replied. "Let's check out that house on Harlandale."

"Okay. By that time, Torres may have a lead from Sandy's cell phone."

Sandy's despair was growing. They'd left the highway and were now traveling along on a farm-to-market road. Nobody would think to look for her way out here. She needed a plan. But what?

Discounting the wimpy Lena, she was still up against four men. *I need to focus on stalling for as long as I can. Zeke will find me. I know he will.*

Cabrini spoke, his voice lazy. "You're awfully quiet, Alexandra. Are we boring you? Perhaps we should try harder to amuse you." He turned to the girl beside him. "Lena, Alexandra is bored. Give Gordon a blow job."

Sandy's mouth dropped open, and she felt the thug to her left stir.

Without saying a word, Lena got up, crawled across the car to Ex-Marine and crouched in front of him.

He spread his legs wide, and the girl knelt at his feet. She reached up to unfasten his pants, but he brushed her hands away. While Sandy watched in horror, he unbuttoned and unzipped his slacks, freeing his cock, which was only semierect.

Sandy quickly looked away, but the sight of Cabrini and Queasy grinning lewdly at the tableau in front of them was almost as bad as watching Lena and Gordon. Sandy shut her eyes and prayed.

"Alexandra!" Cabrini's voice was as sharp as a whiplash. "Open your eyes and watch, or I'll fuck you right here."

She opened her eyes, and he continued in a milder voice. "After all, Lena is performing just for you. Be sure to watch her technique. It will help you later."

Sandy slowly turned to look down at the girl. Lena's hands rested on Gordon's thighs, and she was busy licking his cock. Gordon watched her, his eyes a bit unfocused and his hands fisted at his sides. His cock was fully erect now, and Sandy could hear the rasp of his breath.

"Enough foreplay, Lena. Suck him."

Sandy had never wanted to smash someone in the face as much as she wanted to hit Cabrini at this moment. His arrogance, his demanding voice, his sneering expression—she hated them all.

Lena gave no indication she'd heard him, but she used her right hand to guide Gordon into her mouth.

The thug immediately began thrusting forward, wrapping both fists in her hair to hold her head still.

*She's just a convenient receptacle for his cum.* Sandy's skin was prickling with gooseflesh. *This is so wrong.*

The odor of sex permeated the closed car and made Sandy want to gag. Sensing that the sex was exciting Cabrini, she kept her eyes fixed on Lena. She didn't want to give Cabrini a reason to switch his focus to her.

Gordon's hips were pumping frantically now. The slurping sounds of Lena's swallowing were drowned out by his strangled shout. His body froze in the air before collapsing back onto the bench seat.

Lena continued to suck and swallow for another few seconds before withdrawing from his now flaccid cock. She turned her head to look at Cabrini—*Seeking his approval*, Sandy thought.

Cabrini patted his thigh, and Lena crawled back across the car to kneel in front of him. Her slender body brushed against Sandy's legs, and it took every bit of Sandy's willpower not to cringe from contact with the young submissive.

"Good girl," Cabrini said, again sounding like he was praising a dog. He rubbed Lena's hair with an absent hand while studying Sandy's face.

She kept her expression impassive, unwilling to let him see how much he had shaken her composure.

"Did we amuse you, Alexandra? I hope you picked up some pointers. By tonight, I'll have you servicing me . . . and my men."

# Chapter Nineteen

A woman answered the door at the house on Harlandale. She was dressed only in a sheer nightgown. She didn't seem either curious or concerned as to why the police would be banging on her door before eight in the morning. When Ben asked to come in and look around, she didn't argue or ask for a search warrant. She simply held the door wide open and stood there, puffing away on a cigarette.

A quick walk through the house confirmed that she was alone. When Zeke asked her when she'd last seen Cabrini, she looked at him with dead eyes and said, "Who?"

At the doorway, Ben thanked her for her courtesy. She responded by slamming the door on them.

Side by side, the two partners strode down the walkway back to the Plymouth.

"What now?" Ben asked.

"I don't know where else to look." Zeke felt as though a fist were squeezing his heart. "He wouldn't have taken her to a public place like his office, a hotel room or a club."

Ben's cell phone rang, and Zeke had to restrain himself to keep from snatching it out of his partner's hand. He waited impatiently, his palms tapping on the hood of the Plymouth, for his friend to get off the call.

When Ben hung up, he said, "Let's get in the car and head back to Central."

"What—" Zeke stopped himself and climbed into the passenger side of the unmarked car.

When both were strapped into their seats, Ben turned the ignition and pulled away from the curb.

"Damn it, Ben. What did they say?"

"They've found Sandy's cell phone. It was still on, and the company was able to triangulate its location. Our guys found it just off U.S. 75 on the service road leading to Woodall Rogers. Someone had thrown it out a car window. It was wiped clean of fingerprints."

Zeke felt an icy finger touch the space between his shoulder blades. "Jesus, Ben. What do we do now?"

"Hang in there, buddy. We have a few leads. We know from the cell phone that they were heading south. Maybe he's got another house down here in Oak Cliff." Ben's voice was bracing.

"Ben, we have no idea where that imaginary house would be. And we don't know that he didn't discard the phone right there to throw us off his scent." Zeke pounded his forehead with his closed fist.

"Torres has a couple of ideas," Ben responded. "She's pulling the tapes on any cameras along the expressway, and she's got a DA trying to get a warrant for the GPS records on Cabrini's limousine from the company that rents to him."

Zeke felt a flutter of hope. "The limo has a GPS system?"

"Yup. And it will lead us right to that wiseguy fucker."

"Maybe we could go to the limo company and convince the owner to be a bit more helpful," he suggested.

Ben shook his head. "No, Zeke. We've got to do this by the

book. For Sandy's sake." He reached across the seat and patted Zeke's shoulder. "Let's wait till we get back to Central. Maybe they'll have something for us by the time we get there."

The limo crawled along an unpaved road, bouncing and bumping every foot of the way. The big black car rolled across a cattle guard, metal bars over a ditch that farmers used to keep cattle from crossing a road.

Tall pine trees lined both sides of the road. Despite the fact that it was just eight thirty in the morning, the trees cut off the sun and cast shadows on the dirt road.

"We're almost there, Alexandra," Cabrini said. "Just around this bend is the clearing."

The limo maneuvered a tight turn, and the road opened up. Sandy blinked at the sudden bright light that struck the car when the vehicle moved out from the shelter of the pines.

Ahead of them was a lake. On the other side of the lake from the limo sat a sprawling one-story house made of glass and cedar. Circling the perimeter of the house was a wide covered porch with built-in benches.

The small strip of land between the house and the lake sloped down to the water, where two docks—one for a boat and one for fishing—waited.

"Beautiful, isn't it?" Cabrini said, pride in his voice. "I bought it for a steal from a bankrupt dot-com guy a few years ago."

The car slowly navigated the bumpy dirt road that led to the house, and Sandy leaned forward to get a better look. The pines had been cleared in a wide circle around the lake and the house so that sunlight was everywhere.

Large picture windows fronted the lake and promised spectacular views from inside the house. Ducks swam on the placid water, waiting for fish to jump.

"The lake is stocked, of course," Cabrini boasted. "I've caught a twelve-pound catfish with a ten-pound test line."

The incongruity of the situation was not lost on her. He was bragging about the house to which he'd brought her for torture and rape.

"It's gorgeous," she said, not trying to disguise her admiration. "I'd love it if you'd give me a tour of the property."

"Maybe . . . later," he said. "We have other, more important things to do first."

Augie, the driver, parked the limo beside the house.

"Well, here we are, Alexandra," Cabrini said. "Home sweet home."

"What the hell do you mean, they're in Eldon County?" Ben said.

Peter Spenser, owner of Spenser's Luxury Rentals, shrugged and pointed to the GPS monitor. "See for yourself. According to our system, they're somewhere between Jerusalem and Deerhide."

"But why?" Captain Lucinda Torres asked. "What's the point?"

"He needs a quiet place to discipline Sandy," Zeke said. "We've got to get to her as soon as possible."

Lieutenant Jenkins spoke for the first time since they'd arrived at the limo company. "That's outside of our jurisdiction. We either need to call the sheriff of Eldon County or the FBI."

"Please, God, no!" Zeke said. "Don't bring the damned Feebies into it. They'll get her killed for certain."

Captain Torres took Peter Spenser's arm and directed him toward the door. "Thank you for your help, Mr. Spenser. We'll need a few minutes to decide on a course of action."

Once the civilian was out of the room, the discussion began in earnest. None of the police wanted to bring the federal cops into the case. They finally agreed that Jenkins would call the FBI special agent in charge of Dallas and alert him to a missing-persons case without being too specific. There would then be an official record that the FBI had been notified of a possible kidnapping, although Jenkins would be careful to play down the "possible kidnapping" aspect.

"Let's just hope we can settle this today. If not, we're going to have to call the Feds in tomorrow." Lucy Torres was blunt.

"Can we get started?" Zeke pleaded. "It's after ten now. We need to get down to Eldon County fast."

Torres turned to Jenkins. "We can call the sheriff on our way down there."

The lieutenant nodded. "All right. But if we're talking about a possible standoff, we need to bring our SWAT guys along. Eldon County doesn't have the resources for that kind of operation."

"We can't just show up on the sheriff's doorstep with a squadron of officers," Torres argued.

"So, we get him to ask us to bring them along," Zeke said.

"He's not going to want to risk his men going up against a wise-guy like Cabrini. Can we get started now? Please."

"Prada's right," Jenkins said. "It's a two-hour drive. We can work out the details on the way down. Let's roll."

Sandy stood in the bathroom of Cabrini's retreat, looking out the window. She could open it and climb out, but where would she be? In the middle of a freaking pine forest, dozens of miles from anywhere. *I'm just going to have to tough it out until Zeke can find me.*

A little voice whispered, *What if Zeke* never *finds you?* She couldn't contemplate that possibility. The consequences were just too awful.

Queasy—whose name turned out to be Turner—banged on the door. "Get out here now," he ordered.

With a last wistful look out the window, she left the bathroom. Turner escorted her back to the living room, where Cabrini was lounging on a sofa. Gordon stood near a window, looking out at the lake.

A long open counter separated the living room from the kitchen, where Lena and Augie were working.

"Come in, Alexandra, and take a seat." Cabrini waved her into the room, his voice expansive. He held a glass filled with ice and a whiskey-colored liquid. "It's time for us to talk."

Sandy perched on the edge of a large stuffed chair that faced Cabrini's couch, and waited.

"Alexandra, you present a conundrum for me." He paused as though enjoying the sound of the three-syllable word. "You might not think it, looking at the successful businessman that I am, but I've spent years putting my life on the line and trusting my instincts to save me." He swirled the ice in his glass, while he studied her. "And those instincts tell me that you know something I need to know." He paused again.

Sandy had the feeling that he was performing—she wasn't sure whether it was for her benefit or that of his henchman Gordon. She watched him with the same fascination that a mouse must have when eyeing a snake.

Cabrini continued. "On Saturday evening, when we had our chance encounter at Jerry's, you knew who I was."

She shook her head, but he spoke before she could open her mouth. "Please don't bother trying to deny it. Our little encounter in the supermarket—as pleasant as it was—was not arranged just so that I could give you the butt plug. I wanted to see if you knew my name. I knew you recognized my face, and I deliberately signed the card that accompanied my flowers with just my initials. And yet, when we met in the butcher's aisle, you called me 'Mr. Cabrini.' "

Sandy's heart was beating so hard she thought it would leap right out of her chest. *How could I have been so stupid?* She didn't trust herself to speak, so she remained silent.

Cabrini looked at her thoughtfully. "I'd wondered who'd reported me to the police a couple of months ago. I even had a little talk with my neighbors right after that incident occurred. Both of them denied being home that night, and I could see they were telling the truth. I also questioned my building's staff. Of course, they all denied making the report, too." He paused to take a sip of his whiskey before continuing.

"When you so obviously recognized my face on Saturday night at Jerry's, it made me curious. I sent someone to follow you, but my man Farr got attacked and knocked out in my own garage. You can imagine how much that tweaked my interest." He gazed at her over the top of his glass. "Now I was committed to finding out more about you and your companion, who I'm assuming is the Zeke Prada who tried to call you this morning."

*You cannot let him know Zeke is a cop or that the police have had him under surveillance for the past month. He'll kill you where you sit.*

"The next morning, I brought Gordon and Turner in from Houston to question the staff in the buildings directly across from my penthouse. I wanted people who would not be immediately tied back to me. Imagine my delight to learn that you and I were neighbors." He grinned his wolfish smile before glancing toward Gordon.

"You see, I knew something was going on. I'd felt like I was being watched for weeks." Cabrini slapped his thigh with his free hand and chuckled. "Here I'd been thinking the cops were spying on me, and instead, it turned out that I had a Peeping Tom who was also a dirty little snitch." He drained his glass. "I'll have to find a special punishment for you, Alexandra. I don't mind that you were spying on me, but you should never have called the cops." His cold eyes belied the jocular tone of his voice.

Adrenaline raced through her body. She knew what it was: the fight-or-flight syndrome. Her body was gearing up to either fight or run. She forced herself to remain still and to watch Cabrini as though she were merely listening to a lecturer giving an interesting talk at some university.

"Lena, come here," Cabrini called.

The submissive emerged from the kitchen and came into the living room. She sank into a graceful kneeling posture in front of his couch.

He looked down at her with something like affection. "Stand and strip."

Lena immediately obeyed. Within seconds, she had removed her one-piece sweater dress. Beneath it, she was naked. She stood in the middle of the room, wearing only black high heels.

From her position behind the girl, Sandy could see the welts across Lena's shoulders, her buttocks and the backs of her thighs. Bile filled her mouth as she imagined the pain Lena must have endured while Cabrini was beating her.

"Now sit here beside me," Cabrini ordered, patting the cushion to his right. "That's my girl," he praised when Lena sat next to him on the couch. He casually slid his free hand to rest between her thighs.

Cabrini held his glass out toward Gordon. "Fix me another." He waited while the thug went to the wet bar across the room, poured a second drink and returned to hand it to him.

The mobster took a long swallow of the fresh drink. "Excellent, Gordon, thank you." He turned his attention back to Sandy. "Once I had developed my hypothesis"—he slurred the word "hypothesis"—"that you were the snitch, I wanted to know exactly how interested in me you were, and why your companion felt compelled to attack Farr. So I sent you the flowers, giving only my initials, and then I followed you to the supermarket.

"When I asked if you had called the police on me, your face told the truth even though you lied. That's when you called me by name. So now I was really intrigued. Knowing my apartment location, you could, of course, have simply questioned my doorman, as I had yours. However, why would you bother? More importantly, why did your Mr. Prada attack Farr?" He stretched his legs out in front of him. "These are questions you are going to have to answer, Alexandra. Why don't you start right now?"

Sandy pressed her thighs together in an unconsciously protective movement. She was trembling; she clasped her hands together in her lap to try to hide the fact from him. *I can't tell him about Zeke being a cop or about the surveillance operation, but I have to tell him something. The question is, what?*

*Or am I better off keeping my mouth shut altogether? If I do, he'll start by beating and raping me. No, I need to tell him something.*

She ran her tongue along her lips, wetting them. "Mr. Cabrini, you're right. I was on my balcony one night and saw you in your penthouse." She let the memory of that night paint her voice with sincerity. "I'm a social worker. I didn't know what was going on. I'd never seen bondage or discipline before. I thought you were trying to kill the girl, so, yes, I did call the police. My first instinct was to try and save her life."

He nodded approvingly. "Good. Now, how did you learn my name?"

"I was watching when the police arrived. Your lady friend obviously reassured them that whatever you were both doing was consensual. I realized then that you were engaged in sex play." She looked down, not hiding her embarrassment. "I was curious and wanted to know more. That's why I went over to your building to get your name."

"And who in my building divulged private information about me?" Although his voice was silk, he mangled the word "divulged." The whiskey was definitely impairing his speech.

"I don't even remember. It doesn't matter." She shrugged.

"Oh, but it matters a great deal to me. You see, I tip all the building staff very heavily. If one of them betrayed me, I need to know who it was." There was steel behind the words. "You can choose to tell me, or I will beat it out of you. I'm quite eager to see how you respond to a flogging."

Her mouth went dry at the same time her teeth began to chatter. It took two tries before she could say, "I waited until the doorman was busy with another resident, slipped in and checked the mailboxes."

"Ding," he sang out, mimicking a game show buzzer. "Wrong answer, Alexandra. Our mailboxes don't display names, only apartment numbers." He turned to Gordon. "Why don't you and Turner escort my fat little friend to my playroom? I'll see if I can loosen her tongue there."

# Chapter Twenty

Zeke's muscles ached. Adrenaline had been pouring through them for hours, preparing him for physical action. Being confined to the front seat of a car gave him no outlet for all the epinephrine pouring into his bloodstream. He could feel his heart pounding, and he was working on one hell of a headache.

Captain Torres was in the backseat, talking to Sheriff Winston Parnell of Eldon County on her cell. She had repeated herself several times already, which suggested that Sheriff Parnell was not the sharpest blade in the drawer. Zeke wanted to snatch the phone from her and yell into it, "Damn it! We're on our way to your pissant town to do our job. Just stay out of our way and no one will get hurt."

He saw Ben glance sideways at him, a worried expression on his face. Zeke tried to relax his limbs, but they were hard and hurting from all the sugar dumped into his circulatory system by stress. He smiled reassuringly at his partner. From Ben's expression, he knew the smile came out more like a grimace.

Torres snapped her cell phone shut with an audible click. "I was hoping to do this the easy way, but the sheriff wants us to come by his office in Travis to talk."

"Fuck that!" Zeke snarled. "We don't have time to play nicey-nice with some dumb small-town hick. Sandy is in danger."

"Prada—" Lieutenant Jenkins started, but Torres cut him off.

"I know you're anxious, Detective, but we need the sheriff's help. He knows the area. We don't. He knows the residents. We don't. He knows the Piney Woods. We don't."

Jenkins chimed in, his voice hard. "I've agreed to let you come along on this operation even though you have a conflict of interest."

"Lieu, I don't have any conflict of interest—" Zeke started.

"Quiet. You have a personal stake in this operation. *That's* a conflict of interest in my book. If you don't want to be sidelined, you'll keep your mouth shut and take orders. Understood?"

His military training kicked in, and Zeke swallowed his anger. "Understood, sir. Thank you, sir."

The lieutenant's eyes softened. "We'll get her back, son. Just trust the process."

"Yes, sir." Rather than say anything else that might get him thrown out of the car, Zeke shut his mouth. His jaws clenched together so hard that his teeth hurt.

He looked out the window at the landscape streaking by. There were oil rigs and pumps sitting in fields surrounded by cattle, or sharing space with a ranch-style house or a small crop of wheat or corn.

His gaze was fixed on the landscape, but his mind saw Sandy as she'd looked last night at dinner. Only twelve hours ago, he'd promised to keep her safe. Now she was in the hands of a sexual sadist. *His* gentle, funny Sandy, so full of surprises and contradictions, was with Victor Cabrini. *If he hurts one hair on her head, I'll kill him. I swear to God, I'll kill him. I don't care if I go to prison for the rest of my life. It will be worth it. Hang on, honey, I'm coming.*

———

Sandy sat on a tall stool in the center of what must have been intended to be a media room by the builder. A large square room without windows, it was painted slate gray. But any resemblance to a normal home ended there.

Cabrini had called this place his "playroom." Wrist and leg restraints hung from the walls, while whips and floggers were displayed in a large glass and mahogany case. A long, narrow examining table complete with stirrups sat to her left, and some kind of wooden device with chains and pulleys was positioned on her right.

There was something very dramatic and theatrical about the whole place, as if it were a stage backdrop for a play. If Sandy hadn't seen Cabrini with his submissives, she would have thought the room was intended to frighten visitors. However, knowing what she did about him and his perverse tastes, she had no doubt that the room was exactly what it looked like: a torture chamber. The floor was gray slate; it was probably easier to clean blood off stone than carpet.

She was almost past fear. Her body, swamped by the sudden surge of terror, seemed to have shut down. The trembling and teeth chattering from twenty minutes ago were gone, replaced by a kind of clammy repose. In contrast, her brain was on hyperalert, coolly processing everything and making instant assessments.

*Zeke is looking for me. He'll know Cabrini kidnapped me. He and the police will find me. I just need to hold on until then.*

Victor Cabrini prowled around his playroom, picking up sex toys and stroking the chains on the wall. He'd removed his suit coat, rolled up the sleeves of his dress shirt and taken off his tie.

Gordon and Turner stood side by side in front of the room's only door, now shut.

She thought about everything she'd learned about Cabrini over the past months while she'd been watching him. *He's a sociopath and sadist who uses the BDSM scene to gratify his need to inflict pain and to control women. He wants me to tremble and cry and plead. That gives him more pleasure than the actual act of sex itself.*

*My best strategy is to continue to resist, but to let him gradually break me down. If he doesn't get his way, he'll escalate. He could kill me without meaning to—just because he's so determined to win.*

*That shouldn't be hard,* a little voice in her head said. *You're scared spitless. He's going to break you anyway. And he'll love doing it.*

Cabrini picked up what looked like a cat-o'-nine-tails. He caressed the leather thongs in a creepy gesture that Sandy found hard to watch.

*This is all just lead-up, intended to scare me. Okay, it's working, but—like the room—it's for show.*

He swung around and took two steps toward her. "All right, Alexandra. Are you ready to tell me who told you my name?"

"It was a doorman," she lied. "I told him I'd seen you on your balcony, and we'd waved at each other. I asked him if you were married."

"Because you were interested in me?" He leaned closer and rubbed the baton of the cat-o'-nine across her cheek.

She didn't have to pretend the sharp intake of breath she gave.

"Because I was curious. I'd never seen anyone do the things you were doing." That much at least was true.

"And it excited you?" The gleam in his eyes was bad, but not as bad as his very evident erection.

Sandy tried not to cringe. "Yes," she whispered. "It excited me."

"And who was this very helpful doorman? What was his name?"

"I don't know his name. He was just a middle-aged security guard."

"Now, *that* was a lie." He seemed pleased to have caught her in an untruth. He gestured to his two thugs. "Strip her."

She jumped off the stool. "Wait a minute. You can't do this!"

Cabrini didn't answer. He'd turned away to open the display case. He ran his hand over the assorted whips, canes and floggers.

Sandy backed away from Gordon and Turner until the examining table blocked her path. "Stay away from me."

One of them grabbed and held her while the other simply reached out and ripped the garments from her body. It was fast and brutal, and somehow worse for the very impersonal nature of the attack. Neither man wore an expression of pleasure or lecherousness—it was simply business. Sandy's blouse, bra, skirt and panties were soon a pile of shredded cloth at her feet. She was naked and barefoot.

A week ago, Sandy would have been reduced to a sobbing, cowering puddle on the floor, but a lot had happened in the past days since she'd met Zeke. His unabashed admiration of her naked body had given her pride in her appearance. In addition, her intuition screamed that she must not allow Cabrini to sense her fear; if he did, he'd be on her like a shark smelling blood in the water.

Once it was obvious that she was not going to bolt, Cabrini's henchmen released her arms, but remained on either side of her.

Sandy forced herself to stand with her hands at her sides instead of trying to cover her breasts and genitals. She was rewarded by the fleeting expression of confusion that crossed Victor Cabrini's face.

"You surprise me, Alexandra," he said, coming toward her, slapping the end of a rattan cane against the palm of his hand. "I was expecting you to fall on the floor, pleading and sobbing for mercy."

She remained still, ignoring the cane in his hand, her eyes fixed on his. "I'm not one of those poor little submissives of yours."

The instant the words were out of her mouth, she realized she'd made a tactical error. His eyes widened and his mouth twisted into a semblance of a smile.

"Now, that's really interesting, Alexandra. You feel superior to submissives like Lena. Yet you say you're excited by watching me with them. Which is it? Are you excited or not? Or do you have another reason for spying on me?"

Not wanting to make things worse, she didn't answer.

He approached her and shoved the handle of the cane under her chin, forcing her head up.

"Who is Zeke Prada, and why did he attack Farr?"

"I don't know what you're talking about," she said stiffly.

"That's another lie." He looked at her thoughtfully before gesturing to his men. "Take her."

Gordon and Turner grabbed Sandy. Panic seized her, and she fought fiercely against them, kicking and punching.

Her bare feet and fists had no impact on the huge men. She managed to bite Gordon on the arm, and he responded with a hard slap across her face that stunned her.

She dimly heard Cabrini's voice saying, "Bend her over that table, boys."

# *Chapter Twenty-one*

The Dallas convoy had no difficulty in finding the sheriff's office. Like most small Texas county seats, Travis had a central town square built around the courthouse. The sheriff's office was at the back of the courthouse with its own entrance.

Before they entered the building, the group had discussed the best way to handle the sheriff. After the difficulty Torres had experienced communicating with him during the ride down, the team had decided to depend on a strategy in which they let Lieutenant Jenkins do the talking. Torres laughed. "I don't know whether it was the fact I was a woman or a Hispanic that was creating static on the line."

Winston Parnell was a large man, nearly six feet five and weighing at least two fifty. Within minutes, Zeke realized that his judgment of the man as a "dumb small-town hick" was way off the mark.

The sheriff greeted them with typical small-town courtesy, offering coffee and giving directions to the restrooms. All the while, his sharp eyes were busy making his own assessments. During a quiet moment, he leaned near Zeke to ask, "You see much combat in that Middle East?"

Ben asked permission to use the sheriff's desk to set up the laptop loaned to them by Peter Spenser. Parnell watched with interest as the Dallas detective keyed in the data for Cabrini's limo and then overlaid the GPS grid with a topographical map

of Eldon County. Ben pointed to the location of Cabrini's rent-
ed limo.

The sheriff leaned forward in his wooden chair to peer at the
map on the small screen.

"Well, now, there's Dillo Lake and here's the river. If we follow that river to this little feeder stream here, it looks like your
missing vehicle is on the property of one of our newest residents,
Mr. Vincent Cable."

Zeke and Ben exchanged looks.

"What can you tell us about Mr. Cable, Sheriff?" Jenkins
asked in a conversational voice.

Parnell rubbed his jaw, his hand scratching over his chin's stubble. "Well, he arrived about two and a half years ago. Bought a
house that had been built by one of those computer magnates"—
he pronounced it "magnets"—"from down Austin way." The sheriff shifted his hand to scratch his nose. "Way I heard the story,
this guy—by the name of Mathis—lost his shirt in some kind of
corporate takeover. He sold the place for pennies on the dollar.

"One bright morning, along comes Mr. Vincent Cable and
three or four hard types that made me sit up and take notice. I
paid them a courtesy call, of course, and took down the license
plates of all the cars I saw. Did no good. They were all leased to
holding companies."

The sheriff's eyes hardened. "In a nice, neighborly way, I
made it clear that we don't like any big-city shenanigans here
in Eldon County. Now, we've got a few marijuana plots down
here. Nothing serious. Just for personal use. People like Agatha
Carson need their weed to stave off the pain and nausea of can-

cer." Parnell's eyes dimmed for a moment; Zeke thought he saw compassion in them.

Then the sheriff caught Zeke looking, and his eyes narrowed. "We don't put up with none of that crystal meth poison in my county. I explained all that to Mr. Cable. He said he understood." Parnell reached for his hat and brushed a non-existent piece of lint off it. "I suggested that Mr. Cable and his company might want to do their shopping elsewhere 'cause they probably wouldn't find the kind of consumer goods they wanted in our little shops hereabouts." He smiled, an expression totally without humor. "Cable took my meaning all right. He and his people don't bother us none. They come, and they go." He stood and put his hat on his head. "It's been a real good relationship thus far. But I can't say I'll be sorry to see him leave my county."

There was a moment of silence, a tribute by seasoned law officers to someone they recognized as one of their own. Then, Jenkins cleared his throat and said in a respectful tone, "Sheriff, we'd appreciate your advice on how best to approach the house."

Parnell's eyes twinkled, and he said, "I'm sure glad to hear that. There was a lot of cell phone interference during my call with the captain, and I was thinking that maybe you-all wanted me to sit this one out."

This time, the silence was uncomfortable. The sheriff broke it by saying, "I expect it's time we headed on out to visit Mr. Cable. What do you-all think?"

Zeke stood in the doorway, Ben at his side, waiting. At the sheriff's words, they turned and walked out of the room.

*Sandy, I'm on my way. Wait for me, baby.*

Sandy gritted her teeth when the rattan cane struck her buttocks again.

"You're really going to be black-and-blue tomorrow, Alexandra. I have to admit, I like flogging a fatty." She could hear him panting, but couldn't tell if it was from exertion or excitement.

He continued. "With all that padding on your back, I don't have to worry about damaging any organs. Lena's so slim and frail. Not at all like you, my big, beautiful Amazon."

She was standing in her bare feet, bent over the foot of the examining table. Her breasts, her belly and the left side of her face were pressed against the plastic mattress of the table, and her arms were extended above her head with her wrists handcuffed to a set of convenient chains.

Unlike when she was handcuffed to her shower rod, this experience was neither exciting nor titillating. She was sweating all over, which made her skin stick to the table's plastic surface. Her perspiration smelled of fear.

After Gordon and Turner had handcuffed her to the examining table, Cabrini had sent them out of the room, saying he didn't want to be disturbed unless he called them.

Cabrini was not in her limited range of vision, but she could hear him moving around the room behind her. He was whistling the theme to *Gilligan's Island* again. Her brain couldn't reconcile that silly tune with the terrible situation she was in. The words kept running through her mind as he whistled: *Now sit right back and you'll hear a tale . . .*

Cabrini patted her bare ass, and she jerked in surprise. He

chuckled. "You're a little jumpy, Alexandra. Anxious for more?" He moved into her line of sight.

"You are going to provide such entertainment for me, Alexandra. I've never had a fat sub before. Those big tits and wide, white ass of yours are delicious. This will be fun. How would you like to be my house slave? I could keep you chained down here and come visit you on weekends."

She realized with a horrified fascination that he did have an erection. In an attempt to shut the sight out, she closed her eyes.

He moved behind her. The sound of the cane whistled through the air before she felt its crack across her buttocks. She cried out, arching her back and tensing her shoulders at the sharp pain.

"Open your eyes," he snapped. "You don't close your eyes unless I give you permission. Do you understand?"

She panted with shock and outrage, unable to believe he was actually striking her. Another whistling sound made her open her eyes and shriek in protest, "No, please."

Too late. The cane slapped against her skin again. She gasped, tugging at the restraints that held her.

"When I ask a question, I expect an immediate answer. Do you understand, Alexandra?"

"Yes," she whispered.

"What was that? Did you say something?"

"Yes, I understand," she said more loudly.

He moved back into her line of sight. "From now on, you will call me Master. Do you understand?"

Sandy's stomach lurched, and her mind rebelled. She was not

going to call him that. He was going to have to kill her because she was not going to call him Master.

Cabrini smiled, a happy smile. "Oh, good. You want to be stubborn. I'm happy to help you change your mind." He moved, but before the whistling sound of the cane warned her of another strike, she heard a knock on the door to the room.

He screamed, "I told you I didn't want to be disturbed."

Turner's voice responded, "It's Mr. Kingsley on the phone for you, sir. He wants to go over the list you sent him."

Sandy's mind went into hyperdrive. Maybe she could use this opportunity.

"Damn it," Cabrini cursed. "Tell him I'll be there in a second."

He ran a hand lovingly down Sandy's right buttock. "I'll be right back."

"I think you hit my kidney," she said. "I need to pee."

He hesitated, and for a moment, she thought he was going to tell her to hold her water again. However, he shouted, "Turner, get in here and take Alexandra to the bathroom."

"May I take a hot shower to loosen my muscles?" She paused and then said, "Please, Master?"

He chuckled, clearly pleased. "Since you asked so nicely, yes, you may."

Turner entered the room.

"Take my Amazon to the guest bathroom and lock her in so that she can take a piss and a shower," Cabrini ordered.

"Sir, you ordered us to remove the door from the guest bathroom last month."

"Well, then, lock her into the guest bedroom. Do I have to do all the thinking around here?" He stalked out of the room toward the front of the house.

Turner came over to the examining bed. "How're you doing, bitch?"

"Why? Does it matter to you?" she asked as he uncuffed her left wrist.

"Only because of that hit to my balls you gave me yesterday. I was pissing blood all night. I'd like to take a belt to you myself." He leaned across her naked body to unlock the second handcuff. "Come on. Let's go."

Sandy was stiff all over. The only thing that got her moving was the hope of getting out of this monster's lair. She put her palms flat on the damp plastic and pushed.

The pain through her back and shoulders was immediate. She let out a long groan of agony.

"Oh, good, he did hurt you. Come on." Turner grabbed her upper arm and began dragging her toward the door.

"Wait, my clothes," she cried.

"The boss didn't say nothing about letting you have your clothes back." He glanced from her to the door and back again. "Of course, if you'd like to suck my cock, I might change my mind."

"I'd rather die first," she responded.

"Honey, you ain't been keeping score." He shoved his face toward hers. "What do you think Cabrini has planned for you when he's through playing around? It won't be the first time he's left a body in these woods." He straightened. "You might want to think about being nice to me. I may be the last friend you'll ever have. Now come on."

Sandy's brain reeled at the blunt message. She'd known the truth, but hearing it said so baldly was overwhelming.

The bottoms of her feet were slick with sweat, and she slid. Turner automatically caught her. The second time she slipped, he let go of her arm, and she fell to the hard slate floor.

"A friend would have caught you," he reminded her.

She refused to give him the satisfaction of saying anything, even when she slipped a third time and he let her drop again. Without acknowledging him, she picked herself up and let him take her arm again.

He led her to a room at the opposite end of the house from the living room. It was sparsely furnished with a bed, nightstand, dresser and straight-backed chair. The door to the bathroom had been removed.

"There are towels in there for your shower," he said, shoving her toward the bathroom. "You've got fifteen minutes."

"Thanks," she said in a neutral tone.

He closed and locked the bedroom door.

The second the door shut, Sandy ran to the window and looked out.

Nothing had changed since the first time she considered climbing out a window to escape. Nothing, except now she was naked, bruised and sore. Trying to escape through that window was virtual suicide. The house was at least five miles from the farm-to-market road, and she was in her bare feet. Even if Cabrini's men didn't find her, she couldn't run naked in the woods miles from help.

*If I could find a place to hide, I could open the window and let them think I'd escaped.* She looked around the bedroom. There were no hiding places except the closet and under the bed, the two locations they'd check first.

She returned to the bathroom and turned the shower on. While it was running, she did a quick search of the cabinets. Except for some aspirin, which she eagerly swallowed, the shelves were bare.

She moved on to the linen closet. Half a dozen towels and some toilet tissue were the only things on the shelves.

She was about to close the door when she noticed something. Kneeling down, she examined the floor of the closet.

*Sweet mercy. It's a trapdoor.*

Like many houses built in Texas, Cabrini's home had been built using pier-and-beam construction. Sometimes called raised-floor construction, the design included a crawl space below the floor. Sandy was looking at the trapdoor that provided access to the open space below the house. Such crawl spaces were typically about eighteen to twenty-four inches high.

She pried the piece of plywood up and squinted into the open hole. A musty, foul odor rose to greet her.

Dark, dirty, and filled with spiders and rats and their poop.

*So, Alexandra, do you want to hang out with the two-legged rats or the four-legged ones?*

It wasn't even a contest.

Turner would be back at any minute. If she was going to do this, she needed to do it now.

Standing back up, she ran into the bedroom and opened the window. It took only three hard shoves to knock the screen out of the window frame to the ground below.

Next, she wedged the straight-backed chair under the doorknob, blocking the door. It wouldn't hold for long, but it might buy her a couple of more seconds.

Yanking the sheet off the bed, she wrapped it around her body and returned to the bathroom. The trapdoor wasn't very big, and her hips were wide.

"Where there's a will, there's a way. Get your ass down into that hole, Alexandra Davis," she whispered to herself.

The creepiness of the hole and the fear that she'd get bitten by something made her hesitate. If she had a stick or a broom, she could thrash it around to make sure any creepy-crawlies vacated the vicinity.

The doorknob in the bedroom rattled. No more time. She dived feetfirst into the hole, landing on her butt, and then squirmed to get the upper half of her body into the hole, too.

# Chapter Twenty-two

She heard shouting as Turner began banging on the bedroom door. Reaching up, she grabbed the plywood cover and lowered it into the space with her fingertips.

Not a moment too soon. She heard the sound of splintering wood and then running footsteps.

"Damn it, she went out the window," Turner shouted.

"Well, what are you waiting for? Go find the bitch." Cabrini's voice was filled with rage. Sandy's stomach clenched.

The floorboard above her vibrated. Someone had entered the bathroom.

She'd left the linen closet open, hoping it would prevent anyone from examining it more closely.

Someone opened the cabinet under the sink. He was only inches from her hidey-hole. Would he smell the odor from the crawl space? Would he hear her heart beating frantically?

*Please, Lord, don't let them find me. Cabrini will peel my skin like a grape if they do.*

Whoever was in the bathroom walked out. She strained to hear movement. Nothing.

How long would they stay outside searching? Would they come back right away? Should she go, or should she stay? Was she better off waiting here until they returned to Dallas? What if it took days?

Fear immobilized her. She couldn't decide what to do.

Then she heard a small rustling to her right. Turning her head slowly, she saw a pair of orange eyes staring at her through the darkness

*Oh, God!! A rat.*

Decision made, she pushed open the trapdoor and leaped out of the hole, scratching herself on a jagged piece of wood along the way. *Great. Now I'll need a tetanus shot.*

Stuffing the filthy sheet back into the hole, she covered the crawl space before leaving the bathroom. She tiptoed to the bedroom door and listened.

Nothing.

Still naked, she slipped into the hall. The house was silent, although she could hear the men screaming to one another outside.

First order of business was to find a phone. Then some clothes and shoes. And maybe a weapon. Or even the keys to the limo.

Keeping her head down so as not to be seen by anyone from the outside, she crawled around the living room looking for a phone. Not seeing one, she headed toward the kitchen.

There. On the wall. An honest-to-God telephone.

She had just started to reach up to grab the receiver when she heard a noise behind her.

As she swung around, her gaze met Lena's. The girl's eyes were wide and frightened, glancing from the living room to Sandy.

The two women stared at each other for a long moment.

"Please," Sandy begged. "Let me call the police. Please!"

Lena slowly nodded and walked past Sandy toward the living

room. Sandy held her breath as the girl went through the open front door to the porch.

But she didn't scream for help. She was just putting as much space between herself and Sandy as she could. Knowing Cabrini, Sandy didn't blame her.

She reached up again and dislodged the receiver from its cradle. The receiver fell and nearly bumped her on the head. Picking it up, she listened for a dial tone, ready to dial 911.

There was no dial tone.

Thinking she needed to depress the receiver's hook she stood up far enough to reach the cradle and pressed the button. She held the receiver to her ear.

Nothing.

She began pressing keys on the phone: 0 for the operator, 911. Nothing worked.

"Alexandra."

She turned to find Cabrini standing in the middle of the living room, holding Lena . . . and a gun to her head.

Sandy dropped the telephone receiver.

"I told you I had good instincts," he said. "I just couldn't see you running around the woods in your birthday suit. So I sent Gordon, Turner and Augie to look for you, but I stayed right here on the porch and waited." He ran the tip of the gun barrel along Lena's cheek, digging into the skin. The scope left a long, angry scratch on her cheek.

"Imagine my surprise when I saw you crawl into the kitchen and then, a minute later, saw my sweet Lena walk out of the kitchen without raising any kind of alarm." He stuck his tongue out and licked the blood welling out of the scratch on her cheek. "I'm soooo disappointed in you, Lena."

The girl didn't make a sound, but the hopelessness in her eyes was like a knife in Sandy's side.

"It wasn't her fault. She didn't see me. I hid."

"Naughty, naughty, Alexandra. You're lying again. You'll have to be punished for fibbing. You and Lena both."

Lena shuddered, and Sandy's throat constricted. *Sweet mercy, what will he do to us?*

The line of police vehicles and two ambulances traveled without sirens to the eastern edge of Cabrini's property and parked along the road.

Zeke was in the front seat of the sheriff's cruiser. Captain Torres and Lieutenant Jenkins were in the back. Ben was in a deputy's car behind them.

The only indication that someone lived along this road was a wooden mailbox and barbed wire fencing. A corridor of giant pine trees lined the road as far as Zeke could see.

"Here we go," the sheriff said. "The house is about four miles up that dirt road, in a clearing back behind all those pines."

"So they'll see us approaching?" Jenkins asked.

"If we drive up there, sure." The sheriff nodded. "I was thinking maybe we ought to sneak up there on foot, real quiet-like."

Lucy Torres spoke. "I'm a little uneasy about a covert approach when we don't have a warrant."

The sheriff cleared his throat. "Well, as to that, after I finished talking with you on the phone, I called Judge Burton and asked him if he'd let me have a warrant. Old Judge Burton isn't too concerned about things like probable cause. I got a blank warrant right here. Just got to fill in the name and address." He pulled a crumpled piece of white paper out of his back pocket and waved it at Lucy.

She stared at him in silence for a count of three and then said, "Sheriff Parnell, will you marry me?"

The sheriff—at least twenty years older than Lucy—grinned at her. "Well, now, if my Cora ever tells me to pack up and leave, I'll sure come looking for you, Captain."

Anxious to get moving, Zeke interrupted their comedy routine. "So, we do what? Walk up this road and hope they don't see us coming?"

The sheriff tugged at his right ear, like he was milking a cow. "Be a real shame not to use them SWAT boys, since you brung them all the way from Dallas with you."

He looked at Lieutenant Jenkins. "This road's the only way in or out of the place by car. There's a thirteen-acre lake blocking egress from the house to the north. I was thinking maybe we'd split your team up into two groups. Send half with one of my deputies 'round behind the house to the south. Then we could send the other half with another deputy to come in from the west. When everybody's in place, I'll just drive up the road and come in from the east." He grinned. "Be kind of like one of them pincer movements they liked to use during wartime."

The three Dallas cops exchanged looks. Zeke was the first to speak. "I want to go in with you, Sheriff."

Torres and Jenkins said "No!" in unison.

The captain spoke first. "Detective, Cabrini's already seen your face. If you show up with the sheriff, we lose the element of surprise."

The sheriff interrupted before Jenkins could add his protest. "Well, now, seeing as how this detective's sweetheart is locked up in that place, seems to me he's earned the right to come in the front door." He looked hard at Zeke. "You'll stay on the floorboard of the front seat until things get under way?"

"Yes, sir," Zeke responded.

"Let the detective come with me. I'm an old man, and my reflexes aren't what they used to be. I'll be glad for the company."

They got out of the cruiser, and the sheriff spread a map out on the hood of the car. Sergeant Gomez, head of the SWAT team, listened as Parnell outlined his proposed plan.

"Sounds good to me," Gomez agreed.

"We'll leave a deputy here with the ambulances at the mouth of the road just in case something goes wrong and Cable—or Cabrini, or whatever you call him—manages to drive his limo off the property."

Everyone put their phones on vibrate and synchronized their watches. Zeke and the sheriff would wait until the two teams were in place before starting up the road.

The teams headed off into the woods and the sheriff leaned back against the front fender of his cruiser.

"Won't be long now, Detective. You'll have your sweetheart back."

"I hope you're right, sir. I pray that you're right." Zeke paced back and forth in front of the sheriff's car.

"Have you told her that you love her yet?" the sheriff asked.

Zeke stared at him. "What? No, I haven't."

"Maybe that's part of the reason you're so agitated. You haven't told her how you feel yet."

"I just want her safe," Zeke said. "None of this would have happened if it weren't for me."

"Horseshit," the sheriff said, folding up the map they'd used. "You want her safe because you love her. Be a man and admit it. You love her, and it's eating you up inside that she's in danger. Believe me, I know."

His voice took on the cadence of someone telling an oft-repeated story. "Back when Cora and I were dating, she was a nurse up at the prison in Huntsville, where I was a guard. There was a break one day, and four prisoners took Cora and two other staff members hostage." He shook his head. "I like to died when I realized Cora was one of those taken."

He rubbed the back of his neck. "I made a promise to God that day. I told Him that if He'd give my Cora back to me, I'd marry her and keep her safe for the rest of my life." He grinned at Zeke with twinkling eyes. "And I'm still serving that life sentence. Going on fifty years."

Zeke laughed because the sheriff expected him to do so.

Parnell sighed and opened the car door. "We've still got some time to wait. If you don't mind, I'm gonna take me a little nap right here in my cruiser. Anything happens, you wake me. Okay?"

He quickly dozed off, sitting in the driver's seat of his car.

Zeke continued to pace: back and forth, up and down. His

mind wouldn't rest. He remembered Parnell's story, and although he hadn't prayed since childhood, he found himself praying now, the same refrain over and over.

*God, I know Sandy and I didn't exactly meet at a church social. But if you'll keep her alive, I swear I'll do right by you. I'll ask her to marry me, and if she says yes, I'll keep her safe for the rest of her life. Just take care of her this one time for me. Don't let her die. Let her come back to me.*

When his cell phone began to vibrate, he nearly jumped out of his skin. It was Torres' team checking in to advise they were in place.

Ten minutes later, Jenkins' team called in.

When Zeke opened the passenger door of the cruiser, the sheriff opened his eyes. "Ready, son?"

Zeke used his tongue to moisten his dry lips before replying, "Ready." He crouched down on the floorboard of the vehicle.

Parnell turned the ignition, and the car slowly began rolling down the bumpy dirt road.

The ride seemed to take forever.

"Okay, we're coming in sight of the lake," the sheriff said. "I'm gonna park and then walk up and knock on the front door. I'll park at an angle so that they won't easily see you coming out of the car on your side. You let yourself out and wait.

"They're used to me stopping by to check on them. I'm gonna tell them there's been some vandalism of weekend homes, and I'm just doing the rounds, checking on everyone.

"Give me two minutes. Then send Torres and Jenkins in through the back door and the garage. Cabrini will be focused on watching me leave. It will take him a second or two to refocus.

Meanwhile you get yourself up to that front door to help me. Got it?"

"You're taking an awfully big risk, standing there in the open at the same time Jenkins and Torres are coming in from other directions."

"Naw. I'm guessing Cabrini's never been in a real gunfight before. He won't know what to do with himself. Just get up there and help me."

The sheriff pulled up, parked and opened the door. "Let's do it."

# Chapter Twenty-three

Zeke opened the passenger door, crawled out and crept to the back bumper of the car. The lake was in front of him just like the sheriff had said. He peered around the tire in the direction of the house.

Parnell stood in front of the threshold, tapping lightly on the door.

Zeke pulled his cell phone out and hit the redial button. Torres answered on the first ring. "He's at the door," Zeke whispered. "Give it two more minutes."

"Got it."

He disconnected and dialed Jenkins. "He's at the door," Zeke repeated. "Torres is going through in about two minutes. When you hear her, go on through."

"Will do," the lieutenant responded.

Normal police protocol demanded that the police do a "knock and announce" when serving a warrant. In this case, the metal battering rams would provide the knock.

Parnell seemed to be taking an awfully long time. Zeke couldn't see to whom he was talking. "Hurry up, damn it," Zeke whispered.

Finally, he heard the sheriff say, "Y'all have a good visit now. 'Bye."

A male voice responded, "Thanks for stopping by."

Parnell came toward the cruiser. Before he'd gone thirty feet,

Zeke heard the first battering ram. The second blast came so close on the heels of the first it sounded like an echo.

The sheriff dived for the ground.

Zeke came running out from behind the cruiser, tearing toward the house. He was expecting gunshots from the front door. Instead, the guy at the door raised his hands and stepped out.

"Don't shoot, don't shoot. I'm not armed. I'm just a driver."

Zeke grabbed him, patted him down and was about to cuff him when the sheriff came running toward him.

"I've got this one. Go get your lady."

Zeke surged forward into the house.

The large house was decorated with lots of leather and heavy dark furniture. There was no one in the living room, dining room or kitchen. Zeke heard voices and raced toward the sound. He found four of the SWAT team in the hall. With them were two large thugs, now in handcuffs.

"Where's Cabrini?" he shouted at the tactical cops.

One of the men pointed farther down the hall. Zeke ran in that direction.

A knot of cops ushered Cabrini out of a room. His hands were cuffed behind him, and his face was dark with rage. He looked at Zeke. Recognition filled his eyes.

Zeke grabbed Cabrini's shirtfront and pulled him forward. "Where is she? Have you hurt her?"

The mobster's face twisted in a sneer. "Your fat little slut is in my playroom. Too bad you showed up when you did. I'd have had her pleading to suck my cock in another ten minutes."

Before anyone realized his intention, Zeke slammed his fist

into Cabrini's face. He pulled his fist back for a second blow, and the SWAT members grabbed his arm.

"Hey, guy. Don't waste time on this piece of shit. Your girl needs you in there." The tactical leader pulled him off Cabrini and pushed him toward the doorway.

In his years with Vice, Zeke had seen a lot of Dom/sub setups, so the gray room didn't surprise him. All he cared about was finding Sandy.

She was naked and chained to some kind of medical bed. Gomez and another cop were on one side of her. Zeke leaped forward.

Her face was frozen; she looked like she might be in shock. He stepped to the right side of the bed and leaned over so she could see him.

"Sandy, it's me, baby. I'm here. It's okay. Everything's gonna be all right."

She lifted her head, turned toward him and blinked. He saw recognition flow into her eyes. "Zeke, is it you?"

"Yes, baby. I'm here. We're going to have you free in just a second." He looked at Gomez. "Goddamn it! Where's the fucking key?"

"Right here, man." Gomez handed him a key ring, and Zeke fumbled to unlock the cuff on his side. Gomez rubbed Sandy's left wrist, trying to restore her circulation.

She whimpered: small, hurt animal noises. Zeke thought his heart would break. "It's okay, baby. It's all over now. That bastard will never touch you again."

He got the cuff open and reached to help her stand upright.

That was when he saw the welts. There were at least a dozen, decorating her back from just below the hairline to her ass.

"Son of a bitch! I'm going to kill that bastard with my own hands."

Sandy stood upright and immediately sagged forward. He caught her, being careful not to touch the angry red marks that would soon turn into ugly black-and-blue bruises.

Another cop came into the room, carrying a lightweight blanket. "Here, you can cover her with this. Found it in a bedroom closet next door."

Zeke wrapped the blanket around Sandy's body. She began to shiver, and he said to Gomez, "Get that ambulance down here."

"On the way. I'll go find the liquor cabinet. She could probably use a shot."

"Lena," Sandy whispered. "Is she okay?"

For the first time, Zeke noticed the submissive chained to the wall. Two cops were unlocking her restraints. The girl was sobbing.

"She's okay, Sandy. She's crying."

Sandy looked up into his face. "It's really you. I knew you'd come for me." And then, she started to cry in earnest. The tears became sobs and the sobs became gulping wails.

Zeke held her tenderly, not touching her sore back or sides. He pressed his lips to her temple and forehead while keeping up a steady patter of comforting noises: "It's okay. You're gonna be fine. We'll get you out of here in just a second." He steered her toward the door and down the hallway.

Cabrini and his henchmen were gone by the time the couple

reached the living room. Zeke led Sandy to a leather ottoman and tried to get her to sit down. She took one look at the ottoman and cried out, "No, I won't sit there. Not where he puts them!"

Zeke suddenly remembered Cabrini's penthouse and the ottoman where he placed his submissives. "Okay, baby, we won't sit here. Let's go wait in the dining room."

In less than a minute, two paramedics bearing a stretcher entered the house.

When Zeke would have stood and moved out of the way so that the paramedics could examine Sandy, she clutched at his arm and begged, "Please don't leave me." He stayed with her, holding one hand while the ambulance crew took her temperature and blood pressure and checked her pupils.

"She's shocky," one of them pronounced. "We'd better take her down to the hospital." He glanced at Zeke. "Do you want to ride with her?"

"You bet. She's not getting out of my sight again."

Sandy refused the stretcher, opting to walk to the ambulance rather than lie on her back. The small procession moved past the waiting cops and tactical team and out of the house. Sandy wouldn't get into the ambulance until she saw Lena being carried out on a second stretcher.

"She's going to be okay, isn't she?"

"Yeah, baby. She'll be fine," Zeke said, hustling her into the first ambulance.

The last thing Zeke saw as a paramedic slammed the ambulance doors was Cabrini being hustled into a waiting squad car.

———

The regional hospital in Jerusalem handled the influx of cops and deputies and the two new patients with aplomb. Nurses shooed everyone out but Zeke, who refused to leave Sandy's side. The fact that Sandy wouldn't release his hand also helped.

The hospital staff treated Sandy and Lena like VIPs, giving them side-by-side cubicles. The ER nurses fussed over both women, cleaning their wounds and bruises with gentle care.

Lena had taken the brunt of Cabrini's anger. Sandy explained that the submissive had tried to help her escape. Cabrini, furious at the mutiny, had used a lash on her.

Zeke grew angry all over again, seeing Sandy's bruises. He sat beside her bed, wishing he could lay hands on Cabrini.

Sandy seemed to recover quickly from the daze he'd first seen her in. She wanted to talk, to tell him everything that had happened. Knowing that she would have to give a statement sometime, Zeke asked for a stenographer to take down what she said.

He listened with astonishment to her story of knocking out the window screen and hiding in the crawl space below the house. "You're freaking amazing," he told her.

The ER doctor who examined Sandy insisted that Zeke step outside the cubicle while he did so. Zeke waited impatiently for the exam to be completed. When the doctor finally pushed back the curtain to admit him again, Zeke asked, "How is she?"

"She's going to be very sore for about two days, and she's going to resemble a rainbow for even longer. But she's fine." The doctor smiled and patted Zeke on the shoulder. "She kept telling me that you saved her. You're her hero."

Zeke's eyes filled with unexpected tears. "I'm no hero," he said. "She's the one who deserves all the credit." He cleared his throat. "When can I take her home?"

"Back to Dallas? Not today. Her back and buttocks are pretty tender. I don't want her riding in a car just yet. Let us keep her in the hospital overnight, and you can take her home around noon tomorrow." He signaled the nurse. "I've given her something for the pain, so she may be a little spacey for the rest of the day."

"That's fine, Doc. Thanks for your help."


It was early evening before Sandy was transferred to a hospital bed. By then, the pain medication had knocked her out.

A deputy brought Zeke Sandy's handbag, and he used her insurance card to officially check her into the hospital.

Later, he sat beside her bed, making phone calls. He contacted Leah to let her know what had happened. He explained that while the police would do everything they could to protect Sandy's privacy, the story was bound to hit the news. Because of the sexual assault factor, the media would not release Sandy's and Lena's names. However, that wouldn't stop them from trying to interview everyone Sandy knew. He and Leah discussed whether to contact Victoria Davis. Leah voted to wait, and Zeke was happy to take her advice.

He was sitting in the dark, looking out the window when Sandy woke around eight p.m.

"Zeke," she cried.

"Right here, baby." He stood and moved to her side. "How are you feeling?"

"Dopey. Can you lie down with me, please? I want you where I can touch you."

"Sure, honey." He kicked off his shoes and hung his empty holster in the closet with his jacket. He'd had to hand his gun to security when he entered the ER.

She scooted over to make room for him in the bed. She was lying on her side to keep pressure off her wounds. He lay down facing her on the narrow mattress.

"Have you heard how Lena is doing?" she asked.

"Yeah, I checked on her about six. She was sound asleep."

"I want to try and help her, Zeke. She risked a lot to help me."

"Whatever you want, baby, we'll do." He brushed her hair out of her eyes.

"What about Cabrini? Where are he and the others?"

"They're cooling their heels in the Eldon County Jail," he replied. "Sheriff Parnell is offering them some Piney Woods hospitality." He grinned. "You'll like Parnell. He's a crusty old fart, but he's straight as an arrow. I'll introduce you to him tomorrow before we leave town."

"Will I have to testify against Cabrini?" she asked, her eyes darkening.

"Yeah, babe. If you want him to pay for what he did to you and Lena, you will. But we don't need to think about that now."

He ran his finger down her nose, tapping the tip. "And when the time comes, I'll be there with you."

She nodded. "I want to testify. I want to see his face when I tell the whole world what I think of him."

"That's my girl. My brave, wonderful girl. The cops haven't been able to get enough on him to put him away, but now you're going to do it all by yourself." He shook his head. "Ben was pretty impressed when he heard about you climbing into that crawl space."

"Ugh." She shivered. "I can still see that rat's little orange eyes staring at me."

"Yeah, Ben wanted to know if you had a sister. He said he could use a girl with guts like yours."

"I do, but she's taken. Tell him he'll have to find his own girl."

"God, Sandy, it's so good to see you smile again." He touched her cheek gently. "For a while there, I didn't know when—or whether—I would ever see you again. I've never been so scared."

She nodded. "Me, too. I was so frightened. But I kept telling myself, 'Zeke will come. Zeke will find me.' And you did." Tears were in her eyes, and she touched his shoulder.

Zeke felt answering tears struggling to escape his eyes. "I haven't prayed in years, baby, but I prayed to God to protect you until I could get there."

"And he did. We'll have to go to church to say thanks." Her smile was watery.

"That's not the only reason why we'll need to go to church." His mouth felt as though it were filled with cotton.

She tilted her head. "What?"

"Well, you see, I made this promise to God. I told him if He kept you safe, I'd take care of you for the rest of my life."

Her eyes widened. "Are you asking me to marry you, Zeke?"

"Yeah, Sandy, I am. And you have to say yes. Otherwise, God might strike me dead with lightning."

"So that's the only reason you want to marry me?" she asked.

"Sandy, I'm asking you to marry me because I damn well don't think I can stand to live without you." He leaned forward and gently kissed her. "I love you, babe."

In a tumble of sheet and elbows, she threw her arms around him. "I love you, too, Zeke. So much."

Their kiss was tender and long, interrupted only when the nurse entered to check Sandy's vitals.

Zeke hopped off the bed and waited while the smiling RN took Sandy's pulse and temperature.

"One thing, though, babe."

"What, Zeke?"

"*You're* gonna have to call your mother. Leah tells me I need to stay as far away from your mom as possible."

Her happy laughter could be heard all the way to the nurses' desk.

# Chapter Twenty-four

*Six months later*

Sandy stared at her reflection in the restroom mirror. Although it had seemed impossible, the bridesmaid dress really did look good on her. The rose color complemented her pale skin and dark hair while the low neckline showed her bust to advantage.

Of course, it didn't hurt that she'd lost almost twenty pounds in the last six months. Maybe she needed to think about writing a weight-loss book based upon having fantastic sex on a daily basis.

It had been an amazing few months. She'd testified before the grand jury that indicted Cabrini for kidnapping, and she was scheduled to be the star witness at his upcoming trial.

Although she'd had a couple of sessions with a therapist after her ordeal, Sandy had bounced back faster than anyone expected. Zeke had hovered over her like a mother hen, and his tender care had gone a long way to helping her heal.

The restroom door opened and Tricia entered, sweeping the train of her wedding gown ahead of her.

"There you are," she exclaimed. "Mom's looking for you."

"Oh, great. What is it now?"

"I didn't ask." Her sister grinned. "I was too happy not to have her focusing on me. One of the side benefits of getting married is that she's being nice to me for a change."

"Lucky you." Sandy sighed. "Guess I'll go see what she wants." She leaned into the mirror and, after pinning a loose curl in place, picked up her decorative bag and turned to leave.

"Wait, Sandy," Tricia said, holding a hand out to stop her.

Sandy looked at her younger sister. "What?"

"We've never really talked about Josh and me. I mean I wanted to, but you would never discuss it." She hesitated, obviously uncomfortable. "I didn't mean to fall in love with him, but—"

Sandy interrupted, "But you did, and you two are perfect for each other." She hugged Tricia. "Josh loves you, not me. And that's okay."

"And you love Zeke, don't you?" Tricia asked anxiously as she pulled out of the hug to look into Sandy's eyes.

She nodded. "And he loves me. So everything worked out just the way it needed to."

"Thank you, sis. That's the best wedding gift you could have given me." Tricia's eyes filled with tears. "I'm so happy for you."

"And I'm happy for you." Sandy smiled. "Come on. Let's go find Mom so she can get in her daily minimum requirement of nagging."

Arm in arm, the two sisters left the restroom and returned to the hotel ballroom, where the wedding reception was in full swing. They hadn't gone far when Victoria Davis—resplendent in an icy blue Empire-style gown—intercepted them.

"There you are. Everyone is looking for you, Patricia. The photographer is waiting."

"Then I guess I'd better go find my husband," Tricia said,

glowing with pride as she said the words. "See you in a bit." She patted Sandy on the arm and took off across the ballroom floor.

Victoria turned to her older daughter. "Alexandra, whatever possessed you to wear your hair up with all those curls hanging down? You're far too old to wear that style."

Sandy grinned at her mother. "I like it this way, and so does Zeke."

"And that's another thing." Victoria narrowed her eyes. "When are the two of you going to get married? A social worker shouldn't be living in sin with a man. Can't you get him to propose?" She shrugged. "Although why he would, I don't know. He's already got the milk, so why buy the cow?" Taking her eyes off Sandy, she looked at something beyond her daughter's left shoulder and frowned.

Sandy felt her smile beginning to slip. Before she could say anything, two warm hands grasped her bare upper arms.

"Hi, honey." It was Zeke. She turned in relief to look at him over her shoulder.

"Mom was just asking me when we were going to get married, Zeke."

"Oh?" He nuzzled her left ear. "I've already asked Sandy to marry me, and she's said yes."

Sandy turned to face her mother. "I didn't want to steal Tricia's thunder. Zeke and I are planning to get married soon. When we decide on a date, we'll let you know." Her voice was even and matter-of-fact.

"Well, I think—" Victoria started when Zeke cut her off.

"With all due respect, Victoria, what you think doesn't count. It's what Sandy thinks that matters. Now, I'm ready to hit that buffet. Ready, honey?"

"Ready," she said, touching his cheek with one hand. "We'll see you later, Mom."

The two walked off, hand in hand, leaving Sandy's mother staring after them, dumbfounded.

"Thank you," Sandy murmured. "I was about to lose it when you walked up."

"No, you weren't," he assured her. "Just remember, she's a middle-aged harpy and you're a beautiful young dish. You don't need to fight with her. You're already winning."

Sandy stopped dead in the middle of the room and turned to face him. "Have I told you today that I love you?"

He grinned. "Yeah, but you haven't done anything to show me."

"Just what did you have in mind?" she asked with a smile.

He leaned forward to whisper in her ear, "While you were in the restroom, I was checking the layout of this place. There's a stairwell leading upstairs to the guest rooms. How about a quickie?"

She stared at him. "You're kidding!"

He shook his head. "Nope. I've been keeping track. We've done it in a car, on a plane, in my boss' office, in your office and in your mother's backyard. No stairwells yet."

Sandy giggled. "But someone is sure to catch us."

He grinned. "That's what you said about the stacks at the library. No one caught us there."

She felt the familiar rush of warmth between her thighs. "All right. But let's hurry. I don't want to miss the cutting of the cake."

He grabbed her hand and dragged her out of the ballroom, down a hall and through a heavy fire door.

On the other side of the door was a landing in a gray stairwell. Sandy looked up to see stairs leading to the upper floors. There was also a single flight heading down to the hotel's basement.

"I don't know, Zeke. Someone could come through that door or from upstairs or downstairs. It seems too risky."

He pulled his pocketknife out, selected the screwdriver and made an adjustment to the iron-bar handle of the door. "Okay. I've locked the fire door. No one's coming through here." Turning toward Sandy, he asked, "What are you wearing under that dress?"

She laughed at the now familiar question. "A garter belt and hose. Nothing else."

"Oh, baby."

His erection gave Zeke some difficulty in undoing the fly of his cream and gray suit. When he finally got the zipper down, his penis leaped out, ready for action.

"There he is," cooed Sandy. "My poor baby all cramped up in that awful suit."

"Kiss him and make it better," Zeke suggested.

She looked down at her beautiful gown and then around the dirty stairwell. "Go up three steps and I will. I don't want to ruin this dress by kneeling on the ground."

Zeke almost tripped over his feet in his rush to get up the stairs. She put her handbag down before turning her attention to him.

In his new position, Sandy was able to reach his cock by just bending forward and bracing herself with her hands against his knees. She began by running her tongue up the slit in the tip of his penis.

"That's it, honey," he moaned, closing his eyes. "Oh, yeah. That's good."

She stopped to look up at him. "Just remember, bucko, you'll owe me one."

He opened his eyes. "Hey, this is foreplay. You'll get yours."

"Promises, promises," she muttered, opening her mouth wide and taking the knob of his penis inside.

Above them, a door slammed and footsteps came pounding down the stairs. Sandy straightened while Zeke pushed her forward.

By the time the two teenage boys reached the landing Sandy and Zeke were on, she was standing in front of Zeke, hiding his open fly and bobbing penis.

"Hi," the kids said as they ran past the two adults and shoved on the fire door.

"It's locked," Zeke volunteered. "You'll need to go down one flight and out through the basement."

The boys didn't question him; they just continued down the stairs, their tennis shoes pounding on the metal runners of the steps.

When the basement door slammed shut behind the kids, Sandy and Zeke burst out laughing.

"I told you," she insisted, turning to face him. His naked penis jutted into the front of her gown. She looked down at it and giggled. "He looks so silly."

"I'll show you silly," Zeke growled in mock ferocity. He began grabbing fistfuls of her silk dress.

"Wait! Zeke, what are you doing?" she shrieked. His hands tunneled under her gown and grabbed her bare ass cheeks. In one smooth movement, he lifted her up.

"Zeke!" She gripped his shoulders to steady herself.

"Wrap your legs around my waist," he demanded.

Realizing what he was trying to do, she complied, kicking at the yards of fabric to free her legs. He swiveled and pushed her against the wall while she circled his waist with her thighs. The cement blocks were cold and hard on her bare shoulders, but anticipating his cock, her pussy was warm and wet.

With Sandy's back anchored, Zeke was able to free one hand. Seizing his penis, he shoved it into her vagina. They both groaned with pleasure as he pushed his flesh inside her body.

"Ohhhhh," she sighed.

"Ahhhhh," he moaned.

Zeke didn't wait. Moving his hips in a rapid piston-fired movement, he began pounding into her. He pushed until she could feel the slap of his balls and then he pulled, drawing his penis nearly out of her body.

The friction created by his huge cock combined with the

excitement of sex in a public place brought Sandy to readiness almost immediately. Her position on the wall put her chest even with Zeke's face. She used one hand to yank the front of her dress down, exposing her breasts. He opened his mouth and seized her right nipple. When he bit down with his teeth, she screamed and came.

Her orgasm pushed him over the edge. He drove into her one last time, stiffened and exploded, shooting hot cum deep inside her.

Sandy collapsed forward, resting her chin on top of Zeke's head. She could feel his face pressing into her chest, his gasps heating her skin.

Bodies pressed to the wall, they hung there in the dimly lit stairwell, panting but fulfilled.

When she could get her breath again, Sandy said, "Guess we can check 'stairwell' off that list of yours."

"Yeah," he agreed. "On to 'restaurant.' "

"What? Are you out of your mind? We can't fuck in a restaurant."

"That's what you said about the library and the stairwell," he reminded her.

She started to laugh. "Put me down, you maniac."

He stepped backward and his penis slipped out of her sheath. "Ohhhh," she said as her vagina was once again left empty. "I hate it when we separate."

"Me, too," he agreed, putting her back on her feet. "That's why I want to marry you. How about it, my little Peeping Thomasina? No more stalling. I love you and want to spend the next fifty years with you."

"All right," she sighed. "I'll marry you this fall on the anniversary of our first date." She tucked her breasts back into the built-in bra of her dress.

"This fall! No way. That's another six months. If I wait too long, you're going to find another man and blow me off."

"Not going to happen, Prada. You're stuck with me." She picked up her handbag from the stairs. "If you'll agree to a September wedding, I'll let you pick the place for the honeymoon." She kissed his chin. "Deal?"

"Deal. With the trial starting in June, Cabrini should be in prison by then." He grinned. "But you need to agree to fuck in a movie theater and a department store before we get married." He feathered kisses along her cheekbone.

"Only if the theater has a balcony." She pulled out of his arms and pointed to the fire door. "They're probably ready to cut the cake. Let's go."

He used the screwdriver from his pocketknife to unlock the door and they returned to the ballroom, holding hands.